# Dr. Dumany's Wife

*By*

MAURUS JÓKAI

*Translated from the Hungarian*

*By*

F. STEINITZ

**Fredonia Books**
**Amsterdam, The Netherlands**

Dr. Dumany's Wife

by
Maurus Jókai

ISBN: 1-4101-0458-3

Fredonia Books
Amsterdam, The Netherlands
http://www.fredoniabooks.com

# PUBLISHERS' NOTE.

THIS, the latest story from the pen of Hungary's great man of letters, Maurus Jókai, was translated directly from the manuscript of the author by Mme. F. Steinitz, who resides in Buda-Pest, and was selected by him for that purpose.

Maurus Jókai is now sixty-six years of age, having been born at Komaróm, in 1825. He was intended for the law, that having been his father's profession but at twelve years of age the desire to write seized him. Some of his stories fell into the hands of the lawyer in whose office he was studying, who read them, and was so struck by their originality and talent that he published them at once at his own expense. The public was as well pleased with the book as the lawyer had been with the manuscripts, and from that tender age to the present Jókai has devoted himself to writing, and is the author of several hundred successful volumes. At the age of twenty-three he laid down his pen long enough to get married, his bride being Rosa Laborfalvi, the then leading Hungarian actress. At the end of a year he joined the Revolutionists, and buckled on the sword of the patriot. He was taken prisoner and sentenced to be shot, when his bride appeared upon the scene with her pockets full of the money she had made by the sale

of her jewels, and, bribing the guards, escaped with
her husband into the birch woods, where they hid in
caves and slept on leaves, all the time in danger of
their lives, until they finally found their way to Buda-
Pest and liberty.    This city Jókai has made his home;
in the winter he lives in the heart of the town, in the
summer just far enough outside of it to have a
house surrounded by grounds, where he can sit out of
doors in the shade of his own trees.  He is probably
the best-known man in Hungary to-day, for he is not
only an author, but a financier, a statesman, and a
journalist as well.

# CONTENTS.

# CONTENTS.

# DR. DUMANY'S WIFE

# DR. DUMANY'S WIFE.

## I.

### THE DUMB CHILD.

IT was about the close of the year 1876 when, on my road to Paris, I boarded the St. Gothard railway-train. Travellers coming from Italy had already taken possession of the sleeping-car compartments, and I owed it solely to the virtue of an extraordinarily large tip that I was at last able to stretch my weary limbs upon the little sofa of a half-coupé. It was not a very comfortable resting-place, inasmuch as this carriage was the very last in an immensely long train, and one must be indeed fond of rocking to enjoy the incessant shaking, jostling, and rattling in this portion of the train. But still it was much preferable to the crowded carriages, peopled with old women carrying babies, giggling maidens, snoring or smoking men, and hilarious children; so I made the best of it, and prepared for a doze.

The guard came in to look at my ticket, and, pitying my lonely condition, he opened a conversation. He told me that the son of an immensely wealthy American nabob, with an escort well-nigh princely,

was travelling on the same train to Paris. He had
with him an attendant physician, a nursery governess,
a little playfellow, a travelling courier, and a huge
negro servant to prepare his baths, besides several
inferior servants. These all occupied the parlour-
car and the sleeping compartments; but the little
fellow had a parlour, a bedroom, and a dressing-room
all to himself.

I did not pay much attention to the talk of the
gossiping guard, and so he departed, and at last I
could sleep. On the road I am like a miller in his
mill. So long as the wheel turns, I sleep on; but the
moment it is stopped, I start up and am instantly
wide awake. We had reached a smaller station
where the train usually stops for a few minutes only,
when, to my surprise, there was a great deal of pushing
and sliding of the cars backward and forward, and we
halted for an extraordinarily long time. I was just
getting up to learn what was going on, when the
guard entered, lantern in hand.

"I beg your pardon, sir," he said, "but there is
something amiss. The linch-pin of the parlour-car
has become over-heated, and we had to uncouple the
car and leave it behind. Now we are obliged to find
a convenient place for the little American, until we
reach some main station, where another parlour-car
can be attached to the train. I am really sorry for
you, sir, but this is the only suitable place we have,
and the little fellow and his governess must be your
travelling companions for a while."

"Well, when a thing can't be helped, grumbling

is unreasonable, so good-bye sleep and quiet, and let us prepare to pay homage to the illustrious youth and his lady attendant," said I, smiling at the guard's earnestness. But still he hesitated.

"And pray, sir, what is your religion?" stammered he; "I have to tell the governess."

"Indeed!" My good-humour was rising still, and I continued smiling. "Tell the lady that I am a Swiss Protestant, and I hope she will not object, as I shall not try to convert her or her charge if they are of a different creed. Is there anything else you want to inquire into?"

"Yes, sir. The little gentleman's physician would also like to accompany his charge, and stay at his side."

"But there is only room for three."

"I know; but, sir, the doctor is a very liberal gentleman, and he told me that if anybody would be willing to exchange places with him, he would gladly repay his whole travelling expenses."

"That's liberal, certainly, and I have no doubt the fireman of the engine will thankfully accept his offer. You can tell him as much. And now go!"

The man went out, but right after him came the doctor—a very pleasant and distinguished-looking young man. He apologised for the guard's bluntness and his misinterpretation of his message. He had not meant to offend a gentleman, and so forth. He introduced himself as Dr. Mayer, family physician at the house of the so-called "Silver King," Mr. Dumany, the father of the little "Silver Prince." After

learning that I did not smoke, and had no objection
to children, he inquired my nationality. My astrachan fur cap and coat-collar made him take me for a
Russian, but, thanking him for his good opinion, I
stated that as yet I was merely a Hungarian. He
did not object; but asked if we were free from
small-pox, diphtheritis, croup, measles, scarlet-fever,
whooping-cough, and such like maladies in our
country at present. After I had satisfied him that
even the foot-and-mouth disease had by this time
ceased, he finally quitted me, but immediately returned, assisting a lady with both hands full of
travelling necessaries to climb up into the carriage.
After the lady came a grand stately-looking negro
servant, with gold-braided cap and overcoat of
white bear's fur, and on his arm, bundled up in rich
velvet and costly fur, he carried a beautiful five-
year-old boy, who looked like some waxen image or
big doll.

The lady seemed very lively and talkative, and had
a host of languages at command. With the doctor
she conversed in German; to the guide she spoke
French; the negro she questioned in English, and to a
maid who brought in some rugs and air-pillows she
spoke Italian. All these languages she spoke excel-
lently, and I am certain that if a dozen persons of
different nationalities had been present she could
have talked to them in their various dialects with the
same ease and fluency. Of her beauty I could not
judge, for she wore a bonnet with a thick veil, which
covered her face to the chin.

Taking her seat at the opposite window, she placed the child between us. He was a pale, quiet little boy, with very red, thin, tightly-compressed lips, and great, melancholy dark-blue eyes. As long as the negro was occupied in arranging the rugs and pillows, he looked wholly unconcerned, and the smiles from the great black shining face did not impress him at all; but when the swarthy giant caught the two fair little hands in his own great black palm and wanted to kiss them, the boy withdrew his hands with a quick gesture and struck the ebony forehead with his tiny fist.

At last we were seated. The negro was gone, the guide went out and locked the door after him. Seeing that the open window was disagreeable to the lady, I volunteered to close it. She accepted gratefully, and at the same time expressed her regrets that, in consequence of the accident to the parlour-car, she had been compelled to disturb me. Of course, I hastened to say that I was not in the least incommoded, and only regretted that it was not in my power to make her more comfortable. She then told me that she was an American, and pretty well used to railroad accidents of a more or less serious character. Three times she had been saved by a miracle in railway collisions at home, and she assured me that in America about 30,000 persons were every year injured in railway accidents, while some 4,000 were killed outright.

We conversed in German, and, as the lady became more and more communicative, talk turned upon the subject of the child between us. She told me that Master James was deaf and dumb, and could not understand a word of our conversation; hence restraint was unnecessary. I asked her if he was born with this defect, and she said, "No; until the age of three he could speak very nicely, but at that age he was thrown out of his little goat-carriage, and in consequence of the shock and concussion lost his power of speech."

"Then he will possibly recover it," I said. "I knew a young man who lost his speech in the same manner at the age of five, and could not speak up to his tenth year; then he recovered, and now he has graduated from college as senior wrangler."

"Yes," she said. "But Mr. Dumany is impatient, and he has sent the boy to all the deaf-and-dumb boarding-schools in Europe. Even now we are coming from such an institution in Italy; but none of all these different masters has been able to teach more than sign-talk, and that is insufficient. Mr. Dumany wants to give the German Heinicke method a trial. That professes to teach real conversation, based on the observations of the movements of the lips and tongue."

Of this method I also knew examples of success. I was acquainted with a deaf and dumb type-setter, who had learned to talk intelligibly and fluently, could read aloud, and take part in conversation, but in a piping voice like that of a bird.

"Even that would be a great success," she said. "At any rate, little James will be taken to the Zürich

Institute, and remain there until he acquires his speech."

During this whole conversation the little fellow had sat between us, mute, and, to all appearance, wholly indifferent. His little pale face was dull, and his great eyes half closed. I felt sorry for him, and with a sigh of real compassion I muttered in my own native Hungarian tongue, "Szegény fincska!" ("Poor little boy!") At this I saw a thrill of surprise run through the child's little frame; the great blue eyes opened wide in wonder and delight, and the closed cherry lips opened in a smile of joy.

I was struck with surprise, and did not believe my own eyes. The lady had not noticed anything, since she still kept her bonnet on and the thick veil tightly drawn over her face.

I took pity on her, and offered to go out into the corridor to smoke a cigarette, so that she might make herself a little more comfortable until we arrived at some large station, where she would enter another parlour-car.

She accepted thankfully, and, to my utter astonishment, the little boy raised his tiny hand, and caressingly stroked the fur collar of my coat. I bent down to kiss him, and he smiled sweetly on me; and when I got up and signed to him that he could now occupy both seats and stretch himself upon the little sofa, he shook his head, and crept into the corner which I had quitted. And there, as often as in my walk up and down the corridor I threw a glance into his corner, I could see the child's large dark-blue eyes

following all my movements with an eager curiosity;
the white little face pressed to the window-pane and
the tiny hand never losing hold of the edge of the
curtain, which he had purposely lifted, for the
governess had pulled the curtain down the moment
I left, possibly to take off her bonnet.

Mine was not a very pleasant situation in that
corridor. I watched the rising and sinking of the
moon, which phenomenon repeated itself about twice
every hour, according to the serpentine windings of
the road. I looked at the milky mist which surrounded the icy pinnacles of the great mountains,
and grumbled over the intense darkness in the many
tunnels, in which the roar and noise of the train is
tremendously increased, thundering as if Titans were
breaking out of their prisons below Mount Pelion.

As if they had not broken through long, long ago!
What if the old Grecian gods should come to life?
should leave their marble temples, and gaze about on
the world as it is at present? If Pallas Athene were
told of America? If Helios Apollo could listen to
Wagner's operas, and Zeus Jupiter might look into
the great tube of the London Observatory, wondering
what had become of that milky way which had been
formed out of the milk spilled by Amalthea? If we
could show him that we had caught and harnessed
his heavenly lightning to draw our vehicles and carry
our messages, and that, with the help of fire-eyed
leviathans, we break through the rocky womb of his
great mountains? And yet, how easy it would be for
them with a simple sneeze of their most illustrious

and omnipotent noses, to raise such a tempest that earth and sea would rise and destroy man and his pigmy works at one fell stroke! I wonder if they never awake? I rather think they sometimes get up and shake their mighty fists at us. These cyclones look very suspicious to me!

The huge iron leviathan turns and twists itself like a Gordian knot; disappears and reappears, almost on the same spot, but higher up on the mountain, and then glides rapidly on along the brinks of fearful abysses, over long iron bridges looking like some fanciful filigree work, some giant spider's web, extending across great valleys, chasms, and precipices, over which great mountain rivers splash down, roaring and foaming in gigantic falls. What giant power has cleft the way for these waters—Vulcan or Neptune? Or was it laid down in Euclid's adventurous age, when the Titans went into bankruptcy?

The train increases its speed to regain the time lost in uncoupling the disabled parlour-car, and this increased speed is chiefly felt at the tail of the great iron dragon. I have to cling tightly to the brass rod in front of the windows. We pass the central station without stopping, the locomotive whistles, the lamps of the little watch-houses fly past like so many jack-o'-lanterns, and all at once we are enveloped by a thick fog rising from beneath, where it had rested above the sea, and when the train has twice completed the circle around the valley, the noxious, dangerous mist surrounds us entirely.

But once more the creation of human hands

B

conquers the spectre, and, puffing and whistling, the locomotive breaks through the dark haze. Once again the iron serpent disappears into the bowels of the rock, and as it emerges it crosses another valley and is greeted by a clear heaven and a multitude of brightly-glistening stars.

We are on the Rossberg. A devastated tract of the globe it seems. Our eyes rest on barren soil devoid of vegetation. Beneath a large field of huge boulders, imbedded in snow and ice, the Alpine vegetation thrives. The whole valley is one immense graveyard, and the great rocks are giant tombstones, encircled by wreaths of white flowers meet for adorning graves. At the beginning of the present century one of the ridges of the Rossberg gave way, and in the landslide four villages were buried. This happened at night, when the villagers were all asleep, and not a single man, women, or child escaped. This valley is their resting-place. Was I not right to call it a graveyard ?

Above this valley of destruction the train glides on. Upon the side of the mountain is a little watch-house, built into the rock ; a narrow flight of steps hewn in the stone leads up to it like a ladder. The moon, which had lately seemed fixed to the crest of the mountain, now plays hide-and-seek among the peaks. A high barricade on the side of the Rossberg serves to protect the railroad track against another landslide.

On the high ridges of the mountain goats were pasturing, and not far from them a shepherd's fire was

blazing, and the shepherd himself sat beside it. I
remember all these accessories as well as if they were
still before my eyes. I can see the white goats
climbing up and pulling at the broom-plants. I can
see the shepherd's black form, encircled by the light
of the fire, and the white watch-house with its black
leaden roof, the high signal-pole in front of it, above
which all at once a great flaming star arises.

## II.

### THE DARK GOD.

I was gazing at that shining red light, when all at once I felt a concussion, as if the train had met with some impediment. I heard the jolting of the foremost cars, and had time to prepare for the shock which was sure to follow; but when it did come, it was so great that it threw me to the opposite wall of the corridor.

Yet the train moved on as before, so that it could not have been disabled, as I at first thought. I heard the guards run from carriage to carriage, opening the doors, and I could see great clouds of steam arise from the puffing and blowing engines. The friction of the wheels made a grating noise, and I leaned out of the window to ascertain the nature of the danger. Was another train approaching, and a collision inevitable? I could see nothing, but suddenly I beheld the figure of the shepherd, and saw him raise his staff aloft. I followed the motion of his hand, and with a thrill of horror I saw a great ledge of rock sliding downward with threatening speed, while at the same time a shower of small stones crashed on the roof of the cars.

I did not wait for the guards to open my door. I had it open in an instant. From the other carriages passengers were jumping out at the risk of life and limb, for the train was running at full speed.

I hastily ran into the coupé to awaken my travelling companions, but found them up. "Madam," I said, "I am afraid that we are in danger of a serious accident. Pray come out quickly!"

"Save the child!" she answered; and I caught the little boy, took him in my arms, and ran out.

The train was gliding perpetually on, and I bethought myself of the recommendation of one who is jumping from a running vehicle, to leap forward, because in jumping sideways or backward he invariably falls under the wheels. So I followed the recommendation and leaped. Fortunately, I reached the ground, although my knees doubled up under me, and I struck the knuckles of my right hand a hard blow. The child had fainted in my arms, but only from fright; otherwise he had received no harm. I laid him on the ground in a safe place, and ran with all my might after the train to help the lady out. She was standing on the steps, already prepared for the jump. I extended my hand to her, impatiently crying "Quick!" But instead of taking my proffered hand she exclaimed, "Oh! I have forgotten my bonnet and veil," and back she ran into the coupé, never again to come forth.

At that moment I felt a tremendous shock, as if the earth had quaked and opened beneath me, and this was followed by a deafening uproar, the clashing of stones, the cracking of wood and glass, the grating and crushing of iron, and the pitiful cries of men,

women, and children. The great mass of rock broke
through the protecting barricade and rushed right
upon the engine. The huge, steam-vomiting leviathan
was crushed in an instant, and the copper and steel
fragments scattered everywhere. Three of the wheels
were shattered, and with that the iron colossus came
to a dead stop, the suddenness of which threw the
carriages crashing on top of each other. This fearful
havoc was not all. Through the breach which the
great rock had made in the barricade, an incessant
avalanche of stones, from the size of a cannon-ball to
that of a wheelbarrow, descended upon the train,
crushing everything beneath into fragments, pushing
the unhappy train into the chasm below, into the
valley of death and destruction. Like a huge serpent
it slid down, the great glowing furnace with its feeding
coals undermost, and then the whole wrecked mass of
carriages tumbled after, atop of each other, while
cries of despair were heard on every side. Then I
saw the rear car—that in which I had been sitting—
stand up erect on top of the others, while on its roof
fell, with thunderous violence, the awful shower of
stones. Mutely I gazed on, until a large stone struck
the barricade just where I stood, and then I realised
that the danger was not over, and ran for shelter.

The stones were falling fast to left and to right,
and I hastened to gain the steps which led to the
little watch-house. Then I bethought me of the boy.
I found him still insensible, but otherwise unharmed,
and I took him up, covering him with a furred coat.
I ran up the steps with him, so fast that not a

thought of my asthma and heart disease slackened my speed.

There was nobody in the house but a woman milking a goat. In one corner of the room stood a bed, in the middle was a table, and on one of the walls hung a burning coal-oil lamp.

As I opened the door the woman looked up, and said in a dull piteous moaning—

"It is none of Jörge's fault. Jörge had shown the red light in good season, and yesterday he specially warned the gentlemen, and told them that a ridge of the Gnippe was crumbling, and would soon break down; but they did not listen to him, and now that the accident has come, they will surely visit their own carelessness upon him. It is always the poor dependent that is made to suffer for the fault of his superiors. But I will not stand it; and if Jörge is discharged and loses his bread, then——"

"All right, madam!" I said, "I saw the red light in time, and I shall testify for Jörge in case of need. Only keep quiet now, and come here. You must try to restore this child. He has fainted. Give him water or something; you will know best what to do."

In recalling these words to my memory and writing them down, I am not quite certain that I really spoke them; I am not certain of a single word or action of mine on that fearful night. But I think that I said the words I am relating, although I was so confused that it is possible I did not utter a word. I had come out of the house again, and saw a man running up and down on the narrow rocky plateau, like one crazy. It was Jörge the watchman; he was looking for the signal-post, and could not find it.

"Here it is, look!" I said, turning his face toward the high pole right in front of him. He gazed up wistfully, and then all at once he blubbered out—

"See! See, the red light! I gave the warning. They cannot blame me; they dare not punish me for it. It is not my fault!"

Of course, he thought of nothing but himself, and the misfortune of the others touched him only in so far as he was concerned.

"Don't blubber now!" I said. "There will be time enough to think of ourselves. Now let us learn what has happened to the others. The whole train has been swept down into the abyss below. What has become of the people in it?"

"God Almighty have mercy on their souls!"

"Yet perhaps we could save some of them. Come along!"

"I can't go. I dare not leave my post, else they will turn against me."

"Well then, I shall go alone," said I, and hastened down the steps.

I heard no screams, no cries, not a sound of human voices. The poor victims of the catastrophe were exhausted or frightened out of their wits, and gave no utterance to the pain they felt. Only the never-ceasing clatter of the falling stones was heard, nothing else. Awful is the voice of the elements, and dreadful their revenge on their human antagonists! The thundering heavens, the roaring sea, are awful to behold and to listen to; but most fearful of all is the voice of the earth, when, quivering in wrath, she opens her fiery mouth or hurls her rocky missiles at pigmy men.

From the wrecked train a great many travellers had jumped like myself; but not all with the same happy result. They had mostly reached the ground more or less bruised, but at the moment of escape from the clutch of death we do not much feel our hurts. These unhappy victims, frightened as they were, had managed to creep and hide behind the untouched portion of the bulwark, and happy to have escaped from immediate death, sheltered from the tremendous cataract of stones, they remained quiet, trembling, awaiting the end of the catastrophe and the ultimate rescue. But what had meanwhile become of those who had stayed in the falling carriages?

There came a terrible answer to that question, and out of the old horror arose a new and still more terrible spectre. A demon with a cloudy head, rising from the darkness below, and with a swift and fearful growth mounting up to the sky—a demon with a thousand glistening, sparkling eyes and tongues, a smoke-fiend!

The great boiler of the locomotive had gone down first. There it fell, not on the ground, but on a large fragment of rock, which pierced it completely, so that the air had free access to the fire. Upon the top of both boiler and tender, the coal-van had been turned

upside down, and these had pulled all the carriages
one on top of the other in the same way, so that the
whole train stood upright, like some huge steeple.
This dreadful structure had become a great funeral
pile, the altar of a black pagan idol whose fiery
tongues were greedily thrusting upward to devour
their prey.

Then, as the smoke became blacker and blacker, a
heart-rending, almost maddening sound of shrieking
and crying rang out from that devilish wreck, so loud
and piercing that it drowned the clatter of stones,
the crackling of the fast-kindling coals, and the
crushing noise of the metals. At the cry for aid of
the doomed victims, all who had escaped and hidden
behind the bulwark came forth, creeping or running,
shrieking and gesticulating, forgetful of their own
danger and pitiful condition, thinking only of those
dear lost ones there in that abode of hell, and
maddened at the impossibility of rescuing them. It
was a wild hurly-burly of voices and of tongues,
of despairing yells, hysterical sobs, heart-rending
prayers; and as I stumbled over the twisted and
broken rails, that stood upright like bent wires, and
stooped over the bulwark, I beheld a spectacle so
terrible that every nerve of my body, every heart-
string, revolted at it. Even now they quiver at the
ghastly recollection.

As the fire lighted up the horrible pile I could see
that the first carriage atop of the coals was a shattered mass, the second crushed flat, while the third
stood with wheels uppermost, and so forth to the top,

and out of all of them human heads, limbs, faces, bodies, were thrust forward. Two small gloved female hands, locked as in prayer, were stretched out of a window, and above them two strong, muscular, masculine arms tried with superhuman force to lift the iron weight above, to break a way at the top, until the blood flowed from the nails, and even these strong arms dropped down exhausted. Half-seen forms, mutilated, bleeding, were tearing with teeth and nails at their dreadful prison. Then for a while the smoky cloud involved everything in darkness. A moment after, the red fiery tongues came lapping upward, and a red, glowing halo encircles the fatal wreck. The first and second carriages were already burned. How long would it take the flames to reach the top? How many of the sufferers were yet alive? What power in heaven or earth could save them, and how?

The hollow into which the train had fallen was so deep that, in spite of the erect position of the ill-fated pile, the topmost car—that containing the poor foolish American governess, who had lost her life in running back for her bonnet—was ten mètres below us, and we had not even a single rope or cord with which to hazard the experiment of descending. A young man, one of those few who had come forth unharmed, ran up and down the embankment, shouting madly for a rope, offering a fortune for belts, shawls, and cords. His newly-married bride was in one of those carriages, and hers were the tiny gloved hands that were stretched out of the window. "A

rope!" cried he; "give me anything to make a rope!"
But who heeded him?

A young mother sat on the tracks, fondly hugging
a plaid shawl in her arms. Her babe was there in
that burning pyre, but horror had overpowered her
reason. There she sat, caressing the woollen bundle,
and in a low voice singing her "Eia Popeia" to the
child of her fantasy.

An aged Polish Jew lay across the barricade wall.
His two hands were stretched downward, and there
he muttered the prayers and invocations of his
ancient liturgy, which no one there understood but
himself and his God. The ritual prayer-bands were
upon his thumbs and wrists, and encircling his forehead. His forked beard and greasy side-locks dangled
as he chanted his hymns, while his eyes, starting
almost out of their sockets, were fixed upon one of
the carriages. What did that car contain? His
wife? His children? Or his worldly goods, the
fortune hoarded up through a life-time of cunning
and privation? Who knows? Forth he chants
his prayers, loudly yelling, or muttering low, as the
ghastly scene before him vanishes in smoke and
darkness, or glows out again in fearful distinctness.

Every one shrieks, cries, prays, swears, raves.

No; not every one! There, on the barricade, his
legs doubled up Turk-fashion, sits a young painter
with Mephisto beard and grey eyes. His sketch-book
is open, and he is making a vivid sketch of the
sensational scene. The illustrated papers are grateful customers, and will rejoice at receiving the sketch.

But this young draughtsman is not the only sensible person in the place. There is another, a long-legged Englishman, standing with watch in hand, reckoning up the time lost by the accident, and eyeing the scene complacently.

Some noisy dispute attracts my attention, and, turning, I behold a man, trying with all his might to overcome a woman, who attacks him with teeth and nails, biting his hands and tearing at his flesh, as he drags her close to him. At last he succeeds in joining both of her hands behind her back, she foaming, writhing, and cursing. I ask indignantly, "What do you want with the woman? Let her alone!"

"Oh, sir!" he said, showing me a sorrowful and tear-stained face, "for Heaven's sake, help me! I cannot bear with her any more. She wants to leap down and kill herself. Pray help me to tie her hands, and carry her off from here!"

By his speech I knew him for a Pole, and the woman's exclamations were also uttered in the Polish language. She was his wife; her children were there in that infernal pile, and she wanted to die with them.

"Quick! quick!" gasped the man. "Take my necktie and fasten her hands behind her." I obeyed; and as I wound the silken strip tight around the unhappy woman's wrist, her despairing gaze fixed itself in deadly hate upon my face, and her foaming lips cursed me for keeping her away from her children. As her husband carried her away, her

curses pierced the air; and although I could not
understand the words, I understood that she spoke of
the " Czrny Bog," or, as the Russians say, " Cserny
Boh," the " Black God " of the Slavs—Death.

By this time the horrible tower was burning
brightly, and the night was all aglow with the glaring
light, and still those terrible shrieks from human
voices resounded to and fro.

The young artist had a picturesque scene for his
pencil, and kept making sketch after sketch. The
burning wreck, the flying cinders, the red mist around
the black pine woods on the rocky wall of the mountain, and that small span of star-lit heaven above;
all those frightened, maddened, running, crouching,
creeping men and women around, with the chanting
Jew, in his long silken *caftan* and dangling locks,
in the midst of them, made a picture of terrible
sublimity.

But still the god of destruction was unsatisfied,
and his fiery maw opened for more victims. The
unhappy young husband had succeeded in tearing up
his clothes and knotting the strips together. A com-
passionate woman had given him a shawl, which he
fastened to the bushes. On this he descended into
that mouth of hell. The perilous attempt succeeded
so far that, with one mad leap, he landed on the top
of the uppermost car with its pile of stones, and then,
with cat-like dexterity and desperate daring, he
scrambled downward to the third carriage. Quickly
he reached the spot, and the poor little gloved hands
of his darling were thrown in ecstasy around his neck.

Someone had drawn up the cord on which he had let himself down, fastened a stout iron rod to it, and suspended it carefully. Happily it reached him, and with its aid he made a good-sized breach, widening the opening of the window; he worked with desperate strength, and we gazed breathlessly on. Now we saw him drop the rod again. The tender arms of his bride were around his neck, a fair head was thrust out, the whole form was emerging, when with a tremendous crash, and a hissing, spluttering, crackling noise, the whole fabric shook and trembled, and husband and wife were united in death.

The great boiler had burst; the explosion had changed the scene again, and the young painter might draw still another sketch.

## III.

### THE ENGLISHMAN.

THAT long-legged son of Albion whom I had previously observed, strolled up to my side and asked—

"Do you understand German, sir?"

"Yes, sir, I do."

"Then call for that shepherd. I want him."

I obeyed, and the shepherd, who had complacently eyed the scene as something that was of no consequence to him, came slowly and wonderingly up.

He was in no hurry, and my coaxing "Dear friend" and "Good friend" did not impress him at all; but when the Englishman showed him a handful of gold coins he came on quickly enough.

"Tell him," said the Englishman, "to run to the next railway station, give notice of the accident, and return with a relief train for succour. Tell him to be quick, and when he returns I will give him two hundred francs."

"Yes," said the man; "but who will take care of my goats meanwhile?"

"How many goats have you?"

"Six."

"And what is the average price of a goat?"

"Fifteen francs."

"Well, here is the price of your goats in cash. I

give you one hundred francs—ten more than your goats are worth. Now run! How far is it?"

"A good running distance, not very far." The man pocketed his money and turned, when an idea struck him. "Could you not take care of my goats anyhow, till I return?" he asked.

Smart fellow! He kept the money for his goats, and tried to keep the goats into the bargain.

"All right," said the Englishman, "I will take care of them. Never fear. Go!"

"But you must take my stick and my horn; the goats will get astray when they do not hear the horn."

"Then give it to me, and I will blow it," said the Englishman, with admirable patience, and, taking the shepherd's crook and horn, he gave the man his red shawl to use as a signal-flag.

As the shepherd at length trotted on and disappeared, that unique, long-legged example of phlegm and good sense sat down by the shepherd's fire, on exactly the same spot where the shepherd had sat, and began watching the goats.

I returned to the mournful scene which I had quitted when the Englishman came up to me. It was a terrible one, and no marvel that even the painter had closed his sketch-book to gaze upon it in silent awe. The entire valley below showed like a giant furnace, or some flaming ocean of hell. Huge fiery serpents came hissing and snarling up to the barricade, and great flakes of fire were flying about everywhere, scorching and kindling as they fell. The

c

chill, keen, mountain air had become heavy and
warm in spite of the winter, and a loathsome, penetrat-
ing odour arose and drove us away from the horrible
place. No one remained but the Polish Jew. He did
not move away. He had risen to his knees on the
barricade wall, and his hands, with their prayer-bands,
were uplifted to heaven. Louder and louder he
chanted his hymns, raising his voice above the
thundering roar of the crackling fire, the rolling
stones, and the last despairing cries of the doomed
ones. The fur on his cap, his forked beard and dangling locks were singed by the falling cinders, and his
skin scorched and blistered, yet still he chanted on.
But when at last he saw that his prayer was in
vain, all at once he sprang up, and seemed to strike
at the flames with both palms; then, spitting into the
fire " pchi !" he fell down senseless.

By this time the heat was so oppressive that it was
dangerous to stand anywhere near the barricade, and
even for the sake of saving a man's life from such a
horrid fate, it was impossible to venture among the
falling cinders and rolling stones. All that the few
of us who had escaped with sound limbs and bodies
could do was to carry our less fortunate, wounded
or maimed fellow-travellers up into the little watch-
house.

This we did, and then came those seemingly endless minutes in which we waited for the relief train.
Once the Englishman blew the horn for the goats,
and we thought it was the whistling of the expected train. How terribly that disappointment was

felt! and what sinful, subtle, and sophistical thoughts crowded into our heads, burdened our hearts, and oppressed our spirits in those awful minutes!

What terrible thing had these poor victims done to deserve such fearful punishment? What heinous crime had they committed to be sentenced to death and destruction by such a painful, torturing process? Whose sin was visited on the guileless heads of little infants and innocent children who had perished in those flames? Could not they have been spared? or that loving and beautiful young couple, just on the brink of life and happiness, and now sent to eternity together by such a fearful road, into the mouth of hell when they had thought themselves before the open gate of Paradise? What had that unhappy mother done? or all these old and young men and women, in full health and spirits, enjoying life and happiness, surrounded by happy relatives, full of happy plans and hopes? What had they done to deserve this fate, those poor servants of the public convenience, the guards, the engineer, and the other officials, who could have saved their own lives easily, and in good time, if they had abandoned their fatal posts, and had not preferred to die in doing their duty? Why had not these been saved for the sake of their wives and children, now widows and orphans, abandoned to the charities of a merciless world? Who and where is that awful Deity into whose altar-fire that conjuring Jew had spat, because He would not listen to his invocations? What dreadful **Power** is it which has pushed down that rock-colossus **to**

destroy so many human lives ? Is it the Czrny Bog
of the Samaritans, the Lord of Darkness and Doer of
Mischief, whose might is great in harm, whose joy is
human despair, and who is adored with oaths and
curses ?

But if such a power exists—if there is a Czrny
Bog, indeed—then his deeds are befitting his name—
dark and black. But why should I, who am human
myself, and have a heart for my brethren and a sense
of their wrongs, why should I in this fatal instant,
although full of pity and commiseration, yet inwardly
rejoice that this misfortune has fallen upon others
and not upon me ? Why should I feel that although
others have perished, all is well as long as I am
safe ?

Is this not shameful ? Is it not an everlasting
stain and disgrace upon my inner self ? What right
have I to think myself the chosen ward of some
guardian angel or tutelary spirit ? In what am I
different from those lost ones ? In what better,
worthier than they ? And if not, why had I been
saved and not they ? Here ! Here was the Czrny Bog,
the dark god, in my own breast.

At last day was dawning, and, in the grey morning
light, the horrible picture looked ghastlier still, when,
to our intense relief, the long-expected train came, and
physicians with their assistants, firemen with their
manifold implements, police, and all kinds of labourers,
arrived upon it. The train stopped at a safe distance, and then the work of rescue began. Wounds
were dressed, the insensible restored, watchmen and

travellers were interrogated by officials. Ropes and rope-ladders were fastened and suspended, and brave men, magnanimously forgetful of the threatening danger, went down into the flames, although the hope of success was small. True, the two or three upper-most cars had not as yet caught fire; but who could breathe amid that suffocating smoke, that lurid loath-some atmosphere, and yet live?

The labourers set to work at the breaches of the barricade and the line of rails. The engineers dis-cussed the best way in which a protecting barrier ought to be built so as to shut out every possibility of such an accident; and from the plateau before the watch-house some men were incessantly calling for a "Monsieur d'Astrachan."

At last one of the labourers called my attention to these repeated shouts, and, turning in their direction, I observed that this title was intended for me. The watchman's wife, not knowing my name, had de-scribed me as wearing an astrachan cap and coat-collar, and accordingly I was called "Monsieur d'Astrachan." Now for the first time I remembered the child I had carried thither. I had completely forgotten it, and the occurrence seemed such an age away that I should not have been surprised to hear that the boy had grown to be a man.

I hastened up the steps, and observed that some official personage in showy uniform was expecting me quite impatiently. "Come up, sir," he said; "we cannot converse with your little boy."

"To be sure you can't!" said I, smiling, in spite of

the dreadful situation. "Neither can I, for the boy is deaf and dumb; but I have to correct you, sir. The boy is not my own, although I took him out of the carriage."

"That boy deaf and dumb? About as much as we are, I judge. Why, he is talking incessantly, only we can't make anything out of his prattle, as we do not understand the language," said the officer.

"Well, that's certainly a miracle!" I exclaimed, "and it bears witness to the truth of the old proverb, 'It is an ill wind that blows nobody any good.' Assuredly, the shock of the accident restored his power of speech. What is he saying?"

"I told you we can't make it out. It's a language that none of us understand."

"Then I hardly suppose that I shall be cleverer than all of you."

"Whose child is it, if not yours?"

"Some rich nabob's. I can't at the moment recall his name, although the governess told me, poor soul! We were thrown together by chance, and the poor woman perished in the flames. Has no one of his many attendants and servants escaped?"

"It seems not. But pray come in and listen to him; perhaps you will understand him."

I went in, and found my practical Englishman beside the child, but incapable of arriving at a mutual understanding. The injured travellers and the hysterical women passengers were already snugly stowed away in the ambulance carriages and well taken care of. The goats were again under the protection of their legitimate shepherd, and that temporary official, the long-legged son of Albion, was addressing all kinds of questions in English to an obstinate little boy.

As I entered, and the child caught sight of me, the little face lit up at once. He extended both his little arms in joy. "Please come," he said; "I will be a good boy. I will speak!"

It is marvellous enough when a dumb child speaks; but what was my surprise when I recognised these words, uttered in my own native Hungarian tongue! Just imagine the five-year-old son of a wealthy American, whose entire *cortège* had been German, French, Italian, and English, speaking Hungarian!

I took the little fellow up in my arms, and he put both his little arms around my neck, and, leaning his soft cheek on my bearded face, he said again, "I will be good, very good; but please take me to my papa. I am afraid!"

"Who is your father, my child?" I asked. "What is his name?"

As I uttered these questions in Hungarian, he clapped his hands in gladness, and then, after a little meditation, he answered—

"My father is called the 'Silver King,' and his name is Mr. Dumany. Do you know him?"

"Oh!" said the Englishman, as he heard the name, "Mr. Kornel Dumany, the Silver King; I know him very well. He is an American, and very rich. He lives mostly in Paris. If it is more convenient for you to get rid of the child, I can take care of him and bring him to his father."

"No, no!" protested the little one, clinging tightly to me. "Please, do not give me to him! I want to stay with you; I want to go with you to my papa!"

So he knew English well enough, since he understood every word of the Englishman's. In this case he could not have been deaf at all, but obstinate, hearing and refusing to talk. Was not such unheard-of obstinacy in a child of such tender age some malady of the mind or soul?

"I wonder how this child comes to speak Hungarian?" said I, turning to the Englishman. "Ours is not a language generally spoken by foreigners, least of all by the young children of American nabobs."

"I never wonder at anything," said he, coolly. "At any rate, I should advise you at the first station to telegraph to Mr. Dumany; I will give you his address. So you will be expected when you arrive in Paris, and have no further trouble. Since you are the only person able to talk to the boy, it will be certainly the best thing for him to remain with you. Now I think it is time for us to take our seats in the carriage, or else the train will start and leave us behind. Come on, gentlemen!"

## IV.

### THE NABOB.

THE train from Zürich arrived at the Eastern Railway Station at seven o'clock in the morning. In Paris the day has at that early hour not yet begun, and but very few persons, mostly travelling foreigners and labourers, are seen on the streets. Since it has become the fashion to use the moving train for suicidal purposes, the perron is locked, and only those travellers admitted whose luggage is undergoing examination by the customs officials.

I was lucky enough to have sent my luggage one day ahead of me to Paris, and so it had not been lost in the accident. I had nothing with me but a small satchel, which I had saved, but which contained nothing to interest the custom-house officers, and so, taking my little charge in hand, I stepped out into the hall. I had hardly gone two paces, when the child dropped my hand, and crying, "Papa! dear, darling papa!" ran to a gentleman who, with a lady at his side, stood by the turnstile.

I had never before seen the lady, yet I recognised her at once as the mother of my little charge, so striking was the resemblance between them. She had the same large, dark-blue eyes, the same dimpled chin, aquiline nose, and pretty, shell-shaped, little mouth as he, and she could hardly have been more than four-

and-twenty, so young and girlish did she look. The husband was a large-made, well-shaped, and distinguished-looking gentleman. His bronze complexion had a healthy flush, and he wore side whiskers, but no moustache. His head was covered with a round soft beaver, and a long, rich fur coat was thrown lightly over his shoulder. In his scarf I saw a large solitaire. The lady at his side was very plainly attired in black, and wore no jewellery at all. The age of the gentleman was, according to my judgment, about forty.

As the child ran toward him, with both his little arms stretched out, and crying, in Hungarian, "Apám! Drágo édes apám!" ("Papa! dear darling papa!") the gentleman hastened to meet him, caught the boy up in his arms, and covered the little face, hands, eyes, and hair with a shower of kisses. The father sobbed in his joy, while the child laughed, caressed his father's cheeks, and called him "Édes jo apám!" ("My good, sweet father!") in Hungarian, and the father called him, crying and laughing, "My dear little fool"—in English.

Then I saw the father whisper something to the child, and in an instant the whole little face became rigid and dull, all child-like mirth and sweetness had vanished. He looked around, and then clung tightly to his father, as if in dread of something, and I saw his lips move in appeal. The father kissed him again and carried him to the lady, who all the while had given no sign of animation or interest, but had looked on, cool and indifferent.

"Look, my pet, here is your mama!" said the gentleman to the boy, approaching the lady and holding the boy toward her. Now, according to the law of nature, according to all human sentiment and experience, we should expect a mother who receives back her own offspring, saved from a fate too horrible even to contemplate, her own child who had gone from her mute and comes back to her speaking, I say we should think it natural in such a mother to seize this child, and, in the ecstasy of her love and joy, half suffocate it with her kisses and caresses. Not so here. I could see no glad tear in the lady's eye, no smile of welcome on her face. Her hands were snugly stowed away in a costly little muff, and she did not think it necessary to extend them to her child. She breathed a cold, lifeless kiss upon the boy's pale forehead, and the tiny hand of the child caressed the fur trimming on her jacket, just as he had done with the astrachan lapel of my coat. What a strange behaviour in mother and child after such a reunion!

I had watched this family scene out of a strange curiosity, which was wholly involuntary. Presently I recollected the situation, and turned to leave the perron. Perhaps, if I had saved some honest cockney's son from a like danger, I should not have avoided him, but, with a friendly pressure of the hand, expressed my pleasure at having been able to be of service to him. Then we should have parted good friends. But to introduce myself to an American nabob as the rescuer of his child was impossible! Why, the man was capable of offering me a remuneration!

No, I would have nothing to do with aristocrats like these. They have their child; it is safe; and so good-bye to them!

However, as I turned to leave, I was surprised to hear some one pronounce my name, and, to my astonishment, I found that it was Mr. Dumany. He still held the child on his arm, and, coming toward me, he said in French, "Oh, sir! you do not mean to run away from us, surely?"

"Indeed I must!" said I, bowing. "But, pray, how is it that you know my name? You cannot know me personally?"

"Well, that is a question which must remain to be answered later on. At present it is sufficient to tell you that the telegraph service has been very full and exact, even in personal description. However, I beg you to revoke that 'I must,' for indeed I cannot allow you to depart. To the great favour you have done me, you must add the additional favour of being my guest for the time of your sojourn in Paris. Promise me to accept of my hospitality—nay, to regard my house as your own. I shall be ever so happy! Come, pray, do not hesitate, and give me leave to introduce you to my wife!"

With that he took my arm, and holding it tight, as if in fear I might break loose and run off, he led me to the turnstile, where the lady was standing as quiet and composed as before. He introduced me to her by my proper name and title, naming even the district which I represented in the Hungarian Parliament; and all these he pronounced perfectly and correctly, as I never heard them pronounced by a foreigner before. How could he know all that? True, I had shown my passport to the frontier officials; but were these also subject to the Silver King?

The lady bowed politely as her husband said, "This gentleman has saved our little James from being consumed by the flames at the Rossberg catastrophe"; and for a moment I felt the slight pressure of a little gloved hand in mine. It was a very slight pressure, the faintest possible acknowledgment of a duty, and if I had saved her little pet monkey or dog, instead of her child, she might well have afforded me a warmer recognition. Indeed, I had seen women go into raptures on account of such animals before this, but never before had I seen a mother value the life of her own child so cheap. She did not hold it worthy of a single expression of gratitude; she had not a word to spare for him or me. Was this woman a human monstrosity and void of all natural feeling? or else was it part of the American etiquette to suppress all outward signs of emotion?

What puzzled me most was the boy. He was so different from the happy, talkative little fellow he had been with me and with his father some minutes ago, and he looked just as dull and inanimate as when I had seen him first on the railway. Was it because he could only speak Hungarian? But then, how could he speak to his father? Who had taught the boy to speak that peculiar language, dear to me and my compatriots, but wholly unintelligible and of very little use or advantage to the world at large?

I observed that Mr. Dumany held a short conversation with a tall liveried footman behind him, and I
understood that he ordered him to take out my
luggage. I protested and tried to escape. I like
hospitality at home; but when I come into a foreign
country, I prefer the simplest inn or the obscurest
hotel to the most magnificent apartments of a palace
of a prince of the Bourse, because independence goes
with the former, and of all slavery I fear that of
etiquette the worst.

But Mr. Dumany did not mean to give way to
my polite protestations. "Just surrender nicely,
pray!" he said, smilingly. "It saves you trouble.
Look! If you insist upon going to some hotel, I
promise you that all the reporters of every paper we
have, daily and weekly, will be sure to pester you day
and night with interviews, besides the reporters of
foreign papers here, of which we also have an abundance. Every word you speak will by each reporter
be turned into a different meaning, and by to-morrow
the papers will be full of your intimations, although
you do not say anything at all. And then the photographers: how will you escape them? Don't you
know that every penny paper will appear with your
picture in front to-morrow, and, wherever you go, it
will be thrust before your eyes? You will hear your
name pronounced in all languages, and in every way,
and you will not know how to escape this unsought-
for and unwelcome notoriety. But if you accept my
invitation, nobody will be able to stare at you or
interrogate you, and you shall live as quietly and

peacefully as if you were in some herdsman's hovel in
Hortobágy at home."

I stared at him quite stunned. How, in the name
of all that was wonderful, could he have learned of
the existence of a herdsman's hovel in Hortobágy?
How could he know that it was my favourite spot?
And how he pronounced that Hortobágy! Just as I
myself! He smiled at my astonishment, but offered
no explanation. But now he had caught me in my
weak point—a writer's curiosity—and I gave in,
willingly enough.

Mr. Dumany ordered the carriages. In one magnificent landau Mrs. Dumany was to go with little
James, in the other Mr. Dumany and myself. But
the child obstinately refused to leave his father's
arms, and clung to him more tightly than ever. So
the lady was obliged to go alone, and we two men took
the boy with us.

I confess that the gentleman puzzled and interested
me very much. Not because people had given him
the name of "Silver King." I do not covet, and I do
not admire wealth alone, pure and simple. I know
how to describe a vine-embowered cottage, or even a
thatch-roofed hut, with a garland of gourd blossoms
around its small windows, and I can appreciate the
beauties of a picturesque church or castle. But all
my descriptive faculties desert me before the marble
and gold luxury of a modern palace, and its gorgeous
splendour has no charm for me. The interest I felt
was due to the man himself, and, most of all, to the
connection existing between him and my own home.

How came this American Crœsus to be acquainted with the nomenclature, customs, and topography of my own country and language? How came the latter upon the lips of his five-year-old boy? In my childhood I had known a five-year-old boy, the son of a count, who could speak only Latin, and not a word except Latin. But, then, Latin is taught throughout the world, and no education is considered as finished without a more or less perfect knowledge of Latin. But where in a foreign country is the professor who teaches the Ugro-Finnish tongue, even if there were some whimsical parent who wished that his son should learn to speak it?

During the drive Mr. Dumany acquainted me with some particulars regarding the customs of his house. He told me that the hour for breakfast was nine, and that for lunch one o'clock. Dinner was invariably served at six, and I was entirely at liberty to put in my appearance or stay away. They would not wait for me, but my place at the table would be kept reserved; and if I was late, I should be served afresh. The cook should be entirely at my disposal. If the excitement and fatigue of the journey should make me wish for a day's rest, I was free to retire to my rooms at once, and should not be disturbed by anybody.

In answer to all this I said that I had no habits whatever; that I was able to eat, drink, and sleep at will; was never fatigued, and would with pleasure put in my appearance at his breakfast-table that very morning.

"That will be nice, indeed!" he said. "But I must beg your pardon in advance for my wife. On ordinary days she is up and presides at breakfast; but to-day she bade me apologise. She has been up all night from excitement, and now I have told her to lie down and rest a few hours. After that she usually spends some time in the nursery, superintending the children's ablutions, prayers, and breakfast, and only when all these matters are accomplished is she ready for her duties as hostess and mistress of the household."

"So little James is not your only child?" I ventured to ask.

"Not by many; we have two more boys and two beautiful little girls—quite a houseful."

"But the lady looks almost too young to be the mother of so many children. Little James is the eldest, of course?"

"Yes, he is her first-born, and she is not yet twenty-four. We have been married six years, so christening has been an annual event with us."

Well, I was more puzzled than ever. I had met with a good many English and American gentlemen before, but all had been rather reserved in speech and manner, quite different from this Crœsus; and, regarding the lady, I was altogether at a loss, as all my conjectures were entirely at fault. She was not without feeling; she was apparently a good mother, and little James was her own child and not a stepson, as I had guessed. Her behaviour at the station was still an enigma to me.

D

At last we arrived at the Silver King's residence—a
large, well-built, and rather comfortable than brilliant
mansion, filled with a host of servants, of whom each
knew and fulfilled his particular duty.  A *valet de
chambre* showed me into a very splendid and comfortable suite of rooms, consisting of a reception-room,
sitting-room, work-room, bed-, dressing-, and bath-
room, all furnished in the choicest and most practical
way, and I was delighted to see that, although all
was rich and costly, none of the offensive and
pretentious pomp of the ordinary millionaire's house
met my eye.

The valet, an Alsacian, who talked to me in German—perhaps with the notion of paying me a compliment—informed me that he was entirely at my own
service.  He showed me a beautiful escritoire in the
work-room, with everything ready for writing purposes, and told me that, in the reading-room attached,
I should find an assortment of newspapers.  He then
quickly and skilfully prepared me a bath, unpacked
and arranged my things, and helped me to dress.  He
was altogether a wonderfully nice fellow.

When the valet left me, I went into the reading-
room, and looked at the newspapers.  I found quite a
number of them—French, English, Italian, and one
German; but still I was a little disappointed.  I had
half expected to find a Hungarian paper, and there
was none.

The library contained a choice collection of books;
works of science, philosophy, history, poetry, and
fiction—of the latter, only a small and select number.

Here also was no Hungarian author to be found; not
even the translation of a Hungarian book could I
detect, although I looked into every one—French,
German, English, and Italian, and even some Spanish
and Danish ones.

From the reading-room opened the billiard-room,
a handsome apartment. Its walls were covered with
beautiful frescoes, betraying the French school of art
in the delicate colours, and in the Norman, Basque,
Breton, and Kabyle scenes and types represented.
Of Hungary I could see nothing. The Hortobágy
herdsman's hovel, of which my host had spoken, was
not to be found.

In another room I found a sort of ethnographical
museum, full of relics and rarities from all countries
except Hungary; and yet, if that man had ever been
in my country, he would certainly have brought some
token of remembrance with him. Hungary is more
rich in curiosities than a good many of the countries
represented here.

Mr. Dumany came in to see if I was ready for
breakfast, and I followed him into the tea-room, passing a little, semi-circular, ship-cabin-like apartment,
with small, round windows, between which, in beauti-
fully-sculptured, round frames, of the size of the
windows, hung very handsome landscapes, apparently
American.

In the breakfast-room I recognised a tiny Meisso-
nier, in a gold frame of twice its size, and an Alma
Tadema. Mr. Dumany, observing my interest in
the pictures, informed me that these two were there

only temporarily, pending their shipment to New
York. There, in Mr. Dumany's real home, was his
picture gallery, containing works of art of the highest
standard.

I ventured to observe that we Scythians, bar-
barians as we were held to be, had also some painters
worthy the interest of a Mæcenas, and not without
fame, too.

"I should think so," he said, smiling. "And in my
New York gallery you will find Munkácsy *genres*,
Zichy *aquarelles*, a Benczur, and some other equally
fine Hungarian pictures. Here I keep only French
and German pictures of lesser value."

Our conversation turned to art in general, and Mr.
Dumany surprised me again by an allusion to the
Hungarian witticism that when we speak of Hungarian art we cannot omit Liszt (for the name of the
great musician is also the Hungarian word for *flour*);
and Mr. Dumany remarked that Americans travelling
abroad have learned to appreciate both the Hungarian
specialties. The great artist, and the product of the
soil and mill converted into fine cake, are equally
esteemed by them.

We talked about commerce and exports, and he
observed that although American wheat was sure to
inundate the European market, yet Hungarian flour
was unrivalled in quality, and would increase in consumption throughout the world. Then we spoke of
financial matters, and here Mr. Dumany was completely at home. The Hungarian rente had at that
time just been introduced into the market, and Mr.

Dumany predicted for it a fair success. He prophesied the rente conversion scheme and the four per cent. bonds, and from this topic we diverged to politics. He was a very fair politician, and I was pleasantly impressed by the apparent interest which he took in Hungary. He admired Andrássy, and spoke well of his Bosnian policy. Of Tisza he entertained great hopes, and he felt sorry for Apponyi, because he had allied his great talents with the Opposition. He spoke of Kossuth, and said it was a pity to see the grand old man's name misused by the extreme faction. I tried to turn the conversation to Hungarian literature, but on this point I met with but little interest. Still, I noticed that he knew more about us than foreigners in general do. He did not think the Gypsies the ruling race in Hungary, and he did not believe us to be a sort of chivalrous brigands, as some foreigners consider us; but he did not show any particular sympathy with either the country or the people, and certainly used no flattery on the subject of our special virtues.

Our conversation was interrupted by the entrance of Mr. Dumany's valet, who handed his master two letters. "Will you give me leave to read them at once?" he asked, turning to me. "They are of some importance, being answers to two dinner invitations I sent out this morning."

"Certainly," I answered; "pray do as you wish."

He opened and read the letters, and, replacing them again on the silver salver upon which the servant had brought them, he ordered him to hand them over to

the chambermaid so that Mrs. Dumany might receive
and read them.

After the valet had left, Mr. Dumany said to me—

" I have invited these two gentlemen to meet you
at dinner.  One of them is secretary of the Department of the Interior, the other an old Catholic priest,
the parson of St. Germain l'Auxerrois.  It is very nice
and pleasant that both of them accepted, and so I
hope you will not object to make the acquaintance of
two whole-souled and intelligent gentlemen."

" Quite the contrary," I hastened to say; "I shall
be very happy to meet them."

Just then the valet returned, and, deferentially
bowing, he said to me—

" Madame la Comtesse begs to inform monsieur
that she would be grateful if monsieur would be kind
enough to see madame in her apartments."

## V.

### A REPUBLICAN COUNTESS.

"MADAME LA COMTESSE!" A Peruvian or Argentine countess? Or have these plutocrats of the great republic some special distinguishing titles, such as "Silver King," "Railway Prince," etc., and was this exotic countess the daughter of some such lord of the money market? At any rate, I had to obey her polite commands, so, throwing away my cigar, I bowed to Mr. Dumány and followed the lead of the valet.

In crossing a long suite of tastefully-furnished rooms, I noticed the entire absence of family pictures. They had no ancestors, or did not boast of them. No farthingaled, white-wigged ladies in hooped skirts and trailing brocade robes; no mail-clad, chivalrous-looking gentlemen, with marshals' staffs, keys, and like emblems of rank and high station; or else these, too, had gone over to New York to subdue with their haughty grandeur the eyes of less high-born mortals.

There was something else I missed in these beautiful chambers—the usual obtrusive, caressed and pampered pet animal of a great lady. No paroquet, no monkey, no little, silken-haired lap-dog, no St. Bernard or Newfoundland dog, no cat, not even a little canary bird, was to be met with; and not a single flower, real or artificial, greeted the eye.

At last we came to a room with beautiful heavy
brocaded draperies, evidently veiling the entrance
into some other apartment. As the servant stepped
up and drew the hanging aside, I could not suppress
an exclamation of admiration and surprise; and for a
moment I stood transfixed at the lovely and exquisite
scene, deeming that fairyland had opened to me, and
that Queen Mab was expecting me in her own en-
chanting bower.

The room which I now entered resembled to some
extent the Blue Grotto of Capri. It was flooded with
a magic blue light. Just opposite to the entrance
was some kind of bower, with honeysuckle, wood-
bine, and other blooming and fragrant vines inter-
twined. This bower was prolonged in the rear into a
spacious and seemingly endless tropical garden, with
wonderful blooming exotic plants and trees; and in
this East Indian paradise, gaily-plumed, sweet-voiced
birds of different size and colour were chirping,
hopping, and hovering above their nests, among ever-
green bushes and glorious flowers. The whole winter-
garden received its light from above, and this light,
falling through large panes of blue glass, threw that
peculiar, fairy, grotto-like hue over the little boudoir
in front.

To prevent the luscious odour of the winter-garden
from pervading the air of the boudoir and becoming
oppressive, a fine, translucent film separated the bower
from the garden. But this film was not of glass or
any other transparent but solid substance; it consisted of a beautiful, clear waterfall, transparent as a

veil, and noiseless as a fine summer rain. At the touch of a spring, this softly-pouring waterfall might be shut off and the entrance into the winter-garden thrown wide.

In the little boudoir, at the opening of the bower, stood a couch, and opposite this a little settee and two small gilded and embroidered chairs; while two large sculptured frames, one containing a splendid mirror, the other a life-size portrait of Mr. Dumany, completed the appointments.

Mrs. Dumany, or, as she was called, the countess, wore a loose morning-dress of raw silk, with rich embroidery. Her rich, dark hair was uncovered and wound around her head in three thick coils, like a tiara.

Her graceful figure was as slender as that of a girl, and she looked so young and childlike that no living man would have supposed her to be the mother of five children.

In the peculiar blue light of the boudoir her naturally fair face appeared so white that I was almost startled. It was just as though some marble or alabaster statue had moved, looked at me with those large dark-blue eyes, spoken to me with those finely-chiselled, ruby-coloured lips.

"Pray pardon me for troubling you to call on me," she said, in fluent and precise French, although with a somewhat foreign accent and manner of speech; "I should not have done it were you not the only trustworthy person from whom I can learn the necessary particulars of the terrible Rossberg accident.

My husband, as perhaps you already know, has
invited two gentlemen to dine with us. One is a
government officer of high rank, the other a kind and
benevolent priest. My husband's intention is to
spend a considerable sum of money for distribution
among those who were injured in the Rossberg
catastrophe, or their destitute relatives. They shall
at least not suffer actual want, and although I daresay
that money is a poor compensation for a lost or
crippled husband and father, or son and brother, still
it is the only possible consolation we can offer them,
and in providing for their own future and that of
their dependents, we at least relieve their hearts of one
burden. Of this my husband wants to talk to the
government official. The priest was invited by me,
and I want him to hold a requiem for the souls of
those who perished, and to superintend the erection of
a memorial chapel at the place of the terrible accident.
Mr. Dumány is ungrudging in his charity, and
ready for any sacrifice of money ; but, you see, we know
really nothing about the particulars. How many
were lost, and how many died afterward in consequence of their injuries ? Who were they ? Of what
nation, faith, quality, and circumstances ? How many
were saved, and in what condition ? Have they
somebody to attend to them, to support them in
case of need ? And then those belonging to ourselves, our dutiful servants, I might call them our
true and faithful friends, has not one of them escaped ?
Have they all perished together ? You can tell me
best, and therefore I made bold to call you to

me. Do not hesitate, pray, but tell me all that happened, and in what manner it happened, from the dreadful beginning to the pitiful end—the whole catastrophe, with all the particulars you can recall to memory."

"Madam," said I, "pray do not wish that. These particulars are much too dreadful to relate—much too horrible for the ear of a lady. It requires strong nerves and an iron heart to listen to such a tale as that."

"And what of that?" she replied. "True, my nerves are not a bit less sensitive than those of any other woman, but I have learned to suppress them—to hold them down. Never fear me! Never spare me! If the scourge hurts me, I shall think it a penance. Go on! You hold the scourge—strike! Go on, I say!"

There was an impatient, almost fierce resolution in her voice, and I obeyed.

If this woman regarded the act of listening to the dreadful tale I had to tell as a penance, then, indeed, she allowed it to become a torture. I was obliged to recount the smallest incident of the ghastly event, and she drank in every word, shuddering as at some deadly poison. Again and again she questioned me with the skill and zeal of a professional cross-examiner. Nor would she let me omit a syllable. And when at the most fearful and heartrending point, her soft, dimpled chin sunk down on her breast, and her fair, babyish hand knocked at the tender bosom' *Mea culpa!* Oh, *mea culpa!*"

When she heard that the uncoupling of the parlour-car had caused a delay, she groaned. " Then all this terrible mishap is due to our own vanity ?" she cried. "A consequence of our own presumptuous pride! If our dependents had sat with the boy in a common carriage with other decent travellers, the train would have passed the fatal spot long before the landslide was in motion! But, of course, the Silver King's son is far too precious a creature to breathe the same air with other creatures of God's making. He must needs have a separate parlour to himself! And this sinful, detestable vanity of ours must cost the lives of so many good, brave, happy, and useful persons. Oh, hell itself must mock at our folly!"

Now this commination, unexpected as it was from a lady of wealth and position, was not altogether unwarranted, and so I went on.

As I drew near to the catastrophe I could hear the beating of her heart, and her breath came short and gasping. When I related how I had caught hold of the governess's hand, she was trembling, and an almost deadly pallor overspread her white face. "Alice! oh, Alice!" she cried; and when I told her how the lady ran back to the coupé for her bonnet, just at the last moment for escaping, she broke out into a painful hysterical laugh. "Just like her! Her bonnet! Yes; ha! ha! She would have come down to dinner in her bonnet, the foolish prude! She was so afraid to show her bare ears to a man! Oh! oh! Alice!"

At last the tears came to her relief, and she sobbed

pitifully. "If you had only known her goodness," she cried, "her self-sacrificing devotion, her pure, kind heart! She was the best friend I ever had, and how she loved that unhappy boy! She was more his mother than I, for she gave him all a mother's love and all a mother's care and attention. Why did I let her go with him? Why did I not keep her back from him?"

I told her how the poor woman's first thought had been the safety of the child.

"And you have not seen her again? You do not know what has become of her?"

I denied having seen her again. I could not describe to her the horrid spectacle of the poor woman as I had seen her last, when taken by the brave firemen from that infernal pile; for, strong as she forced herself to appear, this would have been more than she could bear; so I told her that the relief train started with the rescued before we could learn anything of the rest; but of the certainty of their death there could not be the slightest doubt.

"What a misfortune!" she sighed, wringing her hands. "Why, that boy had an escort with him like a prince royal! The honest Dr. Mayer, such a refined, generous young man; and Tom, the negro, my best servant, and the truest! He saved me from an alligator once, and killed him with an iron bar. He was severely wounded by the ferocious reptile, yet he laughed at his pains."

I remembered the grin on his broad black

face in the moment of death, as I had seen him
at the carriage window. He had laughed then
also.

"And poor little Georgie?" she asked again,
"James's playfellow and foster-brother? Georgie's
mother was James's nurse. How she begged of me
to take care of her darling, to bring him up well,
to make a priest of him! And how well I have kept
that promise! I have made more of him than a
priest: he is a saint, and a martyr. Oh, *mea culpa!
mea culpa!*"

When I had explained to her the circumstances
which had made all attempts at rescue impossible
for us, and afterward futile, she nodded. "I know it,"
she said. "On that evening I had not said my
prayers. We dined out late, and spent the evening
there. I could not come home to pray with my
children, and I could not say my prayers there. I felt
the heavy load on my heart, and once for a moment,
when I was not observed by anybody, I heaved a sigh
and said, 'God bless us!' It must have been at the
moment of the catastrophe, for my heart ached with
some vague and gloomy presentiment. Oh, me! our
neglected prayer, and such a fearful chastisement!
Tell me! Who is that terrible being that watches us
so relentlessly, and if he catches us napping but once,
hurls down those we love into death and destruction?"

Her marble-white face, her large wide-open eyes,
gave her the look of a spirit.

"Perhaps," said I, " the single blessing you asked,

saved the life of your dear child. Let this thought comfort you."

"James?" she said. "This child of sin and misfortune? Why, it was because he was on that train that all those pure and good people had to die! Oh, accursed was the hour of his birth! No, no; he is not accursed. I—I, his mother, that gave birth to him, I am guilty! He is innocent; he could not help it. Oh, *mea culpa! mea culpa!*"

She was beating her breast, and rocking herself to and fro, uttering her incessant "*Mea culpa!*" "Tell me more," she said again, presently; "show me more dreadful sights, that I may suffer more. I yearn for it; it will do my soul good—it is like purgatory. Go on!"

I took good care not to feed this religious frenzy further. On the contrary, I spoke of the practical Englishman and his performances, and of the artist who had sat there among all the terrible havoc and had drawn sketch after sketch.

"That picture we must secure, at whatever cost," she said, eagerly. "It shall be the altar-piece of the chapel which we are about to raise in memory of the tragic event and of the souls of the slain."

I had formed my own opinion of Mrs Dumany's state of mind. No doubt she was mentally deranged, and her special craze was religous monomania. From this arose the deep melancholy which held her own innocent babe responsible for the misfortune of others. This made the child repugnant to the

mother, and, no doubt, this was at the bottom of that
remarkable mutual estrangement between mother
and child.

I tried to quiet her. I told her that in a very
short period a great many serious catastrophes, such
as frequent earthquakes, great inundations, and
similar unfortunate and most terrible events, had
shocked the world and buried whole cities, destroyed
the lives and fortunes of thousands upon thousands of
happy and innocent persons. Even this Rossberg
catastrophe had been preceded by another at the
same spot, about the beginning of the present century. Such catastrophes were by no means to be
considered as a punishment from God Almighty, Who
is far too magnanimous to visit the sins of the guilty
upon the heads of the innocent, but simply as the
outcome of geological and meteorological phases of
our globe, depending upon natural laws. If anybody was really to be blamed for the present misfortune, it must be the engineer who had planned and
erected that insufficient barrier instead of a strong
bastion.

Mr. Dumany's entrance interrupted our painful
conversation. He came on the pretence that letters
and newspapers had arrived for me, and with that he
handed me a copy of the *Hon.*

"But I had them addressed to the Hôtel d'Es-
pagne," I said.

"They have been already informed that you are
here," he answered; and then, turning to his wife, he
said—

"Have you drunk deep enough of the bitter cup ?
or do you thirst for more of its contents ?"

His voice was soft and tender, and the wife threw
both her arms around the husband's neck, and, bury-
ing her face on his breast, she wept bitterly.

I took my journal, and, without making my excuses
to the lady, I silently stole out of the room.

E

# VI

## DUMANY KORNEL.

At dinner I was punctual, but nevertheless the two gentlemen of whom Mr. Dumany and his wife had spoken were already present and discussing the question of Mr. Dumany's munificent offer. After a hurried introduction I was soon informed of all that had been agreed on. The Secretary of State had received bonds for 1,000,000 francs, to be taken by the two Governments, the French and the Swiss, for distribution among the injured or maimed of the Rossberg catastrophe and the poor dependents of the slain. The old railroad watchman, who had been discharged by the company, and the canny shepherd, who both sold and kept his goats when he ran for the relief train, each received 10,000 francs, and a considerable sum went to the officials of the relief train as a remuneration for their services. The rest of the million francs was set aside for a memorial chapel on the site of the accident, and for the celebration of masses and a grand requiem in the church of St. Germain l'Auxerrois on the following day—a ceremony which was to be repeated annually.

I have forgotten to mention that although the dinner was sumptuous, and the dishes and wines were excellent, yet it was as stately, solemn, and unsociable a meal as a funeral banquet, and Mrs. Dumany presided in deep mourning. The only jewel she wore was a large cross studded with dark-blue diamonds, only recognisable as such by the rays of blue, yellow, red, and green light which darted from them. This cross was suspended on a chain of black beads resembling a rosary, and giving to the black-robed figure the appearance of an abbess. The Spanish lace mantilla which she had thrown over her beautiful hair served as the veil, and made the resemblance perfect.

At nine o'clock the government official and the priest took their leave, and Mrs. Dumany retired, to put her babes to bed, as she said—a duty which she always fulfilled herself, saying her prayers with them, and watching them until they slept. After the lady had retired, Mr. Dumany told me that even when he and his wife dined out, or were going to the opera, my lady invariably went home at nine o'clock to put her children to bed—a duty which she never omitted; but on the evening of the catastrophe she had been compelled to stay by the company present, and this had given rise to her self-accusations. She was nowhere happy but in the company of her children, who afforded her the greatest delight and amusement. I sighed, and, yes—I think I was actually guilty of the remark that Hungarian ladies of quality were equally good and dutiful mothers.

We went over to Mr. Dumany's bedroom for a cup of tea and a cigar. It was a grand room, lofty and spacious as a church, and if I had been a Chauvinist, I should have said that the rays of light in this room composed a tricolour of the same hues as the Hungarian flag. The beautiful hanging-lamp shed a green light, the glowing coals in the grate threw a reddish tint over the surrounding objects, and the large, richly-sculptured bed-canopy was all ablaze with white electric lights, arranged like a chain of diamonds above the heavy purple velvet hangings which encircled the couch and gave it a cosy and well-shaded effect.

We had hardly finished our first cigar, when Mrs. Dumany, or, as I should call her, the countess, came in. She wore a white wrapper, covered with costly lace and leaving her beautiful arms bare below the loose lace-trimmed sleeves. She led little James into the room, and, turning to her husband, she said—

"This boy obstinately refuses to sleep anywhere but with his father, just as before we sent him to the Institute."

The little fellow was simpering, and tottered drowsily to and fro. He was evidently very sleepy. Mr. Dumany took him up on his lap, unbuttoned his little boots, and pulled off the tiny socks. The mother stood there, looking on unconcerned, and presently she said, " Good-night !" and went out of the room.

The father undressed the child, and put him to bed ; then he drew the curtains aside ; the child knelt in bed, folded his little hands, and evidently said his prayers, for I saw his lips move ; but I could not hear a word. After he had finished, his father kissed him tenderly, covered him up with the angora rug, and, letting down the curtains, returned to me.

He had hardly sat down, when the bed-curtains moved, and the cherubic little head peeped out. "Papa! Papa!" said the child.

"What is it, darling?" his father asked, going back to him.

"I want you to kiss me again," he said, with a little mischievous smile.

After the boy had had his wish, he crept below the covering, and was soon fast asleep. Mr. Dumany observed that my cigar had expired, and that I looked rather drowsy. "You are tired," he said; "let me lead you to your room."

"I have not slept for the last two nights," I replied; "but I shall not trouble you, as I can find my room easily, or else I can ask the valet. Pray stay and rest yourself."

"Well then, good-night and sleep well!"

But however sleepy I had been the moment before, these few words were enough to drive sleep from my eyes for ten nights to come, and to raise my curiosity to the highest pitch, for they were spoken in clear, well-pronounced Hungarian.

I gazed at him in utter astonishment, and he smiled. "You did not recognise me," he said, "but I knew you at once. I knew you very well, too—at one time: we have been colleagues once."

"Indeed? And how is that possible? Pray where was that?"

"In Budapest, in the Sándor Utcza Palace, the House of Commons."

"You have been a member of the Hungarian

Parliament?   When?   And what name did you then bear?"

"The name I bear now, which is my own.   Only I used to write it in Hungarian, Dumany Kornel."

"Still I don't remember.   Neither your name, nor yet your face is familiar to me."

"Naturally enough.   I was in Parliament for only one day; the next day they conducted me out again."

"Ah, now I know you!   You were the dead man's candidate."

"Yes, you have hit it; I was the man."

Well, this was indeed a surprise.   All the drowsiness had entirely gone from me, and, turning back into the room, I asked, eagerly—

"Sir, have I some claim on your generosity?"

"Oh sir! my dear friend!" he cried, extending both hands to me, "I am your most grateful and obedient servant for ever.   I hand you a blank sheet, and, whatever you may be pleased to write upon it, I shall most willingly subscribe to."

"Then tell me how the right honourable Dumany Kornel, a member of the Hungarian landed gentry, and also of the medical profession, if I rightly remember, a rather fast-living bachelor, and rejected Commoner, has been metamorphosed into Cornelius Dumany, the Silver King, the South American nabob, the matador of the Bourse, husband of a beautiful countess, and father of five children, within such a short period.   Tell me this, for it is the only gratification I shall accept."

"And let me tell you, dear friend, it is the highest I could give," was his reply. "In fact, you have presented me such a draft that, in spite of all my wealth, I am unable to pay it at sight. I have to ask my wife's permission first. The story you want me to tell is but one half my own, the other half belongs to my wife, and you must allow me to ask her leave;" and, bowing to me, he left the room.

I was alone. No, not alone. From behind the bed-curtains issued a heavy groaning, as if the little sleeper were troubled with bad dreams. I went to him and lifted the hangings. The glare of the light awakened him, and he cried out, "Apa!" ("Papa!")

"Papa will come presently, my little one," I said in Hungarian, and he smiled happily.

"Oh, the Hungarian uncle!" he said, "that's nice;" and, taking hold of my hand, he caressingly laid his little, soft cheek on it.

"Have you been troubled in your sleep?" I asked.

"Yes," he said; "I was dumb again, although I wanted to speak and tried very hard. A snake was coiled around my neck, and choked me. There is no snake in this room? Or is there?"

"No. Don't be afraid of anything. Try to sleep again."

"You will stay with me?"

"Yes, until your papa comes back."

"Stay always. Papa would like it. He always used to say, 'Speak to me, my boy, only to me! I have nobody but thee to speak to me in our own Hungarian;' and now he has you also. How glad he must be of it! You will stay?—promise!"

I promised him to stay a long time, and, holding fast to my hand, he fell asleep again.

When Mr. Du Many, or rather Dumany, returned to me, I was sitting before the grate, musing over what the child's innocent prattle had revealed to me —the tender, loving recollection this man had of his home and the sweet sounds of our beloved mother tongue.

He came in with an animated face. "My wife has consented," he said. "She told me that it was confession-time. To-morrow she will confess to Father Augustin, and this evening I shall make you my confessor. Now that I have made up my mind to it, I really think that, even from a practical point of view, it would be much better if the truth should be known about us, rather than those wild, fanciful stories reported by gossiping American newspapers."

With that he rang the bell for the servant, and gave his orders for the night. Tea with mandarin liqueur at once, at twelve o'clock punch and fruits, at two in the morning coffee à la Turque, and at five o'clock a cold woodcock and champagne, were to be served.

"I hope you will be able to stand being up all night?" he asked.

"I think so. I am chief of the campaign committee at home."

"I beg your pardon. Then I know your quality. But it will possibly interest you to learn that the bill of fare I have issued consists entirely of products of my own raising. The tea comes from my own garden in Hong Kong. The mandarin is decocted from the crop of oranges grown in my Borneo orchard. The coffee comes from my Cuban plantation, as well as the 'gizr' spirit, obtained from the coffee bean. The woodcock is from my own park; and it is only the flour for the cakes that I have to buy, for that comes from Hungary, and there I own nothing."

"How is that? If I remember rightly, you had a handsome property there."

"Have you not heard that it was sold to pay my debts?"

"And you consented to that?"

"Well, first hear my story. However, I have told you an untruth. I am yet a landed proprietor at home; I own a cabbage-garden in the rear of my former castle. That garden is the only bit of soil I kept, and in this garden fine cabbages grow. Year after year the whole crop is sliced up, put into great barrels, and converted into sauer-kraut. This they send after me, wherever I happen to be—whether at New York, Rio de Janeiro, Palermo, or Paris—and from this, after a sleepless night, my wife prepares me a delicious 'Korhely-leves'" (a broth made from the juice, and some slices of cabbage, with sour cream and fresh and smoked ham, and sausages. This broth is in Hungary frequently served after a night of dissipation;

hence its name, "Korhely-leves," which means "Scamp's-broth").

"And the countess understands how to prepare the old-fashioned Hungarian delicacy?" I asked.

He laughed. "Ha-ha-ha! Why, she is as good a Hungarian as you or L If she speaks French, she only imitates our ladies at home, who think themselves so much more refined when they speak bad French instead of good Hungarian."

This was another revelation, and upset the other half of my fictitious combination. I had imagined that my countryman had won the love of some South American magnate's daughter, and in this way had become the possessor of his innumerable millions. Mr. Dumany might have read my thoughts in my face, for he smiled and said—

"You will presently understand that I did not rob, did not cheat, and did not marry for money, and yet I did not acquire my present great wealth by my own good sense and management, either. I'll show you by what road I have reached it, as a warning to others. May no other man ever do as I did! But I do not believe that such events are ever likely to happen again. I do not believe that there can ever be born another such a pair of thick-skinned, iron-nerved human beings as the heroes of this story, or two other persons able to endure what we endured. I will venture to say that the worldly wealth I have won is not worth the price I paid for it; but I have gained another prize, whose value can never be expressed in figures."

Thereupon we sat down at the little tea-table. Mr. Dumany threw a few logs of odorous cedar wood upon the fire and began his tale. So, from this point, the present romance is not written by me, but by him.

# MR. DUMANY'S STORY.

## VII.

### THE DEAD MAN'S VOTE.

I DO not think it necessary to particularly describe the borough for which I was nominated as a candidate for Parliament. If you know one, you know all. There were factions, of course, ranged into parties, one of which drank deep, while the other drank deeper still. There are a good many nationalities in this particular district, and they are distinguished by the liquor they prefer. The Slavs drink whiskey; the Suabians or Germans, beer; the Ugro-Fins or Hungarians, wine; and the more intelligent and cultivated of all the races show their agreement in matters of taste by drinking, alternately, wine, beer, or whiskey, with equal relish. Jehovah's own chosen people, considering it much more prudent and hospitable to serve the liquid to others than to drink it themselves, furnish all parties with the wished-for fluid, according to individual taste, and find the transaction even more satisfactory and profitable than drinking in itself.

If Dante had visited Hungary, and had seen my particular borough in election-time, he would not have omitted it in his description of hell.

Yet the highly respectable voters expect a substantial confirmation of their patriotic convictions, and some of them are not fully persuaded until four or five angels (golden, of course) come to enlighten their minds. Others refuse to listen even to the sweet voices of these angels, and wait obstinately for the mightier spirits, emblazoned on fifty and one hundred florin bank-bills. Others, again, are to be had only *en bloc*—that is, in company with their friends and connections, and only just at the last moment, when the bidding is highest; and so tender is their conscience that they listen to the persuasions of all parties with equal earnestness, and it takes much to convince and win them over.

It is a matter of course that the nominated candidate of each party is far above such negotiations, and, although he owns that it has come to his knowledge that his antagonist actually stooped to bribery in order to defend his weak cause, yet he himself will never condescend to meet the man on that ground. If his own moral integrity, the lofty standing of his party, and his party's principles, will not secure the victory for him, why, then there is no honesty and patriotism in this decayed age, and the patriotic cause is lost!

At every election, as you well know, are a number of kind, disinterested, active, and zealous party members, indefatigably busy in securing and collecting votes, or, what is more essential, trying to win over the votes of the enemy. These very useful and highly respectable gentlemen are leaders or drum-majors, and they have a number of subalterns, not less useful,

painstaking, and persuasive, only a little less gentle-
manlike and less scrupulous, and perhaps not wholly
disinterested as regards pecuniary gain. These are
the election drummers, plain and simple.

Now at the election of which I am speaking there
were two factions. I, as the champion of the Clerical-
National-Conservative party, stood in opposition to
the champion of the Panslavonic-Liberal-Reform
party, and you may believe that we did all that was
possible to defeat the opposing faction. My own
party emblem was the red feather, that of my adversary the green feather; the national cockade we
sported in common.

At six o'clock p.m. the green feathers were one vote
ahead of us. "This is not to be endured!" shouted
my head drummers, and "This is not to be endured!"
was the war-cry of the subordinate drummers. But
how could they help it? The lists were scrutinised
again, and it was found that Tóth János, the potter,
had not voted. "Where is Tóth János, the potter?
and why did he not vote?" added my chief drummer.
"Beg pardon," said one of the subalterns, "but the
man was buried the other day."

"Well, that was a calamity. Is there no other
Tóth János in the village? The name is rather a
common one."

"There is indeed, and he happens to live in the
same house with the deceased, only he is not a voter,
as he does not pay taxes; he is only a poor poultry-
dealer. Still he is on the list as a carter, and the
thing could be managed."

Tóth János, the poultry-dealer, was sent for, but his voting in his own right was out of the question. So the drummers talked with him a long time, and they had glib tongues, and the aid of the ever-welcome angels. Tóth János the poultry-dealer, who could not vote in his own name, voted as Tóth János, the potter, but he had a great sacrifice to make. The deceased potter was nick-named the "gap-toothed," because he had lost his front teeth in a brawl. Now the poultry-dealer's front teeth were as sound as ivory, yet so great and effective were the persuasions of the "angels" that, in half an hour's time, Tóth János, the poultry-dealer, so closely resembled Tóth János, the potter, in outward appearance that no question concerning his identity was raised, and his vote was recorded.

Still, this was insufficient. True, we were now even with the foe, but we were compelled to show a majority, even if it consisted only of a single vote. If Richard III. could offer "a kingdom for a horse," why should not we offer "1,000 florins for a vote?"

Somebody made the discovery that on the outskirts of the village, in an old tumble-down shanty of his own, lived a poor Jew with a lot of half-starved, forlorn-looking children, and a half-crazed, careworn, hard-working wife. The husband and father had been laid up with consumption for the last few months, and was daily expected to die. This poor wretch, who never in all his life had been the owner of an entire suit of decent clothes—for when he had a hat, he invariably lacked shoes, or when in possession of a coat, he was in sore want of a pair of trousers—this poor fellow had yet a fortune at his call, for he could bequeath to his family the 1,000 florins which we were willing to pay for his vote. All his life he had been as honest as he was poor, earning a miserable livelihood by setting glass panes in the village windows. Nobody had ever thought of getting his vote, still less had he himself thought of attaching any importance to the right he possessed as a tax-payer. Our drummers found the poor fellow just in the act of taking leave of this vale of care and sorrow; but they would not have been the smart fellows they were if they had not succeeded in defeating Death himself, and robbing him of his prey for as long as they needed. The dying man stared vacantly into their faces when they offered him this enormous sum of ready money, while his wife and children broke into a howl of despair that the offer had not come earlier, for how could a dying man leave his bed to vote? But my drummers were not to be beaten. They caught up the bedstead with the sufferer on it, and hastened with it to the tent where the votes were collected. The dying man had been made to understand that the bill of 1,000 florins which he saw would be given to his wife, if he would only pronounce my name when asked to whom he gave his vote, and he held tight to his wife's hand, and met her appealing glance with something like assurance. Happily, he was still alive when brought to the urn, and the drummers announced that "the poor man was

troubled in his conscience, and could not die unless
the opportunity of fulfilling his patriotic duty was
afforded him, so that he had begged them to bring
him to the tent and allow him to vote." This touching little piece of news was received in the spirit in
which it had been given, and just as the poor fellow
in his agony was asked the name of his chosen
candidate, Death came to claim his own. With a last
look of sorrow and affection at his wife he sighed with
his dying breath, "Du mein liebe!"* ("Thou, my
love!"), and expired.

"'Nelly Dumany! Dumany Nelly!' he said," cried
my drummers — "Nelly" being an abbreviation
of Kornel, my Christian name—and since the "Du
meine" really sounded like "Dumany" and not at
all like "Belacsek," the candidate of the other party,
and since the dead man could not be made to repeat
his vote, whereas my drummers were ready to take
their oath of the correctness of their assertion, the
vote was credited to me, and I was declared elected
by a majority of one vote, my suffrages being 1,501 in
number, whereas my adversary had received only
1,500.

The case was afterward contested, and some witnesses endeavoured to prove that the dying man had
not said, "Dumány Nelly," but "Du mein liebe";
yet there was the sworn statement of my drummers
to the contrary, as well as the evidence of his wife
and children that the man had been a devout and

* The Jews in Hungary usually speak German among themselves.

F

religious Jew, incapable of offending Jehovah by
uttering German words with his last breath. He had
simply pronounced my name in Jewish fashion, and
eased his patriotic heart by voting for me. Itzig
Maikäfer's vote was as sound as a nut and could not
be rejected.

Not quite so sound, however, was the other dead
man's vote—that of Tóth János, the potter. We had
sent his substitute, the poultry-dealer, with a cartload
of odds and ends to Galicia, just to have him out of
the way. We managed to make it difficult to prove
which of the two men named Tóth János had been
buried two days before election-day by providing for
the dead man's family, and sending them off to a
remote place; and as the poultry-dealer (who was a
widower without any family) did not return from
Galicia for many weeks to come, everything seemed
secure. But we had reckoned without our host, and
did not take into consideration a possible treachery.
The barber, a miserable wretch, whom we thought to
be a true red-feather man, and who had been more
than liberally paid for extracting the poultry-dealer's
front teeth, and trimming his hair and beard into the
semblance of those of the dead potter, went and
blabbed of his work. A strict examination followed,
the body of the potter was exhumed, and his identity
proved to a certainty. Of course, no one dared to
accuse me of foul play, but a new election was found
necessary, and the day after I had first taken my seat
as a member of the Hungarian Parliament, I was
politely but firmly given to understand that I had no

legal right to its possession, and had better go. This
is the story of how I became to be called "the dead
man's representative," and how I was a colleague of
yours for a single day.

Yet this story I have told you cannot give anyone
a fair or true estimate of me, or my character, or ability.
Anybody who heard or read this story would suppose
me to have been a vain, good-for-nothing sort of
fellow, who had missed his degree at college and
lacked the ability to fill any decent position, and
therefore plunged into politics to make his living,
or perhaps to squander the inheritance he had
received from his ancestors. But, in reality, I had
already, at the age of six-and-twenty, occupied the
position of a well-qualified assistant physician, and at
two-and-thirty the newspapers spoke of me as a
famous specialist and a great light of the profession.
As I was established in Vienna, where the competition
is great, and Hungarians are pushed into the rear
if possible, my reputation could not have been without
some foundation at least. I was respectable and
respected, very much in love with my profession,
and did not care a straw for politics. So, in order
to make you understand the change—nay, the entire
revolution—which my outward and inward man, my
entire existence, had experienced, I must acquaint
you with a portion of my family troubles and domestic relations, and I shall have to speak of my
Uncle Diogenes.

## VIII.

### MY UNCLE DIOGENES.

FIRST of all, I must inform you that my father was a very zealous patriot, and mingled largely in state and political affairs. Of course, in the great insurrection of the year 1848 he took an active share, and after the catastrophe of Világos he was seized and imprisoned at Olmütz. At that time I was a lean, overgrown youngster of sixteen. I was compelled to take charge of the household, and behave as head of the family, for which dignity I had no inclination and but little talent. Study was the great object of my life. After my father's release from prison I was just of an age to decide as to my future career; but that, at the time, was rather a difficult thing for a Hungarian youth, all offices and positions being filled by Germans and Bohemians. I did not wish to follow in my father's footsteps, for I saw that what with his neglect of business matters, what with his liberality in furnishing all patriotic enterprises out of his own pocket with the necessary means, and in extending a wide hospitality to all political refugees, our own circumstances were getting worse and worse, and we were deeply in debt.

So one day I took courage to speak to my father upon the subject, and told him that I thought it was time for me to select a profession.

"Oh! you are going to hunt for some paltry office in the district courts?" he said, with a snarl.

"No! I am going to study as a physician," I replied.

"What? Do you want to be a barber or a veterinary surgeon, or one of those curs who pretend to look after the wounded so that they themselves may keep out of danger when their betters fight? Imagine a scion of the Dumanys, and the last one, too, wanting to be a sick nurse instead of a man! I have a notion to shoot you on the spot!"

"That you can't, for our present ingenious Government takes precious good care that such dangerous persons as my father shall not be left in possession of a rifle or any other shooting-iron; and surely you will not butcher me? Come, father, be reasonable! You know well what I mean to become, and that the calling I have selected is honourable and respected."

"It is not fit for the son of a gentleman and a Dumany. If you dare to follow such an insane course, you may be sure of my malediction, and, besides that, I'll discard you—disinherit you!"

"I am very much afraid, papa, that if our present course lasts awhile longer, there will not be much left to bequeath to your heirs. So I am not afraid of that threat; and as to maledictions, you are much too kind and good-natured to utter such stuff; and, besides, curses are just as harmless and useless as blessings. The Frauenhofer lines tell us all the secrets of hell, and so I am not at all afraid of them. But I am terribly afraid, dear father, that the road which you **have** pursued will lead us to ruin in a very short time."

I had taken precise accounts of all that we possessed and all that we owed. I had computed these accurately, and showed him the result, which was rather alarming; but he waved the document away with his hands, and said, "Don't be foolish; don't worry about these little inconveniences, which can't be helped, and will soon cease to trouble us. Why, there is your uncle Dion, with eighty-seven winters on his head (may God rest him!) and not a soul to leave his large fortune to, but you, his only nephew! Bless my soul! what a nuisance is this boy! Instead of going to this paragon of an uncle, and trying to get into his good graces, as his next of blood and kin, he talks of becoming an apothecary, smearing plasters, mixing poisons, and setting sprained joints. Go to thy uncle, I say, like a dutiful nephew, and doctor him, if doctor you must!"

"I have been to him already, and have told him of my intentions."

"'Pon my word! And then?"

"He gave me the money to pay my preliminary expenses, and I hope to get along afterward by myself."

"Well, to think of Dion giving away anything but advice! It's a treat! And what did he say?"

"That I was right and sensible in providing against the future; for he knows of your difficulties."

"Stuff and nonsense! He can't last for ever, and

then where is the need for your troubling yourself about my difficulties or studying for a profession ? "

" You are mistaken : he will not leave us a penny ;
neither do I care for his money. All I wanted of him
I have got, and there is an end of it."

" Then don't say that I am an unnatural or unfeel-
ing father. I'll give you thir—no, twenty florins ! "
But he never said whether these twenty florins were
meant to be given monthly, or only once for good and
all. However, as I did not ask for them, I never got
a penny, and soon learned to do without my father's
money by giving lessons, coaching less diligent and
capable fellow-students, and contriving to live upon
almost nothing.

But I wanted to speak to you of my Uncle
Diogenes, as he was generally called, although his
Christian name was Dion. He was my father's
brother, but by no means like him. Rather an odd
sort of a fellow, and as keen as a razor. He went even
beyond the old classical types ; he was more cynical
and more of a philosopher than they. Not the oldest
inhabitant remembered the time when the cloak that
covered his stooping shoulders on the street was new.
Daily he went to church, never into church. There,
on the sacred threshold, among the beggars and out-
casts, he paid his homage to his Maker, and then returned to his desolate home. There was a large public
well in the village. To this he himself went with a
large pitcher for his drinking-water. This water he
poured into a large boiler, boiled and strained it, and

then drank it, because then he was sure of the bacilli.
He kept no attendant or housekeeper, for fear of
being murdered; and he was so much in dread of
poison that he never ate cooked food or anything
made of flour, not even bread. He lived on baked
potatoes, nuts, honey, raw fresh eggs, and all sorts of
fruits and vegetables which might be eaten raw, and
which grew in his own orchard and garden. Out of
his large herd of cattle he selected a cow for his stall.
This cow he attended to with his own hand, carefully
examining each stalk or haulm she ate, in order that
no poisonous weed might be consumed by her, and
thus poison the milk. Each morning and evening his
own hands milked her, and he churned all his butter,
and made all his cheese himself. He never ate anything but what I have mentioned, and he never went
out without two loaded double-barrelled pistols in his
boots. He never read any other newspaper than the
Slavonic *Narodne Novine*, which he got from the
village parson; but, before reading it, he held it over a
charcoal fire, on which he had thrown some juniper
berries, to kill possible malarial germs. His land
was all farmed out, and the rent had to be paid to him
in gold or silver, which he locked away in a great old
iron chest. Occasionally, through auctioning off some
poor debtor's effects, he came into possession of bank
bills, 50, 100, 1,000 florin notes. These he rolled up
separately, and pushed one by one into a hollow reed.
Of these stuffed reeds he made bundles, which he
stowed away in a corner of his room. He never lent
a penny of his money; he never put a penny into any

savings-bank, for he called them all humbugs; and
he never gave a penny for charity or friendship.
Such was my Uncle Diogenes or Dion; and now I will
tell you what he had given me. You remember I
told my father that my Uncle Dion had furnished me
with the means of paying my preliminary expenses.
That was true, but I had earned the money, little as
it was, in ciphering, writing, and riding about to my
uncle's tenants at a time when he was ill with a cold,
and would have been obliged to pay a stranger for the
work which I did for him. I said it was little he
gave me. I have not told the whole truth, for he
gave me his advice, and put his own example before me, and that made a small sum go a long
way.

Well, to make a long story short, let me tell you
that I was an established physician when my father
died, and immediately after his death his estate was
seized in bankruptcy proceedings.

I did not care. I was satisfied with my position in
Vienna, and as I had no mother nor sisters or dependent younger brothers, and had long ago relinquished
the hope of coming into possession of our family estate, I tried to forget my former home and live only
for my profession.

After my efforts had made me a name as a clever
and skilful specialist, I was occasionally called to
visit some wealthy patient in Hungary, and then the
papers gave accounts of the diagnosis I had given, and
mentioned the generous fee I had received. I did
not approve of this sort of advertisement, but I found

that it could not be checked, and so grew indifferent
to it.   One day I received a registered letter containing money.  It was stamped all over with the cheapest
kind of sealing-wax, and, on opening the envelope, I
was surprised to find a letter from my Uncle Dion,
with an old, crumpled hundred-florin bill, of a kind
that had long gone out of circulation, and which
showed every mark of having issued from one of the
hollow reeds.  The letter ran about as follows :—

"MY DEAR NEPHEW, DR. DUMANY,—Knowing well
that physicians will not move a step without being
well paid, I send you the enclosed bank-bill, and pray
you to take the trouble to visit me for a few days here
in my house.                 "DUMANY DION."

I took the bank-bill, put it into a fresh envelope,
and wrote the following lines :—

"MY DEAR UNCLE,—One hundred florins will not
induce me to leave my patients, and so I return the
bill; but if you are really in need of a physician, and
want me in that capacity, then please let me know,
without enclosing money, for I should consider it my
duty as a near blood-relation to give you my professional assistance without delay.—Yours,

"DUMANY KORNEL."

By return of post came the answer—"Yes, I wan
you immediately."

I went at once.  It was ten years since I had seen
him last.  He was eighty-seven then; he must be

ninety-seven now. A rare age, indeed! When last I saw him, his long and thick white hair had reached to the middle of his back, and his long untrimmed beard flowed down to his girdle, and was the colour of hemp. His eyes were as sharp as those of any young man, and he did his reading and writing without an eye-glass. Even his grafting he did without an artificial help to his vision. I remembered well the old custom for guests arriving at his house: coach and servants had to be left at the inn, and dinner had to be ordered there. Whoever came to visit the lord of the château, quite a magnificent old-fashioned country seat, had to enter through a narrow garden-gate, just wide enough to admit a single person. The great gate was never opened, no vehicle of any kind was admitted to pass through it, and a thick growth of horse-sorrel, both without and within the great oaken wings, bore witness to the fact. There was a turnkey at the little gate, and an old man—the only servant my uncle ever kept, who served for porter, gardener, and all other purposes—opened the door.

There was yet one tender spot in my uncle's heart, one sprinkle of poetry in his nature. He adored flowers, especially roses, and he did not even grudge money to secure rare specimens. His flower-garden was a real fairy bower, and the old man, with the flowing snow-white hair and beard, pruning and grafting continually, resembled some sorcerer who, with a single touch of his withered hands, could create or destroy all the beauty around him.

I found him there among his roses when I came. He recognised me at once, although the last ten years had considerably changed my appearance. He was looking just the same as he did ten years ago; not altered in the least. He was as dry, as wrinkled, and as white as when I had last seen him, and his eyes appeared by no means less sharp than at the time I speak of.

"Happy to see you, my dear fellow!" he said. "I should have known you wherever I met you. You look like the old boy you were."

"So I do, because of my clean-shaven face, uncle. I do not care for the manly beauty of a moustache and beard. But I must return your compliment. You have not aged in the least, and I can hardly believe in your wanting a physician at all. You do not look like it."

He chuckled. "Well, well, I don't think you are much mistaken; but sit down here in the bower: my room is not quite so pleasant and orderly a place. I must call the gardener——"

"Don't take the least trouble, uncle," I said. "I shall not stay with you, as I ordered a room at the inn and also my dinner. I had a hearty lunch half an hour ago, and so you need not worry about my comfort. Now tell me what ails you, pray, and then I'll see what I can do for you."

"Nothing in the least with regard to my health, for I am not a bit worse than I was ten years ago, and far better than most others at my age. I am ninety-seven, as you know, and that's no trifle. It would be foolish to expect anything better, and you could not prevent my dying about this time next year."

"Oh! you are hypochondriac, I see, and give way to fancies! Come in, and let me examine you professionally, for such fancies are always the result of some serious disorder."

"There you are mistaken, my boy. My heart, lungs, liver, and the rest of it are all right, and I am not melancholy. Neither am I weak-minded or nervous, and you need not look into my eyes or feel my pulse. I have known these four years that I am to die at the time I mentioned, although I am sure, when I tell you how I came to know it, you will call me superstitious. For you fellows of the present day are so sceptical and matter-of-fact that you refuse to believe in anything that cannot be proved by optical inspection or by evidence. It was, as I said, just four years ago, on my ninety-third birthday, when St. John the Nepomuc appeared to me in a dream, and said— 'Dionysius, my good fellow, make the best of your time! There are only five more years for you in store, and then you must die! no help for it!' Since that time he comes to me every year regularly on the night of my birthday, and repeats his warning, each time giving me one year less. Last week was my birthday, and he gave me the last warning. Next time he comes I shall have to go. So——"

"But, my dear uncle," I said, rather vexed, "if you are so much convinced of the certainty of your death, then it was not at all necessary for me to come. You want the priest, and not the physician. I can cure bodily diseases, and release you from the clutches of cholera, or sometimes even of death; but if the saints have got hold of you, and such a tight hold, too, then you had better go to your confessor, for it is his business to be in close connection with all of them. I give you up. Good-bye! I have patients in Vienna, and cannot afford to waste my time on a pleasure trip."

"Good God! what a hot-tempered fellow, and what admirable rudeness! Stay, you unmannerly specimen of honesty, who don't think it worth your while to cajole an old fool for the sake of his money! What do you think that I summoned you for? But none of your impudence, if you please!"

I was amazed, and must have looked so, for the old man broke into a merry laugh, that sounded like two pieces of cracked iron rubbing together. There was a merry twinkle in his eye even after his laugh, and he regarded me with a humorous expression which was entirely new to me.

"Well," he said, "I see that you are somewhat slow of apprehension; not at all as sharp as others of the family. So I must help you out. I am going to make my will. There!"

"Well then, you had better consult a lawyer or a notary. I am neither of the two, and cannot be of the least use to you."

"That's gospel truth. But as you are the only sensible person of the whole family, the only one who is not a prodigal, and have made shift to live decently upon your own earnings, I rather think that I may be of use to you. I like you, because you browbeat me and do not flatter me, and I will tell you the truth; that bank-bill which you returned to me strongly interested me in your favour. There was a time when I was not the shrewd hard fellow that I am, but a true Dumany and a spendthrift. I can show you a heap of signatures from nearly all the members of our family—that is, the elder members—every one given me as security for money I have lent them; but that money was never returned to me, and although I have always believed that spirits will break their bonds and return to their former home, I never believed in a bank-note's return until you showed me the miracle. Therefore I have decided to make you my heir, and I have called you to witness the will and——"

"Not a word more," I said. "I never speculated upon anybody's death, and do not intend to change my habit. I never took the trouble to inquire how much of my poor father's fortune was swallowed by the lawyers, although I know that, after paying all of his debts, there must have been a handsome penny left, and I could have recovered that money if I had cared to see about it. I have earned for myself a respected position and a decent living, and I expect to do better yet. So thanks to you for your kind intention, but I am not the man you want."

"Yes, you are, and the more so because you do not worship the golden calf, and do not want to hurry me into my grave as the others do. To tell you all: I wish to settle everything on you while I live, the

estate, the house, the money, and all—no, don't run
away! I am not crazy, and you need not be afraid
that I want you to live here with me in this old hall
as it is, mouldy and dirty and desolate. Neither do
I want you to share my diet of fruits and raw vegetables, eggs and milk, and baked potatoes. On the
contrary, I want you to come to me and live like a
gentleman, as a Dumany should, and let me enjoy
life with you."

## IX.

### A SLAVONIC KINGDOM.

"You see, my dear boy," continued the old man, fondly taking my hand and pressing it, "it is a princely domain that I offer you, and a princely income. The station I invest you with is that of a king in its way, and not a small way, either. Now listen to me! For a great number of years I have lived here on this spot, like one of those hermits of bygone times, living on roots and other primitive food, and never tasting of a decent cooked meal, because I have never ceased to fear that those who wished to get my money would try to poison me in order to get it sooner. This fear I know no longer. I know well that my time expires next year; but of this one year of life I am assured, and I am resolved to make the best of it. I want to eat nice roasts, good cakes, and other delicate dishes, and I want to drink wine. I have not tasted wine since 1809, when I was studying law and attached as juratus to the Personal. For many years I did not seem to care about it; but now I long for it, and I remember how delicious it used to taste."

"But, my dear uncle, this would not be wise. Such a change would absolutely kill you."

"Tut! tut! Never fear! I am sure of the one year, and am not going to bargain with Death for more. Give me the one year, and let me enjoy it according to my wishes—that is all I ask for. But for a safeguard against extravagances, should not I have a skilled and renowned physician living with me and looking after me daily? Don't you see that your professional attendance will prevent all evil results, so that I shall be perfectly safe? I could not have lighted upon a better plan than making you my heir, and letting you live with me. Of course, I could have taken a housekeeper; but I know womankind. In less than half a year she would have persuaded me to marry her and settle all my belongings on her, and this would not do for a Dumany. But if you come to live with me, everything will be different. I'll let you have the whole mansion, and keep nothing but my old room, of which I am fond, because I am used to it and to the old, dingy, broken furniture that's in it. You should marry, and bring your pretty little wife into the house, and she would sing to me and play the piano or the organ, and would keep pretty little chambermaids that I could pat on the cheeks, and your little wife would let me kiss her fair, soft little hands; it would be delicious! Then I should hear a little scolding and quarrelling in the house, and you would take care that your little lady-wife should not spoil me by too much fondness, and you would order my dinners and select my wearing apparel according to my health. Perhaps I might sleep a little after meals at the open window—a luxury I always longed for, but did not dare to indulge in. This would be life for me, and a slow and sweet transit from the cares and troubles of this world into heaven."

The old man became quite excited over this ideal picture of happiness. "I speak of heaven," he continued, "and this reminds me of the church. Do you know why I say my prayers outside among the beggars, and never go into the church ? Not out of humility, but because at present there is only a simple Slav minister here, and I am not over-anxious to listen to his orations. Besides, the church is always so full of the Slav peasants that you cannot breathe inside of it, such an infernal odour is diffused by them. But if you would come to live here, and bring a gentle little Hungarian lady with you, perhaps the bishop could be induced to send some nice Hungarian priest to preach to us; and I am very fond of a good sermon, especially if I could listen to it comfortably in my pew, as you may wager that not one of these burly peasants would go inside the church if the service were held in Hungarian. And then just fancy the happiness if there should be a christening in the family, and I should be godfather to your son ! Would not that be glorious ? Oh, if I could live to see it ! You must make haste and marry, or I'll put speed into you, you may rely on that ! "

I was ready with my diagnosis by the time he had finished his last sentence. Hallucinations born of religious frenzy; idiosyncrasies with allotriophagical symptoms, a consequence of his ascetical mode of living; nymphomania of old age; hypochondriacal fancies: all symptoms that are frequently found together. To second his morbid intention of changing his diet and habits would be sheer lunacy; nay, worse, it would be actual murder. Yet first I must win his confidence as a physician, so that he may trust me and take my advice. I embraced him, and thanked him most heartily and tenderly for his kind intentions, which I should never forget and should always feel grateful for; but I said, brilliant and splendid as it was, I could not accept his proposition, I could not give up the career I had entered, the profession I had embraced and which I loved, and the independent and honoured position I was proud of. My calling was everything to me—life, happiness, fortune, and ambition; and to give up my profession in order to till my farm, to exchange my study, laboratory, and dissecting-table for the petty cares and troubles of a country squire and a county member, would be physical and mental death to me.

The old man smiled. "You talk so because you cannot comprehend the importance of the position you will fill as the lord of my Slavic kingdom, because you cannot guess the amount of the wealth I offer you. You shall know it, and you are the only person alive to whom I have ever spoken, or shall ever speak about it. You think this old mansion looks as dreary and rotten inside as out; but you are mistaken. This residence of the so-called Slav King is a princely seat, and it hides treasures that monarchs and potentates would be proud to possess. If any one of the family

calls on me, he finds me in my dingy little hole of a
room, which, with an old rotten table, broken chairs,
mutilated chest of drawers, and coarse bed with
bear-skin coverlet, looks poor and inhospitable
enough, and my visitors are generally glad to escape
into the open air again, thinking that the whole
house resembles this room in appearance; whereas,
were I to throw the doors open, and show them the
splendour of the rooms and halls, they would stare in
amazement. Every one of the rooms is a perfect
museum, and contains precious rarities. One is full
of carved furniture of costly woods, inlaid with ivory,
mother-of-pearl, gold and silver, and rich stones of the
time of " Ulászló." The next contains all sorts of
pottery of past centuries—Roman and Etruscan,
Chinese and Japanese, Sèvres and Dresden, old
Hungarian, and so forth. The third room is full
of weapons of all ages—panoplies, coats of mail,
shields, bucklers, saddles. In the fourth room are
gowns and trains and coats of brocade, and artistic
embroidery and tapestry. The fifth room is a picture-
gallery of unlimited value; and then comes a library
that has not its equal on this continent, nor, I may
say, on any other. High up to the ceiling the large
hall is filled with precious and rare old products;
books with clasps that are themselves curiosities of
rare beauty. But those books! If your medical
colleagues had the privilege of entering this library
and peeping into those books, I doubt if they would
be willing to part with them ever after. Why, there
is actually a book to invoke the devil with! I did

not dare to look into it, but you young fellows are
such sceptics that you will deny the existence of God
and Devil presently, and you will take the risk of
reading that book.

"All these treasures were hoarded together by my
father—may God bless and rest his soul! He was
called a miser throughout his life, and he denied himself all comfort in order to spend his income in re-
plenishing his collection of rarities. Shortly after the
birth of his second son, your father, our mother grew
tired of his mania and the sacrifices she had daily to
make, and left him, taking us boys with her, while he
remained alone among his beloved curiosities, which
became dearer to him on account of the high price
he had to pay for them. When we boys—your father
and I—grew up, your father grew daily more like
our mother, while I became strangely infatuated
with the old man and his store of curiosities. He
was also fond of me, showed me all his treasures,
dwelling upon the particular beauty of each. Miser
as our father was, he occasionally gave money to
his younger son, but he never gave any to me,
and I had to consider this as an especial favour,
for had I not the privilege of sharing the main
interest of his life?

"When my father died, there was hardly enough
ready money in his desk to pay his funeral expenses,
and he had left a very strange will. He had kept
minute accounts of the amount he had spent each
day and year for different objects. All the money he
had given to my mother and my younger brother

was reckoned up and subtracted from their share under his will. He wrote that, as he knew that his wife was well provided for, having a considerable fortune of her own, he left her a life-estate in such one of his many domains as she might select. With regard to his two sons, one had never shown him any love, and visited him only when in want of spending-money; the other had never asked for a penny, although he had received less from his mother than her favourite, the younger. Yet, as a dutiful father, he did not wish to be partial; therefore his sons were to divide his lands, goods, and chattels in the following manner :—One was to take all his ready money, bonds, and objects of gold, silver, and jewellery of recent workmanship (meaning the present century), besides his horses and cattle, and the wine in the cellars; while the other was to take possession of all the lands and the residuary estate, on condition that he should reside in this particular mansion and take charge of the museum therein, that he should never marry, never accept any public office, in order that the treasures under his care might receive the full benefit of his resources. He was required to pledge himself to live in exactly the same secluded and frugal way as his father, and to take his oath that during his lifetime and stewardship he would not sell or give away one particle of the estate, whether real or personal, which he received under the will. Further, he must give up all claim on his mother's estate for ever, and must relinquish all that she might give or bequeath him to his brother.

"To say that your father was furious would hardly express his state of mind. I have already said that the whole amount of cash left was barely enough for the funeral expenses. The bonds which were found proved to be so many worthless pieces of parchment. The jewellery of recent workmanship consisted of a set of valueless shirt-studs and a watch that would not have fetched ten florins at auction. Of silver there was a tablespoon, a teaspoon, a ladle, and two or three pieces of tableware, bent, crooked, and broken, hardly worth the mentioning. Of horses there were two lean and decrepit-looking animals, and the cattle consisted of a diminutive black cow and her calf, neither of much value, yet forming no doubt the most valuable part of the whole bequest. This was your father's portion, for as to his taking the other part, giving up the prospect of our mother's goodly store of money and other property, and living a secluded life as guardian of a museum, that was entirely out of the question.

"To tell that I felt pleased or glad on taking possession of the immense wealth my father had left me would be a falsehood. I was young, and not altogether devoid of the passions and inclinations pertaining to that age. But I had interpreted the true spirit of my father's will, and I knew that all this seeming spite and injustice was really a token of his great love for me and of his great wisdom. Had he not stipulated such hard conditions, my brother would have taken and squandered these lands and goods as he squandered our mother's fortune, and I should not

have been able now to say to his only son, 'Stay
with me, and receive at my hands the undiminished
fortune which your grandfather entrusted to my
care.' How immense that fortune is you may
guess, when I tell you that one year's income,
large as it is, was not sufficient to pay the legacy-
taxes. But come, let me show you everything, and
give you an idea of the Slavic kingdom to which
I invite you."

We entered the mansion, an old château built in
the time of King Albert, under the dynasty of the
Mazures. Strong walls of cut stone, like the ram-
parts of a fortress; great projecting, mullioned oriel
windows; everywhere the Dumany coat-of-arms hewn
in stone, wrought in iron, carved in wood. The main
entrance was walled up; the middle portion of the
building contained but one storey; the wings, too,
were low, but in the rear of the house there was a
large, high turret.

A heavy oaken door, beautifully carved, gave
access to this turret, and as this was at present
the only approach to the interior of the house, we
had to cross halls and corridors until we reached
the floor of the main building. As we entered, my
uncle locked the massive portal and put the key in his
pocket. When, in order to do this, he lifted the lapel
of his long zrinyi dolmány (old-fashioned Hungarian
coat), I could see the butts of his pistols, which were
always loaded and ready to his hands. He noticed
the smile on my lips, and said testily, shrugging his
shoulders, "What can I do? I have to think of my

personal safety at all times. Wickedness has not died
out of the world, and a poor lone old man is rather
a temptation to robbers. To keep a manservant for
protection would not do. He would be the very
person to kill me, having me at his mercy all the
time; and as to keeping a dog for the purpose, I
could not think of it. A dog may bite, and there is
danger in that; and, besides, his keep costs just as
much as a man's  He will eat up a fortune in time.
But when you are here, you will have servants and
dogs, and all the rest, and there will be no more need
of my pistols."

My uncle took me directly to his treasures. With
all he had said to excite my curiosity, he had not said
enough. For here were treasures indeed, and I could
readily believe that in these luxurious creations of
long-forgotten ages and races a strong witchcraft was
pent, and that a man might grow to give his heart
and soul to them. My uncle could give me the date
of every object. This statuette is a Praxiteles; this
picture a Guido Reni; Benvenuto Cellini was the
owner of this goblet; and this sword was that of Sultan
Soliman.

It was dusk, and the shadows of night were
falling fast when I quitted the museum. My uncle
and I returned to the narrow turret-room in which
he had taken up his abode for the last seventy years
and more. This room of itself was a sight to see, and
I was slightly faint and dizzy from bewilderment at
what I had already beheld. " You see, my boy," said
the old man again, " I have not lied to you; and when

you are once established here, and open these rooms to your visitors, all the barons, and counts, and princes will stare at them with open mouth, and will cajole you, flatter you, and bring their handsomest daughters for you to choose a wife from; for such is the power of wealth. But do not believe that the rarities I have shown you are all that I can give. For what would be the good of the offer if I gave you nothing else? You would have to lead a miserable existence like mine, for you could not sell these things —no, not to save your life. If once you come to take possession of them, you will find that you belong to them as much as they to you. You will cling to them and neglect the present, only to live in the forgotten past. The beauty of women you will admire in these pictures only; the beauty of Nature in these stones and minerals. For politics you will not care, and home will mean to you this mansion, which encloses your treasure. Oh, the air of these rooms is poisonous to youth, and mirth, and love!"

"Yes, uncle," I said, earnestly, "and to ambition and independence, and all good and right purposes, also; and therefore I cannot stay with you, for I have chosen my path in life, and I will adhere to it in spite of these powerful temptations."

"Oh, you are afraid that they will convert you into a miser and a hermit, as I have become! But I can give you a potent antidote, which was never given to me; that is, ready money. Come, and I'll show you what you have never seen, and assuredly never dreamed of. You see this large iron chest, itself a rare piece of workmanship, and stronger and safer than any of your new inventions? Come, let me show you how to unlock it, for it is difficult; and one who was unacquainted with the secret of this lock might try until Doomsday to force it open, and all to no purpose. See, it turns this way, and at this point you must stop. If in all three locks the keys have been turned to this point, the chest will open. The contents will rebuild this old castle, will buy you horses and carriages, and all the home luxuries of modern times, and will enable you to keep up with the richest and the noblest of them all. Keep up, I say—nay, go ahead of them; and still you will have what money cannot buy for them—your museum. Oh, the Dumanys shall be a powerful race once more, and I shall live to see it!"

He lifted the heavy lid of the chest, and I saw a number of linen bags and an equally large number of bladders. The linen bags, my uncle explained, were full of silver coins, the bladders of gold coins.

"You see," he continued, "there are fourteen hundred acres of ground belonging to this estate—rather a handsome piece of property in this part of the country. It has all been leased out to farmers for many, many years, almost a century, and it has greatly deteriorated. But this money will help you to improve the soil also, and it will yield you more than the twelve thousand acres of Count Vernöczy's estate can do, for half of that land has been turned into a deer-park, and the other half is imperfectly cultivated. Look at the bundles of reeds there in the corner. You have wondered at them, no doubt; and at all those pipes on the shelf yonder. You asked me if I was a smoker. I am, but I do not smoke out of those pipe-stems. Both they and the reeds are money-boxes, every one of them. In them I keep the bank-notes which I have had to take during the last seventy years. They represent a fortune in themselves. I hardly know myself how much money they contain. You can split them, and find out when you come to live with me. I'll settle it all on you in legal fashion, and keep nothing but my own room. You can do with the rest as you please; build and rebuild, buy and furnish, to suit your fancy. Only let me live the one year that remains to me pleasantly and in plenty, and promise me three things: Never to till your acres after the ideas you will get from the text-books; never to do a kindness to a great lord; and never to quarrel or get vexed with a woman."

"I promise you whatever you wish, dear uncle," said I; "but, since I have listened to you for quite a while, you must now listen to me. You have called me in the capacity of a doctor, and as such I must speak to you."

"Do you know a remedy for old age?" was his sarcastic inquiry.

"I do, to grow older still. You do not look a bit older or feebler than you did ten years ago, and there is no positive reason why you should not live for ten

years longer, or even more, provided you do not
change your course of living in the least degree.
The slightest change of habits, of diet, or of dress,
may prove fatal at your age. I know that you are
not afraid of death, and that you also have taken St.
John the Nepomuc's word for the remaining year.
But, my dear uncle, saints are sometimes ambiguous,
and there is something that resembles a living death,
a prospect too horrible to dwell upon, yet dreadfully
near. A single meal of some heavy, unwonted food,
one glass of liquor, may bring it on. It is called
paralysis, and when it comes, St. Nepomuc may stick
to his word and give you a year, but what a year that
would be ! "

He looked at me with a troubled face, and I
pressed his hands and said, " Yes, dear uncle ; you
have to stick to the old, long-travelled road, and then
I may hope to see you ten years hence as hearty as
you are now, or as you were ten years ago. For you
are in perfect health otherwise, and there is no need
whatever of my staying with you. Only beware of
indigestion, and you will be all right. As for myself,
I shall never cease to remember your kindness and to
feel grateful for it, but to accept your offer would be
moral death to me. I have to go back to my
profession, and if you, dear uncle, dislike our other
relatives, and do not want to leave them your property,
then give it to such patriotic and charitable institutions as deserve patronising, and you may be sure
that your memory will be blessed by thousands. Of
me you need not think. I am not the man to

speculate on another man's death, and build my future on a grave."

The old man looked curiously at me; then he sighed, and embraced me. "Thank you, my dear fellow!" he said; "I see you are a truly honest man and no hypocrite. I won't offer you any money: on the contrary, I'll ask a further favour. Before you leave, I'll give you a letter, which you will personally hand to the Prefect at his residence at the county seat, which is on your way to Vienna. I am afraid to entrust this letter to the mail, as there are very valuable papers in it, and you will have to take a receipt for it from the magistrate. This receipt you need not send me, but keep it safe; and if you come to this house again, you may bring it with you."

With that the old man showed me out into the garden, carefully unlocking and re-locking the door, and securing the key. "Thank you for coming to me, my dear fellow," he said. "And since you decline to take anything of actual value from me, let me offer you something that has only fanciful value, yet is dearer to me than all the treasures within the house. See these Remontan roses in their second bloom—for instance, this Sultan of Morocco, the most perfect specimen of its kind? I gave a *Napoléon d'or* for the scion, and this is its first year of flowering. Here, take it!"

With that he actually cut the blossom from the stalk, and handed it to me. It was a magnificent flower, and almost black, with but a slight purple

tinge. It was the darkest-hued rose known at that
time.    Later on  the " Deuil d'Alsace"  came out of
Pandora's box.    At the time I speak of, that box was
in Benedetti's pocket, and more is the pity that the
pocket held it so tight.

# X

## "DEAD."

HARDLY three months after I had taken a tender and affectionate farewell from my Uncle Dion a newspaper item informed me of his death. My prediction that a fit of indigestion would prove fatal to him had come true. His confidence in St. John of Nepomuc had been greater than his prudence, and it was a mercy that the stroke of apoplexy had killed him outright, instead of making a living corpse of him, as is so often the case.

About a fortnight after I had read of the death of the celebrated Slav King, I received a package by mail, containing an official and a private letter. The official letter informed me that the Honourable Dionysius Dumany had recorded a last will and testament in the county archives, in which last will and testament he nominated me, Dr. Kornel Dumany, as his sole heir, upon condition that I should take possession of the property and live in Dumany Castle. But if I should stubbornly refuse to fulfil that condition, lands, goods, and chattels should forthwith pass over to the "Maticza" (Slavic and ecclesiastical literary fund, employed for Panslavonic ends).

The private letter came from the Governor of the county, and referred to the same subject. The Governor declared that it was my unmistakable duty,

H

as a Dumany and a son of Hungary, to take possession
of the home of my ancestors, and not to allow such an
anti-patriotic and dangerous institution as the "Maticza" to do her a mischief on the strength of Hungarian funds, and to turn the ancient halls of my
patriotic forefathers into a meeting-place of daring
conspirators.

I shrugged my shoulders, but had not the faintest
notion of accepting. I did not care for politics, and
knew of the "Maticza" as a purely Slavonic literary
society. If this society was to hold future meetings
in my uncle's museums, I could bear it; there was
very little of Chauvinism or even patriotism left in
me. I was rather cosmopolitan in tendency; and as
to giving up my profession and becoming a country
squire, that was simply ridiculous.

This happened to be the very period when, after
years of degradation and suffering, the Hungarian
national spirit was first allowed to lift its head and
show its colours. Germans and Bohemians, who for
many years had filled all the public offices in Hungary,
were compelled either to learn the Hungarian language
or surrender their places to natives. In most cases
the latter was unavoidable, and these aliens, furious
at being driven from their prescriptive sinecures, went
up to Vienna and did their best to make it hot for
the Hungarians. As every war has its origin in an
inkstand, students are, naturally, the greatest Chau-
vinists, and I was to find that out with a vengeance.
All my friends and colleagues became more and more
averse to me, and even went so far as to take my

patients from me by incensing them against me in every possible manner. Soon they began to drag my name into professional polemics, into professional newspapers; and when I had defeated and silenced them in one place, they began to annoy me in another. At home, in Hungary, the reorganisation of the counties was begun. For twenty years constitutional life in Hungary had been extinct, and now it had to be resuscitated. This was a hard task, and at first it was not even known who were entitled to vote at the meetings.

And now I received another letter from the Governor, again reminding me of my duty, clearly describing the situation of affairs, and telling me how much good every honest and right-minded man could effect, and how much mischief I should be able to prevent. "But," he closed, "if you stubbornly and positively adhere to your unpatriotic resolution, and finally decline to accept your deceased uncle's legacy, I must trouble you to come down in person and give a definite renunciation, with the necessary affidavit, such being your uncle's strict demand."

There was no help. I had to go to get rid of the annoyance. Arriving at the county seat, I paid my respects to the Vice-Governor, the same dignitary to whom I had given the letter which my uncle had entrusted to my care, and which, as I now learned, proved to be the very will in question. I announced my firm resolution to adhere to my principles, and the magistrate replied that that was all right, but before we talked further on the subject, I

had better go to the county meeting, which was to be
held that day.

"But what right have I to be there?" I asked.

"Why, as the present head of the ancient Dumany
family, of course," was the reply. "There is not one of
us provided with a better claim."

So I let myself be persuaded, and went. The great
Hall of Meetings was crowded to suffocation, and
among the local celebrities I recognised a few of those
compatriots who had kindly assisted my poor father
to get rid of his money by feeding them and keeping
their pockets full. There were others who were quite
young men, old schoolfellows of mine; somewhat bad
students at the time, but, since Providence had
furnished them with strong voices, they had taken
advantage of the gift so as to make a noise in the
world, and played the *rôle* of leading partisans. One
of them in particular, a good-for-nothing sort of fellow
who had never come near his degree in any school,
was recognised as a bright particular star, and quite
too smart for anything. If I remember rightly, he
was the head cf the Radical wing.

After much deliberation and a good deal of talk,
of which I did not comprehend anything, it was
decided to read the names of the present county
members. A long list was handed to an official, who
was instructed to pronounce each name clearly; and
each name, as it was read, was followed by a loud
cheer "Éljen!" All at once there came, instead of
the "Éljen!" after one of the names, the unanimous
shout "Dead!" and the person named had to rise

from his seat and leave the room, and his name was erased from the list. This was repeated a number of times, and behind me stood a Slav nobleman, who after each of these utterances of "Dead," added the Slavonic word "Smrt" *—a beautiful word, as bony as the spectre "death" itself.

There was a priest, with a broad red sash, who made himself especially obnoxious to me; for, as often as the "dead" sentence was pronounced, he laughed, and pointed conspicuously with his fat fingers at the expelled man, who, with bent head, made his way to the door. I inquired the reason of these demonstrations, and was told that these men were traitors, who had filled offices under the absolutist government of the Austrians.

Immediately after one of these shouts of "Dead," an old gentleman who sat just in front of me, and of whom I had up to this moment seen nothing but his bald head, which showed an immense scar, evidently an old sword-cut, got up from his seat at the green-covered table, and as he turned I beheld an aged and careworn but honest face, with two big tears slowly rolling down the furrowed cheeks. "That is for the seven wounds I received at Nagy Sarló!" said he, with choking voice; and raising his trembling hand to his eyes, he moved away.

"Seven children the poor fellow has at home, and he had to earn daily bread for them, somehow, so he served as surveyor, and that was his treachery," said one of my neighbours in an undertone. As the

* "Dead."

banished man passed out, I sat down on the seat he quitted. "It is ill luck to sit in a traitor's chair," said a well-meaning man at my elbow; but I smiled and kept my seat.

"Who may that smooth-faced stranger be? and how comes it that he is here?" I heard some of the bystanders ask, referring, of course, to my clean-shaven visage. Nobody in the whole congregation knew or recognised me, except the Vice-Governor, and the fellow-student of whom I have spoken. But, of course, he kept at a distance. Presently my own name, "Dumany Kornel," was pronounced, and "Dead! Dead! Smrt!" was the shout of all around. I had caught the infection, and as the red-sashed priest smilingly and playfully raised a threatening fat finger at me and said, "He is turned into a German, an Austrian," down came my fist upon the green cloth of the table. Philosophy, *sang-froid*, and political indifference were blown to the winds, carrying forethought and resolution with them. I jumped up, pushed the chair away from behind me, and shouted—

"He is not dead! He is here! And what is more, here he shall stay! I am a landed gentleman, as well as the best of you, and as pure a Hungarian as any in this meeting, or in this country either. I am that Dumány Kornel whose name has been read, and I am not dead, but alive, as you shall soon find out!"

There was a dead silence at these words, and some heads were nodded in acknowledgment that I was right. Then there was a whispering and consulting and questioning, until the honourable Vice-Governor said, "Silence, gentlemen! the honourable Dumany Kornel has the floor upon a personal question."

"Hear! hear!" shouted all, some in good earnest, some in order to embarrass me, and the red-sashed parson said, maliciously, "If you are a Hungarian, sir, as you claim, where is your moustache?"

"Out hunting for yours, your reverence," said I, with a grin.

"I am a priest!" was the haughty reply; but that was just what I expected, and looking around at the portraits upon the walls of the room, portraits representing the most celebrated heroes of our national history, I gave them then and there such a barbological sermon, *ex tripode*, that they listened to me in mute astonishment. I told them that the great national high-priests and patriots, Peter Pázmány Prince Cardinal Esterházy, and Thomas Bakács, there portrayed, had worn moustaches, although they were priests; whereas Mathias Corvinus, our glorious, never-to-be-forgotten hero-king, wore a clean-shaven face like mine. The famous Palatinus Illésházy had pronounced Hungary free and independent with smooth hairless lips, and Thomas Nádasdy had carried the Hungarian tricolour to immortal triumphs although his face was as beardless as mine, as everybody might see by his portrait there present. I told them that I did not speak for myself, as I did not care a straw for their opinion, and felt sufficiently strong in my own self-respect and clear conscience, which, perhaps, was more than a good many present could say of themselves. But I was not going to look on when patriotism was made the monopoly of certain people, whereas decent and deserving men were hooted at because they had dared to earn their own bread and that of their family, instead of living upon the bounty of friends and driving them to ruin and death. And then I told them that it was not a time to inaugurate a policy of jealousy and persecution. We had had enough of that under the absolutist government; what we wanted was honest, energetic co-operation for a common purpose, the welfare of country and nation.

I had spoken with all the bravery of a simpleton, who has no idea that if he throws a glowing tinder into a barrel of gunpowder he may blow the house up and himself also. For some seconds I ran the risk of being thrown out of doors, or of getting my hands full of private quarrels and duels, but the concluding sentences met with such unanimous applause that I was heartily congratulated on the success of my maiden speech, and had the additional satisfaction of seeing the majority of those formerly pronounced " dead " restored to the list again, and I was able to give back the seat which I occupied to its former owner, the old gentleman with the seven scars and as many children.

Among those who had congratulated me was one conspicuously handsome and distinguished-looking young man. He fairly embraced me, and said, " You are the man we wanted! Let me welcome you, and consider me your friend; I am Count Vernöczy. Siegfried Vernöczy is my name!"

The Vice-Governor invited me to dinner, and just as we were pushing our way out of the hall, I heard the red-sashed priest and the Slav nobleman, who had always added his "Smrt" to the cry of "Dead!" speaking together in Slav, of which language they supposed me ignorant. The nobleman said to the priest—

"What folly it was of you to vex and excite this blockhead by pronouncing him dead! Had you left him alone, he would have gone off, and left the Maticza in possession of the old miser's fortune. Now we may go and hunt for other fools; this one has escaped us for ever."

"Well, how could I know that the milksop had turned into a fighting bull?" was the reply.

The reverend gentleman was wrong. I was not a bull, but an ox; and a moment's excitement had made me give up fame and ambition, profession and independence, and here I was in the kingdom of Swatopluk, taking possession of my Uncle Diogenes's legacy. It was very foolish, but if I had to do it again—why, I should do it. I was a Hungarian and a Dumany, in spite of my cosmopolitan tendencies and in spite of modern equality.

## XI

So I must needs call him, for dear was his friendship to me; at least, I have paid for it dearly. At
our first meeting he told me that henceforth we
should stick to each other like the Siamese twins.
And the man whom he thought worth catching was
clever indeed if he could extricate himself from the
meshes which encircled him. He was altogether a
wonderful fellow. Of athletic build, striking beauty,
great agility and versatility in all bodily exercises, an
unrivalled fencer, and a perfect marksman. What a
soldier he would have made! But Mr. Schmerling
knew a good many fine tricks, and one of the prettiest
was the prevention of Hungarian youths from entering the army. He took advantage of the prevalent
Chauvinistic sentiments, and put them forward as a
bait. One thousand florins, paid down, protected a
Hungarian youth from serving in the hated army, and
he was free to ride his own horses instead of the king's.
Yet what a general that Siegfried might have been!
He was born to command and direct other people.
All who adhered to him and did his bidding were his
soldiers; all who declined to follow his lead, he
regarded as enemies. The former he compelled to
serve him, the latter he defeated and slew. He was
sometimes high-spirited to eccentricity. At other

times he was discreetly prudent. He spoke almost every existing language, and was a brilliant orator. His addresses were admirably delivered, and he took an independent and imperative tone. His talk was always fluent; and if a Hungarian or a German word failed him, he substituted for it a French, English, Spanish, Italian, Danish, Turkish, or other foreign phrase, never stopping for a moment to consider or even to explain. His Hungarian speeches were rhetorical gems, yet they could hardly be styled Hungarian, for they were delivered in a perfect Volapük—that is, in a medley of all possible languages. He was a strong personality, and a " grand seigneur." His purse was always open, and he spent his money with a liberal hand. He must have been a very rich man, for I never knew him in even a momentary embarrassment for money. When I first felt the pressure of his iron arm, I knew at once that he would dominate me. But such was the fascination he exercised that I submitted at once.

It was at the close of that memorable meeting, and after he told me to consider him my friend. The Vice-Governor had invited me to dine with him, and I wanted to go to my rooms for a change of attire, or at least a white tie and a pair of light gloves. " Nonsense ! " he said, " these rustics will take you as you are, *en plein parade.* Come at once. We will order them to lose no time, but to take up your status in your new domain to-morrow, and have you put in possession of your rights and privileges without delay."

"But to-morrow I shall not be here," I remonstrated; "I have to go to Vienna and provide for my patients."

"What would you provide for them? *Qu'ils attendent, les pauvres bêtes;* death will not escape them. 'We can wait,' is the Austrian parole; don't worry about them. To-morrow you will have the board of commissioners meet on your new premises, and put you in possession of your inheritance, so that you may be placed on the list of voters. This must not be postponed, for if you miss that you are dead indeed—'Smrt,' as that honest Maticza champion said."

Siegfried lost no time, and the Vice-Governor said that he was right. "Yes," he said, "to-morrow you shall have the keys of your castle."

"And that of the famous iron chest," said Siegfried.

"No, that cannot be yet," replied the officer; "the iron chest is under an official lock as yet, for the 'Maticza' has put in a claim to the inheritance. The Slav parish priest in Dumanyfalva, as well as his housekeeper and his sacristan, affirm that your deceased uncle, on the eve of his death, dined with them (in parentheses, the fat pork he partook of and the strong wine he drank brought on the fatal stroke), and there at the table he declared that, even in case you, his nephew, should accept of the inheritance, the Maticza should not be left empty-handed, but should receive all the ready money found on the premises."

"Franca, franca! It's all a lie!" said Siegfried.

"So I think, too. But we have no evidence to prove it. It all depends on the decision of the court, because the Maticza has no documentary evidence, and so the court will decide the question."

"And where is the chest at present?"

"There at the castle, under guard."

"And why did you let it remain there? It ought to be here under your own care."

"Yes; but it is so riveted to the wall that we could not remove it without tearing up the wall also."

"Then why have you not taken the money into your own custody? Some unknown person or persons may force the lock."

"That lock? Why, we tried it in every way, for the tax-commissioner would have liked to examine its contents to make sure as to the amount of taxes due. But we could not find a locksmith capable of using the three keys belonging to the locks in the proper way."

At this I spoke out. "If," I said, "my uncle has indeed willed away his ready money to the Maticza, he must assuredly have instructed them how to get at their money. To me, at least, he disclosed the secret of the lock, and I know how to apply the keys properly."

"Bravissimo! That settles the question. A clearer piece of evidence cannot exist. The court cannot decide otherwise than in your favour."

"Then try to expedite the formalities. You can do it."

"I can't. The parties must be informed at what time the court holds its session; they have to appear before the court, and introduce testimony. All this takes a month at least."

"And how is he to manage until then? Is there nothing in old Diogenes's casket to make money out of?"

"Oh yes, a lot of old rubbish! I daresay it would bring something at least. We have taken an inventory of it, and taxed it; here it is."

With that he took from the shelf an official-looking document, and handed it to me. I was curious to know at what they had appraised my uncle's precious treasures, and looked at the inventory. I was more than surprised—I was amused beyond everything. The contents of the two large halls, ante-chamber, and five chambers were valued at three hundred and seventy-nine florins and forty-five kreutzers. The kreutzers were for an old Gobelin hanging—a rare piece of tapestry.

"Why, this is ludicrous!" said I laughingly. The Vice-Governor smiled knowingly, and Siegfried took the paper out of my hand, and read the items. A Palissy-cabinet was described as a wooden chest, worth three florins; precious old majolica as old earthenware, the suits of armour as old iron, and so forth. "Now this is a masterpiece!" said Siegfried; but I was indignant. "It is hyper-barbarism!" I said. "This inventory enumerates the contents of some dime museum—not of my uncle's valuable collections. If you had looked for it, you might have found an exact schedule, made by my uncle, with the name of each object, statement of cost, etc."

"We could not find anything of the kind," said the Vice-Governor. "But I forgot. Attached to the will was a package, sealed; and addressed to you— 'Dr. Cornelius Dumány.' Here it is."

I took the package, opened it, found the inventory within, and handed it to the official. "Here it is. You see I was right! Here you can see the actual worth of my uncle's museum."

"I have no curiosity whatever," said the Vice-Governor; "this is a private document addressed to you, and, therefore, I have no business to inquire into it."

"But——"

"But it is time for you to go," said Siegfried, slapping me on the shoulder; "never mind that old inventory of your uncle's."

"But I do mind it," I insisted. "I can't have something that is actually worth two hundred thousand florins appraised at three hundred, all in all."

"But can't you see that on the three hundred florins the amount of tax would be seventeen florins, and on the two hundred thousand you will have to pay nine thousand florins as legacy taxes?"

"Is that the law?"

"Of course it is, clear and distinct."

"Then I shall pay according to law. I do not intend to cheat the Treasury."

The Vice-Governor broke into a laugh, and Siegfried took hold of both my ears and gave them a

hard pull. "Oh! you, you, you doctor!" He would
have said you fool, or you simpleton, but he found the
"doctor" more explanatory, and a good deal more to
the purpose. Why, did I not understand that it was
the patriotic duty of a Hungarian citizen to cheat the
Treasury whenever an opportunity to do so was
offered?

"Just you let him alone," said the Vice-Governor,
laughing. "He is an innocent, honest fellow, with
a tender conscience, and nothing so tough and
hardened as you. Come, friend Kornel! tell me,
what do you think of the rate at which the other
things are estimated? For instance, your uncle's
private room? The whole furniture is valued at
twenty-three florins. Do you think that under-
estimated? No? Well, here are his pipes—old clay
pipes, stuck into cane stems. They are valued at
ninety kreutzers."

I laughed. "The pipes are hardly worth more,
but the stems would be well worth the money,
for they and the old reeds in my uncle's room were
his bank-note receptacles, and for all I know they
may be full of hundred- or even thousand-florin
bills."

"Well, if you are not the greatest ass in Christen-
dom, then I am—and no doubt about it," said Siegfried,
vexed. "Here is this fellow actually denouncing his
own money to the police. If you are such an imbecile,
and really do not care for your own profit, then at
least do not talk without being asked."

"Hadn't you better use more civil language?" I

asked. "I really am not used to such strong expressions."

"Oh, of course; I beg your pardon! Only I should like to know what you will do without ready money? Because you have compelled our friend, the Vice-Governor here, to take all the money on the premises, that is, all the contents of the reeds and pipe-stems, of which you blabbed, into his own custody, whereas you might have kept your own counsel, and culled the money out at your leisure, without anybody having an idea of its existence."

"Yes; but that would not be honest. If anybody finds a pocket-book full of money he cannot keep it for himself, but must give it up to the authorities."

"Not if it is his own pocket-book, I should think. But, as you have done it, it is too late to quarrel about the policy of the act."

The Vice-Governor called in one of his office clerks, and drew up a statement containing all I had said about the reeds and pipes, and the actual value of the museum. I had to put my signature at the foot of the document, and then I was allowed to go.

Next day Siegfried took me out in his own chaise, to which four beautiful horses were attached, to Dumanyfalva, and there, with all the ceremony belonging to the occasion, I was inducted into my legal rights as landlord. I was conducted into the mansion, the keys were put into my hands, then they took me out into the field and gave me a handful of soil of each individual plot, or meadow, or pasture. After that they split the reeds and pipe-stems, and ten bills of one thousand florins apiece, two hundred bills of one hundred florins, and sixty-four fifty-florin bills were found, flattened out, made into a package, upon which each of the persons present put a seal, with his own name. Then the Vice-Governor wrote on its cover, " Legacy of the Late Honourable Dionysius Dumany," and handed it over to the trustee.

" Now you see what has come of your blabbing," said Siegfried. " How will you manage now ? "

" Well enough. I have some money in Vienna, and I am going to fetch it. I have to go up to Vienna, anyhow, to arrange my belongings there."

" And I'll go with you, for, thorough Æsculapius as you are there is danger of your escaping us yet."

He kept his word, and we went by his own chaise and four to Nagy Szombat, where we took the train for Vienna. In Vienna he never moved from my side, hardly allowing me time for any business transactions, but taking me to theatres, dinners, cafés, and all sorts of variety-shows and music-halls. I had lived soberly and industriously up to this time, rarely going to the opera or to private entertainments; but I was young and naturally jovial, and did not object to a few days of dissipation, enjoying the manifold diversions which the Austrian metropolis offered.

On the last day, Siegfried helped to pack and send off my furniture to Dumanyfalva, and, as I could not sleep in my empty rooms, he carried me off to a hotel; but not to sleep, for we never closed our eyes that night, and it was with a dizzy head and a confused brain that I found myself in the railway carriage, travelling homeward. Happily, my faithful old servant had gone with the furniture ahead of me, and, on my arrival at home, I found that the practical old fellow had made the best of his time. A bedroom and sitting-room had already been furnished and the old dining-room made serviceable. He had also procured a cook, and for the first time in my life I enjoyed the sensation of sitting at my own table and playing the host, for that Siegfried did not leave me yet will be readily understood.

While at dinner, Siegfried laid down a plan of how the old mansion might be renovated without and within, and I had to acknowledge that his taste was perfect; but—very expensive, as I remarked.

"How much ready money have you?" he asked.

"Something over four thousand florins," I replied.

"That is almost nothing—hardly sufficient to furnish a few rooms, and what becomes of the building? Then there is the grange, the stable, etc., and then you will want to buy two pair of horses; one for your chaise, the other for work. You will have to buy cattle, and grain, and hay, and a good many other necessaries, and you will have to take the distillery away from the lessee, for what will you do with your cattle? What you want is at least twenty thousand florins, and these you have fooled away. It will take months to get hold of them again, and then half of them will be gone, and the time for making all necessary arrangements will have passed. I'll tell you what, you cannot sit here and do nothing, and I am

not going to let you waste time. I'll lend you these
twenty thousand florins." I was surprised at the offer.
"Yes," he said, "I have the money ready, for I intended
to buy a piece of property, but could not make a bargain with the owner. Now the money is of no use to
me at present, and you may have it until your money
is restored to you. Happily, I have the money with
me now. Here it is!"

With that he took out a portfolio, and handed me
twenty bank-notes of one thousand florins each. I
wanted to give him a bond, but he would not hear of
it. "The idea!" he said; "why, we are no Jews, but
gentlemen. Just write upon your card; 'Good for
twenty thousand florins, which I will pay upon
receipt of my legacy.' Here, take my lead-pencil;
that will do."

I was rather embarrassed, but his face showed so
much sincere friendship and regard that I did not
venture to refuse the offer, and, considering the circumstances, he was right, and he had behaved nobly.
Still, I did not like the obligation he had put me
under, and should have preferred to pay interest on
the sum even to a common usurer. I had some faint
presentiment that the interest on such a loan as this
would be much higher than the usual percentage
taken by the professional money-lender; but I had
done it, and could not undo it, as you might
say.

With the money in hand I attended to business.
Siegfried, indefatigable in his endeavours to be of use
to me, assisted me with his practical versatility in

business matters, and with his good taste in the domestic sphere. He purchased the horses for my carriage, he bargained with the mason about the buildings, he made the contracts with my tenants, and he bought my grain and other household necessaries. I could never have got on without his help—at least, not so profitably—and I was naturally very grateful to him.

"You can't pay any visits to your neighbours until you have made your own house fit to receive company; but, as it would be rather hard upon you to live like a hermit until that time, you might drive over to the county town and put in an appearance at the casino. I'll introduce you to the whole set."

The county town was two hours' drive from Dumányfalva. Siegfried drove me over, and my own brand-new and very "pshutt"-looking cab was to wait for me at the casino door. In the casino Siegfried introduced me to about a dozen of young and old local celebrities, and one or two great lights of national reputation. Party divisions there were none; all parties agreed harmoniously, and played with each other their whist, their games of chess or dominoes. I was very cordially received, and in the ensuing conversation I took a very lively and active share, and stood my ground without any of the usual bashfulness of a novice. Siegfried seconded me in all my remarks with an occasional nod and a "Very true, my friend," or "You have hit it exactly," or "You have expressed my own opinion;" "My friend, you are an excellent debater," and other observations of the kind, and soon we were unanimously called "the Dioscuri," for we were never found apart.

At a county banquet Siegfried spoke of me, in a brilliant toast-speech, as of a newly risen star, or rather "a great shining planet," and there was a universal "Éljen!" and shouts of acclamation. It was wonderful how many friends I found, and how much I was sought after! I had a dozen different invitations at once. One invited me to his shooting-box in the mountains, another to inspect his model farm and dairy, a third invited me on a fishing excursion, and so forth.

While driving home from the casino, Siegfried said to me—"I wonder you are not vexed at my never inviting you over to Vernöcze, but I must tell you the truth. I am not the master of my own house and home at present. An aunt of mine is here with my two cousins, half-grown young girls, staying until the bathing-season begins. So the lady has control of the house, and I live in a little pavilion in the park. My aunt will be very much pleased to make your acquaintance—too much pleased, I should say, for she is one of those spirited women who have an opinion of their own, and let you know it. She is never tired of arguing, and you are the very person for her. I verily believe that the two little girls have caught the infection from her, and you would be surprised to hear what a flow of nonsense issues from the aristocratic little mouths. And the number of questions they ask is astonishing! Sometimes I give them an answer in language such as I would not venture to use to a variety singer; but the little innocents come at me, and laugh without the slightest blush; they do not understand the hidden impertinence. I'll some day introduce you to all of them, my aunt and the two girls; but your house must first be put in order For I find it hard, even now, to keep them from rushing in upon you unawares, and introducing themselves. They are positively dying for a peep at you and your museum. Well, I have done enough to excite that curiosity. I am incessantly talking of you."

"Then it will be your fault if their ladyships are shocked at finding out the deception. I am too commonplace a fellow not to disappoint them cruelly."

"Vederemo!" he said. "The Devil is never at rest!"

### INTERMEZZO.

The Devil?

"Do you believe, then, in the existence of a personal Devil?" you ask.

"Has not this story been terribly dull and tedious up to this moment? You have not shown us a single Devil as yet. No, not even a woman."

"Well, I'll show you three of the latter species presently—a strong-minded, argumentative aunt, and two little nieces."

"You won't say that these two little countesses or their aristocratic aunt, or either of them, is an incarnation of the Evil One? Or are you speaking of your dear friend, Siegfried? Why, he is a perfect guardian angel, the personification of goodness and benevolence!"

"Do you know the story of St. Anthony? How he was tempted by the Devil in the semblance of a lovely sylph, until all at once he saw the fiend's hoof appear from under the robe?"

That night, as Siegfried took leave of me, to drive home to Vernöcze, he embraced me and kissed me on the cheek. It is many years since that night, but many a night since then I have lain sleepless in my bed and rubbed that eternally burning and smarting spot, and felt an almost unconquerable temptation to take the operating-knife and cut out the part which had been contaminated by that foul kiss.

## XII.

### THE DEVIL'S HOOF.

One morning my dear friend, Siegfried, came. "My dear Nell," he said, "we held a party meeting yesterday, and it was decided that you should be a candidate for Parliament. In fact, we have nominated you already."

"You are in a jocular mood, I suppose?" said I. "I do not understand an atom of legislation and politics."

"Neither do I; yet I fill my place in the House of Lords, so will you fill yours in the House of Commons. You need not stare at me, for I am not joking. I am fully in earnest, and, now that the chalice is set to your lips, you are bound to drain it."

"But I can't see why," said I. "I am not in the least fit for the position, and am not going to make a fool of myself. I am a doctor of medicine, not a legislator."

"And what does that matter, pray? The department of public health is very much in need of a radical reform, and you are the very man to advocate sanitary measures in Parliament. But this is all non-sense. Hungary is not yet in a position to have all departments represented by experts; what she wants at present is firmness to principle, strict party fealty The demagogues, the heretics, and the Panslavonians

of our country are preparing for a strong contest at
the coming electoral struggle, and we Conservatives
must strain every nerve to defeat them, and cause
patriotism, religion, and aristocratic rights to triumph.
Our party believes that you are the man to represent
these principles, and you can't decline to accept such
an honourable mission. Do you not love your country? Do you want her to become a prey to infidels,
or Panslavonic conspirators, or to the mob? You
would not have the descendants of the Hussites dominate Hungary? Are you not a Catholic Christian?
You are brave; you have strong principles, and you
are an excellent orator. You are the man we want,
and there is an end of arguing."

"Very good! But there is a practical side to the
question."

"Yes. If the other parties come off victorious,
the agrarian movement will grow too fast for us.
The Socialist rabble is preaching the assessment
of all land, the abolition of the congrua taxes,*
and the abolition of our feudal privileges. This
is the prose or practical side of the question, my
friend."

"There is another still," I persisted, "and I must
speak plainly. You know that I have no money for
political enterprises. My own money is in official
custody; but, even if it were not, and I had so much
money at my disposal that I did not know what to
set about in order to get rid of it, I should not

---

* Congrua taxes are the taxes paid by the parish members to their
curates or priests.

waste it in buying myself a seat in Parliament. I remember well what politics did for my father, and how much it cost him. But, besides this recollection, the idea of corrupting the minds of the electors and of making drunken animals out of decent and intelligent labourers for two or three weeks is repulsive to me. It is entirely against my conscience."

"Now listen to me. In the first place, no one asks for a penny of your money, so it is no business of yours to inquire or care about it. What is the use of party funds, I might ask? Then, what have you to do with the details of the campaign? I am head-drummer, manager of the canvass. You need not give a single bottle of wine to anybody, unless you want to regale your friends here in your house; but that is quite a different thing, and has nothing to do with the election. There is one thing you must remember. If you offer venison and champagne to your electors, it is called a banquet, and the papers speak admiringly of your bountiful hospitality; but if you boil a sheep and open a barrel of sixpenny wine or beer for them, then you are bribing voters, and corrupting the minds of the innocent. So never trouble your head with a thought about these things. I have made a bargain with every hotel-keeper or inn-keeper in the whole county for that one day, and the voters may revel as they please—at their own expense; that is, a dinner may be had for two kreutzers, a supper for three, and the wine will be included in that price. Who can forbid an inn-keeper to sell cheap viands ? You will have nothing to do with the whole business. Only, if some decent elector gets his head broken in the spree, you will plaster him up, or sew him up, as may be necessary. Up to the day of election you will not show yourself, and only put in your appearance when they come to fetch you with music and flags and all that flummery, and beg you to come and kindly accept the mandate, which the chairman of the party is dying to hand over to you. Then at the banquet you offer a toast to his Majesty the King, and afterward you will accept of the torchlight serenade, which your voters will give you, and perhaps speak a few gracious words; but that is not essential, and you may hold your peace. At any rate, with that serenade all your duties are ended."

"I should think they began with that—at least, according to my notion. No, I can't accept. I can't afford to loiter about in Budapest, and have everything here go to the dogs."

"What a greenhorn you are! You need not live in Budapest at all. If the chief of the party telegraphs you that some great division is coming on with respect to some important question, you go up, find the seat with your name on it, sit down, and, when your name is called, you shout 'yes' or 'no,' according to the party's views, and then you travel home again, and make your famous 'Lipto cheese.'"

"I have no intention of becoming a voting machine."

"There you are right. You are too spirited and much too talented for that. You will deliver your maiden speech amid universal applause, and become famous at once. You will be hated by the opposite parties, hated and feared, and that will only stimulate your courage. You will be a great man, and a blessing to your country. You can engage a trustworthy man to manage your estate, and do well under such an arrangement; and you will give your talent and your faculties to your country and your party. It is your duty, and you are not the man to shrink from an acknowledged duty. Besides, out of friendship for me, you cannot refuse. I have positively staked my word on your acceptance; and then there is a request from the party, with a hundred and twenty signatures. Look here!"

He showed me a sheet of writing, with a long list of badly-scrawled names underneath a few lines of writing. I still hesitated, when Siegfried smiled, and, taking from his pocket a little bit of a letter, perfumed with heliotrope, handed it to me.

"My aunt sends you this."

I broke the rose-coloured wax, and drew out a tiny piece of bristol-board with the signature of Countess Diodora Vernöczy. Its contents were as follows:—

"Pray accept the nomination."

That was all. But what all the persuasions, all the allusions to country, race, patriotism, and religion had not effected, these few Hungarian words, written in a fine, aristocratic hand, did at once. They persuaded me, and I accepted  Yet I had never

seen the lady who had written these words, and
did not even know whether she was young or
old, beautiful or ugly! She was a woman, and
that sufficed. No! the Devil is not dead; here is
his hoof.

How I triumphed and how I fell I have told you
already. If I had the gift of Virgilius Maro, and could
speak or write in hexameters, in such verses I would
compose the "Æneid" of my career as a belligerent.
As it is, you can read it all, described in somewhat
unflattering language, in the Hungarian newspapers of
the period. There is a whole history of bribery, corruption, intimidation, and similar crimes committed
in my name, related in those papers, and you may
read of the horrible fraud that was practised in offering the vote of a dead man. The epithets "cheat,"
"deceiver," "liar," and so forth were freely and frequently attached to my name; and then followed the
shameful annulment of the election, and I was sent
home—a broken, disgraced, snuffed-out wretch—a
dead man, indeed!

There is something fearful, something terribly
cruel and unjust, in such a moral cudgelling to death,
for those who cast the stones are not a whit better
than their victim. A common criminal, murderer,
counterfeiter, or forger may procure a pardon, and
rehabilitate himself in time; but a man that has
furnished society with amusement and been laughed
to death is never again allowed to hold up his head
and show his face. I was nearly mad with shame and
disgrace. What should I do with myself now—now

that I was nothing but a broken tool—I, who might have been a scientific celebrity, a light in the profession? I could not go back to Vienna for very shame. A flouted, ridiculed man cannot be a doctor. A doctor must be respected, trusted, even revered, like a priest. For me there was nothing but to hide myself in my own house, shut the doors against everybody, and live the life of a hermit—the life of my Uncle Diogenes.

I need not have shut my doors; not a soul demanded admittance. I really think my dear friends made a circuit around my château when they had to pass through my village.

The first day I remained shut up in my room; the second I paced the garden walks in a furious rage; the third I noticed that I had shamefully neglected my uncle's dearly-cherished garden since I had abandoned myself to the mania of politics. The carefully tended Isabella grapes wound their tender twigs up and around an apple tree; the roses were full of water shoots; the American lilies choked up with dead nettles. Wasps' nests were hanging from the branches of the trees, and giant ants had built their pyramids on the foot-path; and the hedgehogs boldly invaded the lawn as I passed. As I strolled, my eye fell upon a little flower which I recognised as a favourite from my dear mother's garden; I observed a glowing alkermes, an Oriental corn-rose, then again an artichoke, overgrown with vile weeds. All at once I found myself working away with garden-knife, shovel, and spade, pruning, weeding, and tying up the twigs and branches, just as Uncle Diogenes had done.

By night I had smoked out the wasps, put the little bower to rights, and, hardly knowing how or why, I had gone into my uncle's turret-chamber instead of my own bedroom. And why not be as he had been? I asked myself. Here at least I could meet with no shame, no disappointment, and no deception. All was well. I should be a gardener in summer and a museum-keeper in winter, and so the time would pass with me as it passed with him. No doubt, in time, this solitary, secluded life would not be so irksome to me as now. The social instinct would die out; and, left to rural pleasures and occupations, the polish would be rubbed off me, and in appearance also I should be as my Uncle Diogenes had been. I gave up shaving, dressed shabbily, and ordered a dinner of pork and potatoes, which disgusted me. I ceased to drink wine, because I was no toper to enjoy drinking alone, and in the course of two or three days I had a hearty indigestion, which at least recalled me from my self-tormenting course so far as my inward man was concerned. In outward appearance I had a beard of a week's growth, wore a pair of coarse breeches and high top-boots, because in low boots I could not ramble about in garden and field as I did.

My valet was in despair; the good old man had known me for years, and was very faithful to me. Of course, he dared not ask questions, but he threw me such appealing glances that I was strongly tempted to

pour out all my burning shame and rage to him, since
I had nobody else to make a confidant of. It was a
very, very miserable time, and it lasted something
more than a week—a week, I say! I thought it a
century at the least.

**3**

## XIII.

### THE VALKYRS.

It was about ten or twelve days after my discomfiture, and a beautiful afternoon. I was standing in my front garden, attired, as I usually had been of late, in coarse breeches, muddy top-boots, a not very clean linen blouse, and a broad, rough straw hat on my head. My face was rough and adorned with bristles. I do not think that anybody coming upon me unawares would have taken me for anything but a Slav garden labourer.

Presently I heard the gallop of horses, and, looking through the new and very handsome iron trellis in front of the building, I saw three Amazons riding up to the house. I did not know them, and supposed them to be strangers in the country, approaching in order to admire the curious old building. They wore long black riding-habits, all three alike, with blue veils tied around their high beavers and entirely concealing their faces. One of them was a real Zenobia figure: tall of stature, regal in gait, a magnificent creature! The second was tall and slender, and slow and stately in movement. The third was a tiny little figure, but full of nervous vitality and energy. Opposite to the verandah of my house they checked their horses, and looked through the trellis at me as if they expected me to run out,

and give them the desired information. The tall,
slender lady rode nearer to the gate and looked
haughtily in, while the little girl-rider cried out:

"*Tu y serais!*" Then she beckoned the groom,
who was waiting behind them, to come nearer and
hand her a little wooden case with a round glass set
in at the front—a little photograph-apparatus.

"Well," thought I, "these are amateur photo-
grapers, and Dumany Castle has apparently pleased
their eye, and they want to immortalise it in the pages
of their albums—an interesting object!"

I was standing near the fence, by the side of a
flowering rose-bush. I held a spade in my hand, and
was just in the act of putting it to its proper use
when the lady directed her camera toward me. I
thought it was rather a clever performance for a
person on horseback.

"*Ne remuez pas, mon cher!*" cried the lady, as I
lifted the spade. Of course the Slav gardener, whom
I resembled, was bound to understand her French
prattle. So there I stood, with uplifted spade in
hand, until the lady had finished her picture, and
then she released me with a "*Merci, mon garçon!*"
and I, hardly able to keep my composure, answered
in Slav, "*Dobri nocz, mladi panyicska,*" which means
"Good night, miss!"

The ladies broke out into a merry laugh, returned
the apparatus to the groom, and rode off, laughing
because the slender lady had been included in the
picture. I laughed also as I looked after them, and I
said to myself, "Now I shall not utterly die, '*non*

*omnis moriar.'*  The Valkyrs have come to pick up
the fallen hero and carry him into their Walhalla,
which in all probability is bound in morocco leather
with silver clasps."

The same evening I had another surprise.  My
friend Siegfried drove up to my house, sprang from
his barouche, and, seeing me, he ran up and embraced
me tenderly.

"So you know me still?" asked I.

"Know you?  It would be no wonder if I had not
recognised you as you look now!  Do you know that
with a week's growth of beard and moustache a man
looks like a gorilla?"

"Well then, I look like the progenitor of mankind,
if Darwin is to be believed."

"I say, it's high time I came!  otherwise you would
cease to be a Christian, and become one of those
detestable naturalists."  With that Siegfried ordered
his coachman to walk the horses about, feed them,
water them, and prepare for the drive home after
supper.  So I had to give orders for a supper, and
remember that I was not yet my Uncle Diogenes, but
his nephew and a gentleman, and this friend of mine
a veritable Count, who expected me to give him a
good supper.  "After supper you must come with
me," said Siegfried, decidedly.

"I!  Where?"

"To Vernöcze, to visit me!  Have you not got my
letter?"

"I received a letter.  I have it in my blouse-pocket
yet; but——"

"You have not opened it, nor looked at it yet?"

"No. I thought that if anybody wrote to me now, he either wanted to insult me or call me to some kind of a reckoning. I thought there was time for both."

"Oh, you stupid fellow! Where is that letter? I want you to read it at once!"

I took out the letter, opened it, and read:—

"DEAR NELL,—Our party decided at yesterday's meeting to support your name at all odds against the ensuing new election, and carry you through at any cost. My aunt wants to inform you of some very serious matter, so she begs you to pay her a visit on Wednesday next.—Yours, as ever,     "SIGID."

The previous day had been Wednesday, and the letter had been in my pocket for the last four days. I confess that I felt a glow after reading these lines. Something like joy, like exultation, filled me, that after all I was not dead and buried there in that house, not an utter laughing-stock, and that my name was not hooted by friend and enemy alike. I still had noble friends. They remembered me, acted for me, endeavoured to avenge me, and rehabilitate me. It was an intense feeling of relief, of pride, of happiness; but I tried to hide my sensations and play the Cincinnatus a little longer. When Siegfried said, "We expected you all day yesterday; but as you did not come I concluded to come over and look after you," I replied, "I had not read the letter; but if I had, it would hardly have been otherwise. I cannot go from home at present."

"Why! what is the matter with you? You are not going to play Uncle Diogenes, are you? Simple civility might have induced you to come over to Vernöcze. You are due there for ever so long."

"You are very kind; but, you see, the Vice-Governor does not send his sentinels to guard the iron chest with the money, and so I have to guard it myself; and then, you see, I am busy budding my 'Marshal Niel' and 'Sultan of Morocco' roses—it is their season."

Siegfried broke into a merry laugh. "The dear boy is actually trying to live after the pattern of that exemplary old uncle of his. Now, don't make a fool of yourself, old fellow, and don't make believe that you like baked potatoes and curds. I tell you I want a good supper, and after that I'll take you with me. You can take your rose-scions with you. My gardener will be thankful for them. We have a lot of water-shoots in our garden."

We had a good supper, and after the first glass of wine I felt the gloom vanish from me entirely. Siegfried had brought me good news. The new election was to take place in twenty days. Our party was firm as a rock, and the enemy was disheartened and short of money, as the Maticza Society, which had given up all hope of driving me away from the estate, would not furnish them with more funds. Now they had resorted to a last desperate method, and their candidate was about to unfold the anti-Semitic flag, in this way driving all intelligent, Liberal voters—or those at least who assumed the name, and all the Jews with their money, influence, and keenness—straight into our arms, so that our success was undoubted. In order to silence all accusations of bribery, of feasting the voters, and so forth, Countess Diodora, Siegfried's aunt, was ready to keep open house in Vernöcze for our political friends, and so there would be no need of engaging any public restaurants or wine-shops. Siegfried told me that Countess Diodora was a very active champion of our party, and very influential, too. Besides, she was very much interested in me personally.

"I am sure I am very grateful to her ladyship, and shall take the liberty of telling her so, to-morrow," I said—"the more grateful, as I really do not know how I could have merited such an interest."

He smiled. "Merit is not everything," he said. "But Aunt Diodora is a little vexed at your want of politeness. You should have come and paid your homage long ago. Her ladyship really threatened the other day that some day she would come over with the two little ones and fetch you, if not personally, at least in effigy. They have photographic apparatus, and are very clever amateur photographers."

I could not suppress an exclamation, and then I related the little adventure of the afternoon. He laughed. "Oh, no question as to their identity! Sure enough, it was my aunt and the girls! That queenly Amazon is my aunt, Countess Diodora. You are surprised? I see, you supposed that an aunt must necessarily be some aged, corpulent lady, fond of her game of 'patience,' and secretly indulging in a sip.

My aunt is but one year my senior, and I am barely
thirty. My aunt is a classical beauty, highly intellectual, and very talented; quite a female phenomenon.
That tall, slender girl is Countess Flamma, a miracle
of beauty and virtue; and that tiny creature was the
little Kobold, Puck, or whatever else you may call her,
Cousin Cenni. She is the most skilful photographer
of the three, and it was she who told you not to move,
and took you with spade in hand. That's the best
joke I ever heard! How vexed Countess Cenni will
feel on discovering the mistake! She is a little vixen,
and full of mischief. If any of the young dandies
tries to court her, she bids him go bear-hunting with
her and show his valour. My woods are full of bears.
I have shot three, but there are a lot of them alive
still, and they do a deal of damage. So, if Cenni
invites you, which no doubt she will, you need not be
afraid of want of game."

I was dazzled, flattered, and surprised. What a
difference between these ladies of the high aristocracy
and the daughters of our country gentry! As if they
really belonged to a different world, lived on a different
planet. One of them assuming the lead in politics,
another bear-hunting and photographing. The third,
that tall, slender, somewhat haughty, but modest girl,
who had approached to admire my roses, pleased me
best; and then, too, their names—" Diodora! Cenni!
Flamma!" The first domineering, imposing; the
second with a touch of the Bohemian or the gipsy;
the third bewitching, enticing, a flame! Oh, what a
moth I should make!

I did not show much further resistance, but was willing enough to go with Siegfried. I did not even take the trouble of locking the turret-chamber, in which the precious iron chest stood, with my own hands, but ordered my valet to perform that duty and take care of the key. I went out into the garden, and cut all the blooming " Sultan of Morocco " roses and carefully wrapped them up with wet moss; and all the way I held them in my hand for fear of injuring them.

So the Valkyrs were indeed taking away the fallen hero to Walhalla, their own abode.

" Where is Walhalla, and what is it like ? Does anybody know ? If only somebody might return and tell us ! "

" Well, I have been there, and I have returned, and I will tell you."

# Part II.

## I.

### THE SEA-DOVE.

FROM Dumanyfalva to Vernöcze the high-road makes a circuit of a two hours' ride, but we took a short cut by a cross-road through Siegfried's deer-park, which is about ten thousand acres in extent. The whole park was fenced in with high iron railings, and this fence alone had cost the neat little sum of one hundred and fifty thousand florins. Yet it was worth its cost, for, before its erection, the Vernöczys had to pay yearly about twenty-five thousand florins for damage done by their game upon the crops in the neighbouring fields. At the big iron gate a ranger with two loaded rifles was waiting for us. He handed the rifles to the two servants, and then took his seat on the box with the coachman.

It was a beautiful wood through which we drove— all of giant larch trees of a century's growth, perfuming the air with ambrosial odours. The bright rays from our lanterns attracted the deer, and they stood gazing at us with their glittering eyes. One of the bucks bellowed at us, and one of the little fawns came almost under the wheels. Pheasants, startled from sleep by the noise of our wheels, soared above our heads. From the depths of the forest mysterious

voices met our ears : the woodcock's hoarse call, the
roebuck's deep bellow, the wild boar's grunt, the
squirrel's chatter, and the shrill cries which announce
the presence of the wild peacock. What a difference between this lordly forest and my small twenty-
acre park! Red squirrels, gray squirrels, gambolling
among the boughs, playing with acorns and hazel-
nuts ; thrushes, blackbirds, nightingales, and green-
finches, chirruping and twittering, were all the game I
had.

In vain we endeavour to bring high nobility and
plain gentry into one class. They are divided by the
game-park. We are only visitors there, kindly invited,
kindly received, but visitors still, and we can never
repay the compliment. Therefore I consider we
should always think twice before we accept the
invitation.

It was past midnight when we finally arrived at
Siegfried's shooting-box, a beautiful pavilion in the
Swiss style, with a large verandah to the east, facing
the magnificent château. Between the two buildings
extended a clear, broad lake, with silvery willows on
the nearer side, and grand old lime-trees on the side
toward the mansion. Graceful white and black swans
swam on the lake, and two tiny little wherries lay
ready for a boating excursion. The south side of the
shooting-box had "altdeutsch" windows of coloured
glass, and wooden shutters with heart-shaped perfora-
tions on the outside. On the nearer side of the lodge
was a beautiful green lawn and a few somewhat
neglected rose-beds.

The shooting-box was a comfortably large and luxuriously-furnished building, and afforded accommodation for thirty guests. The couches in the different sleeping apartments were all covered with deerskin spreads, and the furniture was all in harmony with the purpose and style of the building.

I left my window ajar for the night, so as to be up early, and my plan succeeded. The dew still glittered upon the tender petals of the roses when I was up and sauntering among the flowers. I had brought my "Malmaison" and "Sultan of Morocco" roses with me, and also my budding-knife and the sap for budding. "What a surprise for them," I thought, "when they find these beautiful flowers instead of the wild suckers." I had put my roses into a glass of water, and was now preparing for the performance by cutting off the collateral shoots and removing the inconvenient thorns. Just as I had taken one of the "Sultan of Morocco" roses out of the water, I heard steps on the gravel, and a musical voice cried—

"Gardener, do you hear ?"

I turned around, and beheld two beautiful young girls hurrying toward me. One of them, a tiny little creature, was of the blonde type, with long, golden curls and a face of cream and roses. One startling, bewitching little black mole was seen on one of the dimpled cheeks. Her eyebrows were dense, of a golden-brown, and arched over a pair of large, glittering brown eyes. The corners of her little mouth curved upward in a smile, and the cherry lips were always open and moving. Her little hands were busy gesticulating, explaining, acting, and never at rest; a picture of the entire little personage.

The other girl was a tall, slender, willow-like figure, with raven hair pushed high above the marble forehead. Her skin was clear and transparent, but with hardly a tinge of colour. Her straight, black brows and long black lashes overhung a pair of deep blue, or rather sea-green, eyes, and her little coral mouth was so small that the idea struck me that it must hurt her to speak, and therefore she liked to hold her peace.

Both were in morning dress, appropriate to the country. The blonde wore a dress of some sort of light Japanese silk, covered with a pattern of great painted birds and flowers. The dark girl had a Nile-blue gown of some light material, and in style somewhat resembling the Greek.

The verandah had prevented me from perceiving their approach. Now they hastened toward me with the easy composure with which we meet some old friend, or—a servant. Of course, I had no difficulty in recognising the equestrian amateurs of the previous day, and it was easy to guess that they repeated their mistake of that afternoon, by taking me for a gardener. I had no intention of undeceiving them, and did not take off my hat, but stood with the "Sultan of Morocco" between my teeth, and my hands engaged with the budding-knife.

"Do you hear?" said the little blonde, now coming near; "cut me a bud of these 'Gloire de Dijons.' No! one of these 'Marshal Niels'; not this, the other, that is just opening!"

I was correctly dressed for the occasion, and quite in proper style for a country visit: tanned shoes, knickerbocker jacket, Pepita waistcoat, Madapolam shirt-collar, Bismarck *en colère* scarf, Panama hat. "My darling, does not that content you?" Still these girls took me for a servant. Well, let it pass!

I cut off one of the roses, and began to pare off the thorns with my knife, when she angrily stamped her little foot on the grass. "What are you paring the thorns off for? I don't like a rose without thorns. I want a rose with thorns; this looks stripped!" and, pulling the rose out of my hand, she held it over to her companion.

"*Tiens! Ca m'embête!*"

To her she spoke French; to me, German. The girl took the rose without a word; for her it was good enough without the thorns. I prepared to cut another bud for the capricious fair one, when she asked, "What rose is that in your mouth?"

"A Sultan of Morocco," I said, taking the rose from my lips.

"Give me this," with an imperative gesture.

"This is for grafting," I tried to explain.

"But I want it!" was the haughty reply, and she impatiently held out her bit of a hand for the rose. I handed it to her, and for a moment she buried her little nose in it and then tried to fasten it to her dress.

Presently a thought seemed to strike her, for she lifted the rose to her lips, and then, turning to me again, asked—

"Has the Count returned home?"

"He has," I answered.

"He did not come alone? A gentleman came with him, did he not?"

I answered in the affirmative.

"Are they asleep yet, do you think? Which is his window?"

"Whose? The Count's?"

"No, that I know! The stranger's?"

"The one that is open," I said, wondering what she meant. She looked around, and observed a double step-ladder standing in front of a tree. "Bring that ladder," she said to me, "and put it in front of that window."

I began to perceive her intention, and, much amused, I fetched the ladder. "Shall I hold it?" I asked, with seeming innocence.

"No. Go back to your work!"

I submitted, and went back to my roses, where the other girl was still standing. The little blonde vixen, as Siegfried had called her, went up the ladder, throwing me a haughty glance because I had the impertinence to watch her movements.

As I prepared for work again, I noticed that in the chalice of each flower, two or more green cetonias were to be found. The cetonia beetle is the deadliest foe of the rose, destroying it entirely, and since my boyhood, when I used to practise gardening at home, and

was taught to kill a cetonia wherever I found it, I
could not bear the sight of the glittering, green beetle.
I was just crushing one under my foot, when the dark-
haired girl near me cried out—

"Why do you kill that poor cetonia?"

"Because it injures the roses," I said.

"Well, let them alone! Who cares for the
roses?"

"Who cares for the roses?" Is not that strange?
A young girl taking the side of the harmful destroyer
against the innocent victim!

The blonde descended the ladder, and her face,
her hands, and her walk betrayed that she was vexed.
I was very much amused. Was it not a joke that she
had climbed up to my window to present me with my
own rose, the rose she had taken out of my mouth?
And was it not amusing to see her angry, because I
had had the sauciness to watch the movements of
those tiny slippered feet in pink stockings as they
mounted the ladder and revealed a bewitching little
ankle?

The black-haired girl turned to her and complained—"See, he kills our cetonias!" Whereupon
the little one, with a queenly mien, stepped in front of
me and said—

"I forbid you to do that! Do not dare to hurt
my cetonias!"

I could not repress a smile, as I answered, "I shall
duly obey. I had no right to interfere, as these
cetonias do not belong to me."

"I really think that fellow is laughing at us!"

said the little one, with arching brows, when the other, who had been watching me for some moments, made some whispered remark, and then the fair head and the dark one were put close together in earnest consultation.

On one of my hands I wore an antique carnelian seal-ring, with my family crest, and a large solitaire, the gift of a grateful patient. These rings, rather unusual upon the finger of a common gardener, had caught the eye of the dark-haired girl, and she could not but notice that my hands and nails were not those of a labourer. For a while they looked shyly at me, while they busied themselves in gathering into their garden hats all the cetonias they could, as if afraid that, after their departure, I should avenge myself by a general onslaught on their *protégées*. Presently the blonde stepped up to me, and, touching the carnelian on my hand with her finger, she said—

" Are you a nobleman ? "

I answered by an anecdote.

" A German journalist had to translate an item on sea-turtles from an English paper. He did not exactly understand what a turtle was; but he knew of turtle-doves, which are in German called *Turtel-tauben*, and, as he did not want to trouble himself to look for the expression in a dictionary, *turtle-doves* it remained. He wrote of the bird, that it comes out of the sea to the sand of the shore, lays its eggs in that sand, carefully and safely scratching them in, and smoothing the surface with its front paws. These front paws of a turtle-dove perplexed him, and he did what he

x

ought to have done before: he looked in the
dictionary and found that the sea-turtle was no dove
at all."

"Hem!" said the little one, looking with charming
astonishment at the other girl; and then she turned
to me again, and, lifting a threatening little finger at
me, she said—

"Now, don't you go and betray us to anybody
Promise!"

"You have my knightly word," I said; "*parole
d'honneur!*" But, unable to suppress my mirth any
longer, I broke into a ringing laugh, and both girls
fled as fast as they could.

On returning to my room, I found Siegfried there.
"My aunt's footman has already been here to invite
us to breakfast," he said. "When in the country she
is always an early riser, and so are the children. I
wonder they have not been running about yet. They
used to."

I did not tell him that they had been running
about already; but, stepping up to the window, I
found the rose which the fair girl had laid upon the
sill, and, fastening it in the button-hole of my jacket,
made ready to follow up the invitation for breakfast.

"Wouldn't you rather shave before going down?"
asked Siegfried, with a disapproving look at my face.
"My valet has an easy hand, and is very reliable."

"No, thank you!" I said, and with that I took his
arm and we went down.

Near the lake was a mass of beautiful dolomite
rock, a forerunner of the high mountains further on.

The face of the rock was all overgrown with birch trees, and wild roses and other flowers were peeping out of the thick moss and bush. At the foot of the rock was a clearing surrounded with pines, their drooping foliage forming a shady roof above the little circuit of ground. In the wall of the rock was a grotto, overrun with henna leaves, hedge-plant, and other creepers. Out of one of the walls of the grotto broke, murmuring and rippling, a clear mountain spring, which, meeting with another and uniting with it to form a rivulet, flowed across the flowery plain, emptying itself into the lake by a series of cascades.

In the centre of this space the breakfast-table was set—the shining silver, the glittering crystal, and the creamy china forming a pleasant contrast to the rural simplicity of the chairs and table and the green roof and walls above and around.

Countess Diodora was already there, expecting us. The two girls were in the grotto, pretending to be busy with the preparations for breakfast.

Countess Diodora was strikingly handsome. Tall of stature and fully developed, her movements had all the elasticity of youth and all the majesty of a goddess. Her Creole complexion was in harmony with the great almond-shaped eyes, the Minerva forehead, Grecian nose, and shell-shaped mouth with its coral-red lips. Her head was crowned with a tiara of heavy black tresses, more precious and beautiful than any artificial ornament.

Siegfried led me to her and presented me with the following words—

"At last I am able to introduce my hitherto invisible friend. Do not be amazed at his present resemblance to our common progenitors, the Simians—
that is, if we believe the evolutionists; but our friend
here has no intention of claiming that affinity. His
sprouting moustache and beard are a token of
patriotic zeal, and a sacrifice upon the altar of national
idiosyncrasy. Henceforth he will be known as a
Hungarian in appearance also, and nobody will be
justified in calling him an Austrian."

The lady smiled at the humorous introduction,
and extended both her hands, which were somewhat
large, but magnificently shaped. Could I do less than
kiss both? The smile that flitted over her queenly
features gave her the appearance of a veritable
goddess.

"Is it not odd," she asked, "that we know each
other so well, yet have never met until this moment?"
Her voice was a rich, deep contralto, and very sweet.

"I have already enjoyed the happiness of seeing
your ladyship," said I, smiling.

"Indeed? And where?"

"In my own garden. If I am not greatly mistaken,
your ladyship and the two young ladies, your cousins,
were yesterday at the pains to immortalise me by
taking my photograph."

"Impossible!" she cried. "It could not have been
you! With the spade in hand, and—oh, it is too
odd!" And she broke into a loud laugh.

A laughing Pallas! The two girls ran out of the
grotto to see what the staid Diodora was laughing at.

"Come on, Cenni," said the lady to the little blonde : "here is the gardener of yesterday; the one you have photographed along with his garden."

But by that time the little one knew me well enough; she had recognised the rose in my button-hole, and, with pretended anger, she ran toward me, took hold of the collar of my jacket, and gave it a hearty pull.

"You are an artful and dangerous cheat and deceiver—that is what you are !" she said. "Why did you deceive us this morning, and make sport of us ? Let us treat you as a gardener, and send you on errands ? Why did not you tell us who you were ?"

Siegfried came to my help. "How could he ? He did not know you; maybe he took you for your own maids. If you had told him who you were, he would have returned the compliment."

"But you won't betray us to anybody ?" she said, holding up, as if in prayer, her little hands, that looked like the delicate petals of the white lily. "You won't tell anybody of our conversation at the rose bushes ? If you promise, I'll give you a kiss; I will, indeed !"

"But, Cenni !" cried Countess Diodora, shocked, "what expression is that again ?"

The little one looked like a scolded school-girl, who does not know what crime she has been punished for, and said, poutingly—

"But I want him to keep the secret, and I must give him a reward."

"You always forget that you are no longer a little

girl of twelve years, but a grown-up young lady, although, God knows, you do not look like it!" said the countess, with a humorous shake of the head.

"Now you great debater and future lawgiver, what do you say to this offered reward? Answer *ex tripode!*" said Siegfried, laughingly.

"I say that I am no usurer, and cannot take unlawful interest," I replied.

"Bravo! bravissimo! A usurer! Unlawful interest he calls a kiss! Oh, what a moral fellow!" cried Siegfried; but Countess Diodora observed that breakfast was waiting, and that we had time enough for ventilating academic questions afterward.

At the table I sat between Countess Diodora and Countess Flamma. The latter turned to me, and said in her quiet and sober way—

"But I discovered soon enough that the sea-turtle was not a sea-dove, did I not?"

"What are you talking about sea-doves?" asked the countess; "it seems you have secrets in common already."

I opened my mouth to answer, when the little blonde opposite to me sprang up and put her little shell-coloured hand to my lips. "No betrayal, if you please! You have given your knightly word!"

"I am mute!" I said, bowing to her with a smile.

"I declare!" said the countess, "knightly word, turtle-dove! Why, what mystery is this? Flamma was complaining something about the cetonias."

"Oh, that is nothing," said Cenni, lightly, "and that may be spoken of; but the 'step-ladder,' the

'Sultan of Morocco,' and the 'sea-dove' are strict secrets, and never to be mentioned anywhere."

Siegfried clapped his hands in surprise. "Riddle after riddle! and to think that I myself have brought this boy to the house only last night for the first time in his life, and introduced him not an hour ago, and—talk of his being shy in the company of ladies!—he is head over ears in conspiracy with both of the girls, when I thought he had never seen them, and they did not know him at all!"

## II.

"WE not know him?" asked the little one. "Why, we have his photograph in our album! Only he looks much nicer there. Such a Lord Byron face!"

"Well, this is really audacious!" cried Siegfried, "with such a face to appear before ladies! Coarse and stubby like that of a Slav field-labourer, and yet such a young lady as that calls it a Lord Byron face! Now I see that the old proverb is right, and a man has to be but one shade handsomer than the Devil, for women will find him handsome enough."

"Only that the proverb is a paradox in itself. The Evil One is not ugly; on the contrary, he is beautiful!" said Diodora.

"*Quien sabe?*" answered Siegfried. "I have seen his portrait in the Greek churches, in a large wall-painting, and there he is represented as a bandy-legged, ox-tailed, black-faced monster, with a pair of big horns on his forehead. Then, again, I have seen the Devil in the opera, as Göthe and Gounod's creation of Mephistopheles in *Faust*, and there he wore a goat's-beard and red-feathered cap, was a little lame in one leg, and had a baritone voice. He was not in the least beautiful."

"You ought to read Klopstock, then, and Milton," said Countess Diodora. "Their Devils are enchantingly handsome men, with pale faces, and deep, sorrowful eyes; and that is the real demon-type as given by the classics: for, originally, the Devil was not known as an evil spirit, but was an angel. Only he was haughty and ambitious, and tried to rival and dethrone the Almighty. It was after he was defeated, and due punishment was dealt to him, that he became the representative of Evil, and, after the creation of man, the tempter and seducer."

"So part of the Devil's corruption is due to man kind," said Siegfried, ironically.

"If you read the Cabalists and Gnostics you will learn how sinful pride had its downfall, and the angel fell. Still, in all his humiliation and his banishment from grace and glory, he never lost his beauty, and this is natural; for who would listen to the temptations of an ugly monster? A seducer must needs be handsome. In the old Jewish Scripture, from before Moses' time, the Evil Spirit is represented by a woman, Lilith, the ideal beauty. In the same manner Menander has painted Sybaris, and of Socrates it is said that he lived in intimate friendship with the demon."

Siegfried had made a desperate onslaught on the sandwiches; now he turned in comical vexation to me, and said—

"Friend, brother, help! for this learned woman is slaying me with pandects, and, if the Devil has such a champion, what can poor I do against him?"

It was a difficult task. If I said that she was right, she would scorn me as a simple, empty-headed flatterer. If, on the other hand, I tried to contradict her, she was sure to conquer me with arguments. So I thought I would plead scepticism.

"Indeed, I can't," was my reply. "All I have to say is that I do not believe in the existence of an actual Devil at all. I positively deny the existence of evil spirits or devils."

"Ah!" said the countess, astonished and seemingly dismayed, "do you know that such a negation includes a denial of the fundamental truths of all religion also? Turn wherever you will, and you will find that the Roman Catholic faith expressly commands us to believe in the Devil. The Protestants, with Martin Luther at the head, have in speech and writing gone so far as to compose a whole Shamanism of the Devil's special qualities; and so on in all positive religions. Are you an infidel, a so-called Freethinker, and not a Christian?"

At first I smilingly referred her to Becker's "Bewitched World," which made all belief in an actual Devil completely ridiculous, showing to demonstration that such a being is simply impossible. She answered me with Spinoza. I again spoke of Thomasius, whereupon the countess declared me a Rationalist.

Siegfried smiled, and smoked his cigarette complacently, and the two girls listened innocently and wonderingly to the strange dispute.

"You see, my lady," said I at last, "I am a physician, and I know of no bodily or mental ailment that is without some foundation or reason. I know of miasmata, spores, bacilli, as sources of bodily diseases, of inherited or fancied maladies, infections, contagions, and their proper remedies: vaccination, disinfection, prophylactics; but an invisible, immaterial spirit, which we ought to know by the title of Devil, has nothing to do with any of these. All evil-doers, murderers, etc., are prompted to the mischief they do by some abnormity in their brains, or by some powerful egotistic motive, as jealousy, revenge, greed, ambition, etc.; but the temptation is always material—a benefit they want to secure by their crime—never a spiritual Devil. We may fairly say that all crimes committed without a visible motive are founded upon lunacy, a disorder of the brain. I do not believe in one being, either corporal or spiritual, that would do mischief purely for mischief's sake, out of evil principle, of pure malice. I do not believe that any being exists which would inflict sorrow on others just in order to rejoice at the despair of the victims. The so-called hellish passions and inclinations in man are really created by that which is beneath him, the animal part of him, the material element, and it is superfluous to look to that which is above him, a spirit, for a motive."

As I pronounced this conviction, the four persons present looked at each other and then at me, in wonder and defiance, but without a word. For a moment a chilly presentiment crept over me—a shadowy warning that the declaration I had just made would prove the *fatum* of my life.

As a physician, I had given very much attention to disturbances of the mind; nervous distractions, diseases of the brain. In lunatic asylums I had had frequent opportunity of observing the different manifestations of extravagances of the mind diseased. There are cases in which simulation is identical with the symptoms of actual insanity, others in which it is mistaken for such; but still the simulator is never quite sane. I had speculated about the hidden motives of apparently motiveless crimes. I had seen a gallant youth, whose noble, manly features inspired love and confidence, and who yet had murdered many victims of his bestial desires; had lured them on, and killed them.

I had seen a tender, innocent, pleasant-looking young girl, with a winning smile on her ruby lips, after she had poisoned all the members of her family in turn; and I had known a miracle-working virgin, who had for years and years befooled and deceived aged and experienced men. All these and more I had seen, but all had possessed one common peculiarity which betrayed them as belonging to that large and unhappy class we term lunatics, and their mental disorder was revealed in a clear, glittering glance, cold and keen as a steel blade. The moment that unlucky assertion had escaped me, I saw my companions stare at each other and then at me, and in the eyes of all four of them I clearly discerned and recognised the same cold, keen, and gloomy expression. I felt a shock of terror, and then I laughed at my own folly. A professional habit of mentally examining and distinguishing all persons as sane and healthy, or diseased, I thought, and I tried to joke the matter away.

"Let us make a bargain, countess! We will leave the demon to those who cannot spare him; for there are people who would greatly protest against being robbed of their devils—as, for instance, some Western nations who worship him instead of God. They say God is good, and won't hurt them, anyhow, but the Devil must be bribed by compliments to keep him from doing mischief. Therefore they raise altars to him, and set up his images with many ceremonies. The Yakoots and Chuckches believe in a double creation, and think that all good things are created by God, and all bad things by the Devil."

"It would not hurt you to be of the same creed," said Countess Diodora.

"For instance, to believe that the rose was created by God and the cetonia by the Devil," I replied, smilingly.

"And why those?" she asked. "My niece has complained to me that you crush these beautiful little beetles to death. In what have they offended you?"

"Offended me? Do you hold me capable of such petty malice? I kill the cetonias because they are the deadliest foes of the rose; or, rather, as they love the rose, and in loving destroy the flower, I must call the cetonia the most dangerous friend of the rose."

"However, the beetles are necessary to my nieces, and therefore they must live."

"Necessary?" I cried. "How so?"

The blonde girl went into the grotto and, returning, brought with her a large teak board, upon which a Chinese sun-bird was enamelled. The bird was only half finished as yet, but it was the most artistic, tasteful, and delightful enamel-work I had ever seen, and all of it was composed of the delicate lids of the beetle-wings. The cetonias vary in colour: some of them are red with a tinge of gold; others green and gold; others again the colour of darkened copper, and still others in a metallic blue, like steel. All these were carefully arranged and pasted upon the teak board in a wonderful mosaic, the sun-bird's head and wings consisting of red, its neck of blue, and its breast of green cetonia-wings. I looked admiringly at the work. So, then, they had not protected the cetonias out of some sentimental fancy for them, but for industrial purposes. This changed my conception of the matter entirely; for the better in some respects—in some for the worse.

"So you save the life of the beetle in order to rob them of their wings?" I asked them, reproachfully.

"These are only their winter wings which we take off; their summer wings they keep, and we give them their liberty again. It is summer now; they have no need of their winter wings at present."

Well, this was girlish logic and philosophy: I have taken what I wanted, you must make the

best of what I have left you.   Rather a striking piece
of egotism !

"Do you know that the cetonia contains poison ?"
asked I.

"What kind of poison ?" was the inquiring
response, given with great quickness.

"The poison," I said, evasively, "that gives the
motive to the Bánk-Bán tragedy."

At these words Siegfried puffed a whole cloud of
tobacco-smoke full in my face, and at any other time
I should have strongly resented the insult; but this
time he was right.   The explanation was, even as an
allusion, objectionable in the presence of girls.   Nevertheless I could perceive through the cloud of smoke
that the pale face of Flamma had coloured violently,
and that Cenni pouted and pushed the sun-bird away.
The innocents were not so very innocent, after all.

"Is not this beetle identical with the holy scarabæus of the Egyptians ?" asked Countess Diodora.

"No.   Because the cetonia lives on roses ; and of
the holy scarabæus Herodotus tells us that he dies
of the odour of roses.   As soon as the roses begin to
bloom the scarabæus vanishes."

This interested the girls, and we continued the subject.   I told them of the South American Hercules-
beetle, that is as fond of liquor as any human tippler,
and I really thought that I had succeeded in turning
the conversation from the horned devil to the horned
beetle, when Countess Diodora said—

"You are too much of a naturalist.   This won't do,
and you must try to amend.   To deny God is bad

enough, but He is kind and forgiving, and the infidel
may yet be saved; but to deny the Devil is sure destruction, for the Devil knows no mercy, and he
takes his revenge on the insulter."

I looked up astonished and met her eyes. Again I
detected that bewildering cold glitter, and with an
involuntary shiver I turned away.

## III.

### THE FOUR-LEAVED CLOVER.

THE same day our political friends and partisans came, and we held a conference. From that day on I was a daily guest in Vernöcze, and when occasionally I spent a night at home in my own house, next morning I was sure to feel restless and uneasy, and persuaded myself that political reasons required my presence in Vernöcze, and that I must make haste to go there.

A number of times the illustrious ladies of the Vernöcze castle descended from their lofty situation to pay a visit to my lowly house, and on these occasions I played the host, and set before them what my cellar and buttery afforded. Then I conducted them through the chambers in which were stored my late uncle's beloved curiosities, and I told them of the horrors of the olden time, and the history of this ancient seat of my family. There was the story of a walled-up wife and murdered lovers, and we had our "Woman in White" and our "Red Templar," who, at the stroke of midnight, duly stalked through locked rooms and corridors, and performed all the actions that could be expected of real and respectable ghosts. These phantoms the countess rather envied me, for Vernöcze could boast of no such token of old nobility; yet the Vernöczys were counts and the Dumanys only plain gentry.

Of course, I was an ardent admirer of the three fairies, only I could not exactly tell which of the three I admired most. Countess Diodora's philosophical intellect impressed me as much as Countess Cenni's unruly activity; and Countess Flamma's pensive silence affected me none the less, and I looked at her with the reverential awe of the priest before the Holy Virgin.

Only one thing puzzled me. Here were three beautiful, gifted, high-born, and wealthy young women, and not one of them had a real, earnest, and sincere suitor. Of course, there were a number of young aristocrats paying court to them, and very much inclined to carry on a little bit of flirtation; but all in an easy-going, although certainly very respectful and distant way; but of a real, true attachment I could perceive no sign. Once I had ventured a remark to this effect in Siegfried's presence, whereupon he explained that the two younger countesses were mere school-girls yet, and nobody would have the audacity to think of a serious courtship in that quarter as yet, while, as to Countess Diodora, she would never marry at all. She repudiated the very idea of marriage, and would no doubt, sooner or later, enter a convent as abbess.

This explanation, to tell the truth, did not satisfy me. If the two young ladies were such forbidden fruit at present, why bring them in constant

contact with young men? And, as to Countess
Diodora's intention to become a nun, I had my
strong doubts. True, she was religious, even to
bigotry, but she was not averse to the pleasures of
the world, and I did not believe in her inclination to
give them up of her free will. I rather believed that
men were afraid of her, for such learned and strong-
minded women can be only the wives of yet wiser and
more strong-minded men, or else of fools, who willingly become their slaves.

To me Countess Diodora was conspicuously kind,
and showed me an exceptional preference—that is,
she did me the honour to select me as her antagonist
in debate.

When she supported one paradox, I would
support the opposite, and we kept up a constant
battle with intellectual weapons. She was a great
reader; so was I. She had travelled a good deal; so
had I, and, as it chanced, we had observed the same
countries and scenes. On art, architecture, literature,
I gave judgment with the same startling audacity as
she, only that my opinions were in direct opposition
to hers.

Still in matters of politics our views were har-
monious. I had the same Conservative principles as
she, and I heartily agreed with all that she uttered on
that point. This was the first step to our mutual
understanding. The second step was taken when we
joined each other in defence of our principles against
persons of opposing views; and the third step, which
lifted me not only to a level with my new and

beautiful ally, but even above her, was gained by me
in a controversy on professional science, with especial
relation to physicians. The countess, in a very
spirited bit of banter, ridiculed the whole profession
and its science, stating that, in her belief, our entire
pathology, therapeutic, etc., was not worth the sand
strewn over the prescriptions. She declared that in
the treatment of internal maladies medical science
has made no progress since Galen's time, and our
most renowned professional celebrities are no wiser
than Paracelsus. Our medicines, according to her
opinion, were either baneful poisons, or of no higher
sanative power, at the best, than the waters of
Lourdes. She also was afflicted with bodily pain at
times, but never yet had she submitted to any professional treatment. No physician had ever entered
her bed-room or parted the tapestry hangings around
her bed, and never yet had she tasted of any kind of
medicine.

I listened complacently to her talk, and did not
interrupt her with a word. After she had finished, I
said—

"Allow me to contradict, and, at the same time,
convict you. You have never spoken of your special
ailment to me up to this moment. I have never heard
of it before this, and I need not put any questions
either to you or to others in regard to it. Yet, by
simply looking at you, I can tell you from what you
are suffering—that you are a victim of occasional
nervous attacks of greater or less severity, and I can
tell you exactly how these paroxysms commence,

what symptoms they show, and all the particulars of your ailment."

She stared at me, quite perplexed. "You are right!" she said at last, and there was not a man alive who could boast that she had ever said as much to him. She asked me how I came to know or to guess the nature of her sufferings, and I told her that I had had great experience in the treatment of nervous disorders, and that her case was by no means hopeless. That although it was impossible to entirely and permanently cure the disease and drive away its attacks, yet it might be greatly diminished. The paroxysms might be reduced in duration and violence, and that without administering any poisonous drugs — simply by proper massage.

"Then I am sorry that we have no female physicians as yet; for I would never submit to that treatment from a male physician."

"And do you know that this shrinking is one of the symptoms of the malady, and at the same time its main foundation?"

"How so?"

"Because, if your views of propriety were not distorted, you would apply for help in time, and not wait until you are past cure; but you grow up with the conviction that it is a shame and a degradation to confess your physical weaknesses to a male physician, yet you are by no means ashamed—nay, you consider it a duty and a virtue—to confess your mental and moral failings to a priest, although he is a man as

well as the physician, and the sins you confess are
sometimes more degrading and shameful than the
sores of your body."

She looked at me for quite a while. "Again you
are right," she said, and with that broke off the
conversation.

At that period, every day brought some political
meeting or party conference, and the leaders of the
coming elections, head-drummers, and subalterns
swarmed into Vernöcze, bringing all sorts of news,
asking for all sorts of information, and Countess
Diodora was at the head of everything—presiding at
the councils, assisting them all with her advice, never
tired, never slackening in spirit or courage, and never
forgetting her position as hostess—and a bountiful
hostess, too.

When the discussion approached the financial
question, she said to me with rare delicacy—

"This is no affair of yours; leave that to us. You
can meanwhile go and look for the girls in the
park."

And I, in spite of my professional sagacity, in spite
of the knowledge and experience I had gained, I was
such a greenhorn—such a simple fool—that I actually
believed in the existence of a fund raised for the
especial purpose of sending such shining political
stars, such rare celebrities, as the Honourable Cornelius
Dumany, into Parliament, there to enlighten the
minds of his compatriots, and to be a blessing to his
country; although, if any one had asked me how I
had deserved to be held in such high esteem, I could

not have found an answer! Oh, vanity and conceit!
How easily you are caught in the meshes of cunning
deception!

The "girls," as they were invariably called, were
on the lawn looking for four-leaved clovers, and the
little blonde declared that she was bent on finding
one, for whoever found it first was sure to be married
first. I laughed, and, looking down, I saw one
little quatrefoil just at my feet. I gathered it, and
presented it to the little blonde countess, but she
refused to accept it. "No," she said, "everybody
must keep his own fortune. You have found the
leaf, and you will get married first, and within the
year."

"Ought not I to know something of the coming happiness in advance?" I asked, smilingly.
"Surely I can't get married without my own knowledge!"

"Just you keep quiet. Mockery is not becoming to
you; but tell us in good earnest, why don't you
marry? You ought to."

'Why, then, in good faith, I do not marry because the girls that would not reject me I do not
care for, and those that I might care for would not
accept me."

"How do you know? First tell us what qualities a girl must possess to make you care for
her."

"Well, I suppose I must obey your ladyship's
wishes. In the first place, then, she must be young
and pretty; then she must be intellectual, prudent,

and well educated; and, finally, she must have a kind
heart and a sweet disposition; if she is merry and
bright also, I shall like her the better. Yes, there is
something else: I should like my future wife to be
always elegant and stylish, and I should like to give
her a splendid home and keep her in luxury; but, as
my own little Slav kingdom is not sufficient for my
notion of the term, therefore she must also have a
fortune of her own. Yet, if a woman, or let me rather
say a young girl, should possess all these qualities
at once, which I think unlikely, I would not take her
if I were not fully convinced that she married me for
love. So, you see, with these pretensions I am likely
to live and die a bachelor."

"Not necessarily. I, for instance, know a lady
who answers to your description as if you had drawn
her portrait."

"Indeed? You seem bent on proving that the
four-leaved clover was a true prophet of marriage.
You want to make the match?"

"Why not? But, indeed, I am speaking in
good faith. Why don't you marry Aunt Diodora?"

"Because I have more sense than those poor birds
who shatter their heads and beaks in flying against
the reflected rays of the lighthouse."

"I don't understand the simile."

"Do you know the story of Turandot?"

"No. Novels and comedies I dare not read yet;
but I should like to know, for Aunty Diodora is
nicknamed 'Princess Turandot.' I have often heard

her spoken of by that name. I think that Turandot must be a fictitious creature, who tortures all her suitors to death, for aunty is also very unkind to them. Only that is no fault of hers; it is her misfortune to have nobody sue for her hand except simpletons. All these sweet-spoken, flattering, aping, thought-snatching, cajoling, empty-headed wooers my aunt calls monkeys, and not men. A man must have the courage to oppose her, defend his own opinion against her and all the world, to gain her respect and her confidence. This you have done. Oh, we girls know well enough what impression a man has made on another girl!"

This was a startling confession. Here was a little girl, who was treated and spoken of as quite a baby; yet, in spite of her unacquaintance with novels and comedies, she seemed to be very well versed in all matters of love and matrimony.

"Yes," she continued, "I have noticed it plainly enough, and quite frequently. Whenever you are away she is gloomy, and melancholy, and out of spirits; but, as soon as she sees you or hears your voice, she brightens up and is good-humoured and pleasant. When, the other day, Flamma and I had made some remark about you—some light jest—she gave us such a sermon! telling us that men were all so different, and that you were, among them, like a real diamond among coloured glass. Oh, if I could tell you all! But you are proud and disdainful, I see. Perhaps you want to wait until Countess Diodora Vernöczy makes you a humble offer of her hand, and

then maybe you would be proud, and consider
about it."

"Perhaps I should. Give me leave, ladies, to tell
you a story—the history of a very intimate friend, and
from beginning to the end true to the letter. I shall
invent nothing."

## IV.

As soon as I promised them a story, the two young girls sat down on a low bench beneath a jasmine bush, and I sat down on the bowling-green at their feet; or, rather, I kneeled there before them. Do not think that we were left without a proper guard, for we could be seen from the balcony of the house, and on the mountain-ash tree was an old missel-thrush that kept on chirruping and twittering, "Take care, you boy! take care!"

The young ladies had stripped a heap of the slender Pimprinpáre stalks, from which they began to braid chains and other ornaments, while I related the following story:—

"My friend is a descendant of the noblest families of Hungary, and a count by birth. During the Revolution of 1848 he was one of the bravest and most heroic defenders of the national cause, and his great personal attractions, manly beauty, athletic strength, intellectual power, and high moral integrity, united with an iron will and the tender heart of a woman, made him distinguished above many. Of him it was said that, even as a man, he obeyed every command of his mother, but could never be made to obey that of any potentate of the world."

"Is that paragon of a man alive yet?" asked Cenni.

"He is. Only he is an old eagle now, for our friendship dates from the time when he gave me a ride on his knees, while I blew the whistle he had brought me. During our national struggle for liberty in 1848 he served as a captain of the —— Hussars, and, after the Russian invasion and the final overthrow of the national cause, he made good his escape to England. Of course, his lands and goods were siezed, and he was sentenced to death; but, as he could not be caught and hanged in person, he was hanged in effigy—that is, his portrait was nailed to the gallows.

"The same high qualities which had distinguished him at home distinguished him abroad. A great many Hungarian refugees had found a home in England, especially in that gigantic metropolis, London; and it is said of them, in general, that of all political emigrants they behaved best. They never quarrelled, never grumbled, and never conspired. Everyone hastened to find a mode of earning a decent living for himself, and none of them were too proud or too lazy to work. Every one of them was honestly and diligently engaged in some business.

"My friend had some acquaintances among the English nobility, and he was soon introduced, and speedily became at home in English high life. Among those aristocratic families with which he had frequent intercourse was one in which there was a young girl, an orphan and an heiress. She was beautiful and intellectual, like Countess Diodora, and competition for her hand was naturally high among the young and old bachelors, and marriageable men of their set.

Singularly enough, the young stranger, who never thought of such good fortune, at last felt compelled to believe that the open preference the lady showed him was more than common courtesy, and more than the friendly, even sisterly regard with which most ladies of his acquaintance honoured him. He could not but admire her beauty, her grace, and accomplishments, and he was ready and willing enough to fall in love with so much charm and loveliness. His courtship, if so it must be termed, although the lady was doing the greater part of the wooing, was short and successful, and they were married.

"The marriage took place on the Isle of Wight, at that time the favourite haunt of the Hungarian refugees. Two of the latter, the one a renowned politician, the other a famous general, were witnesses, and the wedding breakfast was quite an event. But when, after the bridal cake had been cut and the toasts drunk, the guests retired, and the young couple were left alone, the fair young bride said to the happy groom :—

"'I beg your pardon for leaving you to your own company, but I must retire to change my dress, for my yacht is waiting, and I shall start for France in two hours.'

"He gazed at her in utter amazement. 'Why, dearest,' he said, 'don't you know that Louis Napoleon denies us Hungarians even the privilege of passing through France, and that for me to go there is equivalent to imprisonment, possibly death?'

"'I know it, and I do not ask you to accompany

me. I shall go there alone. I yearned for independence and liberty, and for the coming years I could
get it only as a married woman. I was in need of a
husband, or of his name, and my choice fell upon
you, because I did not dare to play this trick on one
of our English Hotspurs. Of you I know that you
are too gentle and too noble withal to injure a woman.
So good-bye to you, count, for I do not think that we
shall ever set eyes on each other again!'

"With that the fair goddess left her husband of
two hours' standing, humiliated, stunned, without
money, bereft of his former occupation, to which, as
her husband, he could not return; left him for ever;
and he was such a gentle fool that he did not even
for a moment think of revenge upon the woman who
had robbed him of the last and only treasure he
possessed, his spotless name and honour, and had
ruined him for ever.

"For twenty-five years the poor victim of the fair
deceiver could not with decency extricate himself
from the meshes of the net which she had thrown
over him. After some years he found a good, pure,
and true heart that was full to the brim with love for
the unhappy man—so much so that she sacrificed
position, family, and reputation for his sake, and ac-
companied him from country to country, through
danger and poverty, sharing his cares and troubles,
and consoling him with her love and fidelity. To this
woman, who was his real wife, he could not give the
legal name and position she merited, and the curse
that had been laid on his own life was heavy upon his

innocent children, for he could not carry them to the baptismal font, could not christen them as his own. In England he could not secure a divorce, to France he could not go, and home to Hungary he dared not come. For twenty-five years he dragged these heavy chains on his weary limbs, until Hungary had risen from her prostration, had become a constitutional state with a free Parliament, and had crowned her king, and called home her banished children from the nooks and corners of the world. Then only, when again at home and in full possession of his ancestral castle and estates, then only a legal divorce set him at liberty and left him free to bestow his name upon his faithful, loving companion and their children. But when that time had at last arrived, my friend was an old man with silvery beard and a bald head. The fairy that was the cause of so much suffering had taken nothing of him but his name, of which she was in need; but what is a name? Nothing but the lid, the tender coverlet of the beetle's wing. She did not kill the poor beetle, and she set him free; he was allowed to live with his winter wings."

During the recital of this story, Cenni's rosy countenance was crimsoned through and through, while Flamma's pale face was overspread with an almost deadly pallor, and, as I spoke the final words, the girls looked at each other in silence. "So, you see," I continued, "if such a thing could happen to a man like my friend, the bearer of a great name, noble, brave, accomplished, and handsome, what would be my fate if I should attempt to do what he did—

marry a beauty and an heiress? I, that am nothing but a runaway doctor, an expelled Member of Parliament, and a Slav King! one who, from his appearance, is mistaken for his own subject."

"No! no!" said Cenni, taking hold of both my hands, "there you are mistaken, and—and I am sure you do not know your own worth!"

At that moment the jasmine-bush was parted, and Siegfried's voice asked, "May I take the liberty to interrupt these tender confessions?"

At the sound of Siegfried's voice we all sprang from our seats, and Cenni, throwing the chain she had braided on his neck, said, "You are a great, naughty, good-for-nothing fellow! What do you want?"

"This noble and gallant knight of yours. He is wanted by his executioners—that is, by the election leaders that are to be."

The two young girls laughed, and ran to the little lake for a boating trip, and I asked Siegfried, "What do these men want from me? What is their business with me?"

"Oh, nothing!" he said, coolly. "They have not come; it is I who have business to speak of with you, and quickly, too, for I may be too late already. My dear boy, even a friend has something that he wants to keep for himself and does not want to share with his dearest friend—his love! You are making love to Cenni, although you must have seen that I am over ears in love with her myself."

"I have seen nothing of the kind, and I give

you my word that I never thought of making love to her."

"Possibly so; but then she makes love to you, and that renders matters worse yet."

"I assure you that your jealousy leads you into error."

"Oh! Do you think we have no telescopes in the house? I have witnessed the last interesting scene as if I were on the spot."

"Then I can only wish that your hearing might have been as much increased by some instrument as your vision by the telescope, so that you might have heard our discourse, and not guessed at it by sight."

"Did you not find a four-leaved clover, and offer it to Cenni?"

"Yes, here it is; take it, my boy, and marry your Cenni, with my blessing!"

"Take care! I may take you at your word!"

"And welcome! I'll be your best man."

"That's a bargain. And, now that I see that you are really not going to play the traitor with me, I'll tell you the whole truth. I am mad with love for Cenni; and then, too, she has a million florins from her grandfather, and this money would come in well to help me carry out my plans. But my aunt does not consent to give the girl to me. She says I am a libertine, a *frivole viveur*, etc., and she won't take the responsibility of trusting me with the dear child."

"Tell her you will reform, you will change after marriage."

"That I have repeatedly tried, but she refuses to

M

believe me. Then there is that million. As long as
the girl is unmarried and a minor, my aunt takes her
revenues, and, among her other accomplishments, my
aunt is a very fair accountant. She has found out
that the girl cannot eat figs and candies in a year to
the amount of sixty thousand florins, so she is not
over-willing to part with her at all. But I am not
going to play the Tantalus for years, and run the risk
of having the girl snatched from me by some jackanapes or rascal or another. Pardon!"

"Never mind! I shan't pick up the 'jackanapes'
or the 'rascal.' They do not belong to me."

"Then help me carry out my plan. Do you
promise?"

"By all means."

"Thank you. But let me unfold my plan. Cenni
and I will be married clandestinely behind Aunt
Diodora's back. My aunt is sometimes subject to
severe neuralgic attacks, and, as she never calls a
physician and never takes any remedies for her pains,
she suffers all day. During these paroxysms of her
nerves she remains all day in a darkened room, and
will not allow anybody to stay with her but Flamma.
That kind soul is with her at such times, administering to her comforts, smoothing her pillows, etc., and
in return she is allowed to read Flammarion, or one
of Verne's harmless fictions, in the adjoining sitting-
room. On such days Cenni is entirely at liberty, and
not watched by anybody, because that sleepy governess the girls have is hardly worth mentioning.
Now listen. I keep here, concealed in my shooting-

box, a priest—a Capuchin monk—Father Paphuntius. He seems to be a jolly good fellow, and he has an open hand. In the park there is a little memorial chapel, erected by one of my ancestors in honour of St. Vincent de Paul. In that chapel we will exchange vows. You and Muckicza shall be my witnesses. Now you have given me your promise, will you stick to your word?"

"By all means! Only after the marriage is perfected give me leave to run away as fast as possible; for I should not dare to look your aunt in the face after such perfidy on my part."

"*Au contraire*, you shall not run, for you must stay and help me out further. I have chosen you in your capacity as physician to persuade Diodora to swallow this bitter medicine. She will take much if it comes from you, and I really believe you have magnetised her. It will be your mission to break the fact of the accomplished marriage to her, and persuade her to give her consent, since the matter is irreparable. You see, we cannot afford to quarrel with her, for she has four millions, and is not likely to marry at all."

I hesitated, but he begged and prayed—"My dear friend," "My own Nell," and so forth—until I gave way, and promised to do all that he wanted.

When I had finally promised him he pressed my hands, and then turned away and buried his face in his silk pocket-handkerchief. Was this to hide his tears or—his laughter? *O sancta simplicitas!*

## V.

### HOW ROSES ARE INOCULATED.

THE same day, after luncheon, Countess Flamma turned to me with the question—

"Would you mind teaching me the process of inoculation? I am greatly interested in roses, and should like to see how the scion is set into the stock."

"With ever so much pleasure," I said, pleased that the pale, silent girl showed an interest in my favourites, the roses, and turned to me for a favour. Countess Diodora gave the required permission for the lesson, which was to be given and taken while the others were playing lawn-tennis on the adjacent grounds. Flamma was a bad player, anyhow, so she might take to horticulture meanwhile.

When the whole company were on the grounds, Flamma and I stepped up to the rose-beds, and I began to explain to her how, in the first place, a T-shaped incision has to be made on the stock, when presently she said, in a low whisper, "Take care of yourself."

I thought she meant that I should cut my fingers with the knife, when she repeated her warning again, and more explicitly, "Take care; they mean to play a bad joke on you."

I looked up amazed. What could she mean?

"Who?" I asked.

"Don't look at me, but continue the explanation and demonstration. Never forget I am taking a lesson, for we are closely watched."

"Thank you. So now we take a carefully chosen scion. Tell me, pray, who wants to play that jest on me?"

"This scion is beautifully developed, let us take it —Siegfried."

"Siegfried? What does he intend to do?"

"Keep your hands busy, and do not look surprised. That clandestine marriage, of which you are to be a witness, is a comedy. The Capuchin monk, who is to perform the ceremony, is Seestern, the famous German actor, who is here under an assumed name, as he does not want to be pestered to play or amuse the others."

My hands trembled, but I kept on and said—

"Siegfried has sworn to me that he is madly in love with Countess Cenni, and that he will marry her, come what may."

"What for?"

"What a question! For love, and—because—he wants the million florins of her grandfather's which the countess has."

"Hand me the knife, for you will assuredly cut your finger, and give me that scion, so that I may try to insert it. Cenni is no countess at all, but the niece of Leestern and daughter of an actress, who at one time did my aunt a great service, and, when dying, made Aunt Diodora promise to take care of her little girl. Aunt gave her at confirmation the name of

Cenerentola, which we have shortened to Cenni. Her real name is Klara. She has no other money or dower but what Aunt Diodora will give her, which will not be much, for in money matters she is not very liberal, and Cenni is called 'comtesse' because it suits Aunt Diodora's whims. That million of which Siegfried spoke exists; but it is mine, and not Cenni's. Is this scion well inserted?"

"No. I will show you the whole process again. What is Siegfried's object in the deception?"

"You show too much agitation. Show me how to cut out the germ properly. This is the plan. After the ceremony, on the day when Diodora is confined to her room and I am with her, a festival banquet will be spread in the shooting-box. It will be a noisy, dissolute company that meets there, and Siegfried will drink most, be the loudest and least well-behaved of the set. The bride will pretend to be afraid of the groom, and at last she will break away from his hands, and ask the protection of the only sober, sensible, and decent man present, namely, yourself. The bridegroom will have lost all self-control through drink. He will swear, and use all sorts of bad language, and the bride will sob and entreat you to take her away, protesting that she hated the sight of the vulgar wretch she had just married, but had been forced to do his will, although he knew well that in reality she loved you, and you alone. At last, growing desperate, she will attempt to leap out of the window to escape from this place, even at the risk of her blighted life. You will take pity on her; her tears

and charms will conquer your resistance, and you will
tell her to dispose of you for ever, and take shelter in
your own castle from the ruffian who was not worthy
of the treasure he had obtained. You will order your
carriage, and take Cenni with you; but, as soon as
you have left, the fellow-plotters will mount their
horses, and, by a short cross-cut, arrive there before
you, discover the intended elopement of the bride,
and carry off you and her as criminals. You will of
course offer to fight every one of them, until all, the
bride included, will burst out into Olympian laughter,
and you stand stunned and bewildered. But, pray,
show me how to insert the germ properly into the T-
shape ?"

My whole frame trembled with excitement.

"What is his object in all this ?" I asked.

"To give you the usual 'jump,' as they call it in
our set. If, for instance, a member of some other
class of society—in your case a simple nobleman—is
pushing his way into high aristocracy, he must be
'jumped,' each in his own different way. One is
made to drink until he makes himself obnoxious even
to his nearest friends; another is made to gamble
until he either wins or loses a fortune, generally the
latter; but all must 'jump,' and if they break their
necks, well and good! It was proposed to 'jump'
you in courtship; you refused to aspire to Diodora.
In a duel you are not afraid of a fight, and so this
course was decided on. You had been 'jumped'
already—at the election—but the triumph and your
downfall were not complete. Your vanity—don't

start—was not yet wounded to death, and you will
have to 'jump' once more—once in private and once
at a second election. But this time you will not rise
again. Hopp! Hopp! That's the design. Don't
look at me—that's all!"

I was fairly choked with emotion. "But why do
they play that trick on me? I did not want to enter
their society; in fact, never valued it at all; but I
cared for Siegfried, and he lured me on with protestations of friendship. What was his reason for that?
What have I done to him to merit this?"

"What have you done? You have provoked him—
called him out. You said you could not believe in
the existence of a spiritual or corporal being who
would do mischief without a material motive, simply
for the sake of mischief and the pleasure he found in
the despair of a fellow-being: you did not believe
that there are men who will afflict the innocent with
pain and sorrow, who will degrade, socially and morally
humiliate you, and then laugh you in the face and
make game of you. Stay here, move in our society,
and you will find out your mistake! Why, what a
sight it will be to have the great debater, the candi-
date-elect, the sage and learned doctor, and heir of
old Diogenes caught in the act of robbing another
man of his bride! They will have a painter there to
take a sketch of the fine situation '*en plein air.*'"

At that moment one of the lawn-tennis players
threw the ball just in front of my feet, and Siegfried
came running to fetch it.

"Well, have you profited at all by this lesson on

inoculating?" he asked the girl, and he added a remark which was so vulgar and impertinent that he would not have dared to use the expression in a variety theatre or any other low place of common entertainment.

"I have," said the girl, with low emphasis, and laid down the knife.

I was in such a state of anguish that I did not know for certain whether the spot I was standing on belonged to this earth or was part of the infernal kingdom, for the soil actually burned my feet. Countess Flamma thanked me for the horticultural lesson I had given her, and I was so much embarrassed that I repeated her own words verbally, instead of giving her a courteous reply. Siegfried laughed.

"What an exemplary, bashful young fellow you are! Evidently you are not used to teach young ladies such delicate lessons. Come! come! Don't blush. Try your hand at lawn tennis."

And I went with him and played.

# VI

## MR. PARASITE.

I HAVE never given way to paroxysms of temper;
not exactly because I was naturally cool and collected,
but because my profession had taught me presence of
mind and self-control. Violent wrath, violent terror,
and violent love could not attack me.

Countess Flamma's singular disclosure had made a
twofold impression. My first feeling was a painful
regret that my most intimate friend, in whom I had
placed infinite trust and confidence, was a faithless
deceiver; and my second emotion was that of a
burning curiosity as to why that girl, a close relative
of my cozening friend, had betrayed him to me—a
stranger. What reason had the one to hurt me, and
what was the motive of the other in warning me?
For, as I refused to believe in evil spirits, I also
refused to believe in protecting angels.

"My dear friend, take care!" said Siegfried,
throwing the ball at me. The ball I did not catch,
but the "dear" epithet I picked up; for it struck me
that the same phrase was often attached to my name
as well as to that of other less intimate acquaintances,
and sometimes with a special, humorous playfulness.
Now I caught it. Of course I was their "dear"
friend, for did not I sit there and do nothing, and let
them waste their money on my election?

In Hungarian society, and I think in most other societies as well, there is a certain person whom we call "Potya ur"—"Mr. Parasite." He feeds at every board, sleeps in other men's rooms, is served by other men's servants, uses other men's horses and carriages, and smokes other men's cigars. When playing cards, he has invariably left his money at home; so when he is a loser it does not matter, for he is not accustomed to pay his losses; but, when a winner, he complacently pockets his gains. He never pays for the flowers he sends to his hostess, never pays anything or anybody; yet he is well lodged, well fed, well clad, and in excellent spirits, for he needs them. His wit is his only resource, his sole capital.

Such a Mr. Parasite, I thought, was I to these men, and I determined that I would be so no longer. Surely I, who was formerly a physician in Vienna, had no right to accept a nomination for Parliament in Hungary—at other men's expense. They were right, and I had been an ass and a coxcomb. When Siegfried told me that the party had decided not to take a penny of me, but to secure my election out of party funds, I should have remembered Chinese etiquette. If two Chinamen meet on the street, Tsang will invariably invite Tsing home to dinner, and Tsing will invariably refuse. Tsang will use all possible persuasion, and finally fairly drag the invited one to his house, although the man protests and struggles as much as possible. And well he knows why; because if he should give way to the pressing invitation and go with Tsang, the moment he entered the house his

host would call him a rude, unmannered peasant;
for he must remember well that it becomes the one
to courteously invite, and the other to respectfully
refuse. This is the law of civilisation in China; and
I had forgotten that law the second time.

So, about Siegfried's motive I felt pretty sure;
but what was that girl's motive in betraying the
whole plot? More! She had not only betrayed
Siegfried, her own cousin, to me—a stranger: she had
betrayed Cenni, her origin, her real name, and her
kin; and, finally, what motive had she in informing
me that the million of florins was her money, and not
Cenni's? What was her motive in confiding to me
such a secret in such a mysterious and secret manner?
Was it only kindness, generosity, compassion, that
prompted her, or——? No, I durst not go further
—as yet—only I knew now beyond a doubt that,
from the first, of all the three fairies of the castle
Flamma alone had aroused my interest and sympathy. Her clear, transparent, pale face, her deep,
sea-tinted eyes, and her silent, cherry lips, so lovely
when parted in speaking, had attracted me from
the first.

We were called indoors to partake of some iced
coffee, and strawberries with cream; but this time I
had not forgotten Tsang and Tsing. I refused, saying
that I had a letter from the Vice-Governor, and was
expected by him; so I could not return until next
day in the afternoon.

My excuse was accepted, and I took my leave.
For a second the thought flashed through my mind

that I ought not to return at all, and that this should
be my last visit to the place; but, somehow, to that
rose-scion which I had taught Flamma how to
inoculate I had involuntarily and unconsciously tied
that particular part of my being which is known as
the "soul."

Next morning I drove over to the county seat, and
paid a visit to the Vice-Governor.

Of course, he was as cordial as ever, and welcomed
me as a dear friend. "Well, what have you brought
me?" he asked finally.

"This time a sensible resolution," I said. "I have
come to give in my resignation as a candidate for
Parliament."

The Vice-Governor embraced, nay, fairly hugged
me in his arms. "My dear boy, that's a sensible
thing, indeed: not from the view of the Government
party only—I don't believe that your party could
have carried the day with you—but in consideration
of your own welfare. Just sit down, and let me inform
the President of the Board of Elections of your resolution. I shall do that at once. Not for a world would
I let you reconsider this excellent idea. Perhaps you
might be over-persuaded, and 'jumped' again by your
good friends."

Again I heard the expression "jumped," and I sat
down to meditate over it. "Have you told Siegfried
yet?" asked the Vice-Governor.

"Not yet," I said; "but I think he won't greatly
object."

"Who knows? But you will pledge your word

that you will stick to your resignation against all
persuasion ?"

"Certainly. I'll give you any oath you want, and
—well, here is my hand on the promise. My resignation is final."

"Then allow me to congratulate you, and to convince you, by action, what a sensible conclusion you
have come to. I should have withheld your property
from you until after election, for I feared that generous
nature of yours, and was afraid that, if you had free
access to your uncle's iron chest, your companions
would soon enough have their fists deep in it. But,
now that you convince me of your good sense, here
are the papers which make you lord of the real and
personal property of your late uncle, and here is the
package with the bank-bills. Pray open and count
them over. The county sheriff will go over with you
to take off the seals from everything, and put you in
legal possession."

I thanked him, and put the money, uncounted, in
my coat pocket. Then I returned to our former
theme, and asked the Vice-Governor if he really
thought that my nomination had put my party to
very great expense.

"Think so ?" he exclaimed, "of course, I think so!
Why, my dear friend, you are a new man, and considered almost as a foreigner and a scholar, not a
patriotic politician! But, if you are really interested
in the question, you can find out the exact figure
which your nomination has cost your party. Just go
straight to the County Savings Bank here, and ask

the amount which Siegfried has drawn on bills signed
with his own name and that of his political friends as
security."

I was stunned. "I never thought of such a thing,"
I said. "Siegfried told me that he had money at
home which he did not want for himself at present,
and could easily spare."

The official laughed. "Siegfried, and spare money!
Why, what an innocent you are! If he had money
at all, he would leave it on the card-table, he is such
a gambler. The fact is, he is on such a sandbank,
just at present, that it will be fortunate for him if his
barque ever gets afloat again."

"How is that possible? I thought him very well
off."

"He is more than that; he is very rich. His
domains are large and beautiful, and his income is
princely; only he is of the opinion that it is mean to
keep money, and he spends in six months the income
of a year, and in this way he runs into debt. He has
practised that for a considerable time, and it cannot
go on that way much longer. His only resource is
his maiden aunt, Countess Diodora. It is said—at
least, Siegfried says—that she hates men, and will take
the veil to become an abbess. In that case her estates
will revert to him as next heir."

"H—m; and do you think Siegfried would feel
insulted if I should go to the Savings Bank and pay
those bills of his? Or do you believe that his friends
would be offended if I took up all the bills, and paid
all the expenses I have caused them?"

"No; although they would pretend to be so for a while, in reality I think they would be only too glad. But I will tell you something: you are just such a generous, large-hearted, noble, free-handed fool as your father was, and, if you go on the way you have begun, old Diogenes's hoard will go after your father's fortune. Do you know what the two Ms in the palm of your hands signify?"

"*Memento mori*," I said, smilingly.

"No. Mind money. It means 'Always mind your own money.' It is the best advice I can give you, and the one you stand most in need of."

I thanked him, and took my leave: no more Mr. Parasite, but on the way to earn the title he had given me—that of a fool.

## VII.

### A BRILLIANT GAME.

If I had had a particle of good judgment or common sense, I should have taken the bills I had paid for at the bank to the solicitor who acted both for Siegfried and myself, should have authorised that gentleman to pay the twenty thousand florins Siegfried had lent me when I came into possession of my house, and I myself should have written two pleasant letters—one to Countess Diodora, thanking her for her great and disinterested kindness and hospitality, and the other to Siegfried, notifying him formally of what I had done, and, at the same time, telling him that my resolution was firm, and that no persuasion on his part would shake it. Then I should have thanked him for his friendship, and finally have taken myself off with all possible speed to Heligoland, Ostend, or some other remote watering-place. After an election campaign, or, as in my case, nearly two campaigns, such an invigorating of the system is very commendable.

All this I should have done as a man of good judgment, but, alas! I was not such a man—at any rate, no longer. My judgment had left me, and it would need a whole pathologico-psychological dissertation to explain how the process of inserting a rose-scion into a stock can, in a period of hardly an hour,

N

convert a cool, sensible, and collected man into a stark
raving madman.

For a lunatic I was—no doubt about that. Now it
was I who wanted to play the game to the end, and
to show to those five companions of mine which of us
could "jump" best. An angel had come to warn me,
and had given me a weapon against my adversaries;
now I was bound to show her that I could make
proper use of the weapon. There was already a
sweet secret bond between us—her warning, and I
was burning to find out the cause, the fountain-head,
of that significant partiality shown to me. Why was
the angel an angel? The question was all-important
to me.

On arriving at home with the sheriff I found a
letter from Siegfried, and on the envelope the inscrip-
tion, "*Ibi, ubi, cito, citissime.* N.B. Dr. Cornelius
Dumany, Esquire."

The contents of the letter were as follows :—

"DEAR FRIEND,—Aunt Diodora has her nervous
attack, and is dangerously ill. Pray make haste!
*Periculum in mora.* Bring your electro-magnetic
apparatus with you, and come at once.—SIEGFRIED."

The gamekeeper had brought the letter, and said
that he had strict orders to wait for me, if it was until
midnight. So I despatched my business with the
sheriff, gave orders for refreshments for him, and,
going into my museum, I took out a watch of the
Apafy period, with which I presented him, and made

him perfectly happy. Then I picked out an antique opal bracelet, which Cenni had found exceptionally beautiful, and put it into my pocket as a present for the bride. I would take the ceremony *bonâ fide*, and play my part as naturally as possible.

We drove through Siegfried's game-park, and at the cascades I was expected by Baron Muckicza, the other witness. "You are expected like the Messiah by the Jews," he cried, and leaped up to me without stopping the vehicle. "Cenni and Siegfried are in the chapel already."

On arriving in front of the chapel, an old Gothic edifice, situated in a large clearing in the park, we alighted, and I ordered my coachman not to unhitch the horses, but to drive about, and wait for me at the gate in about an hour or more.

We opened the little gate that led to a large stone crucifix in front of the chapel, and found the vestry-clerk and a boy ministrant waiting for us in the entry. Now they tolled the bell hurriedly and briefly, and gave way to us.

Siegfried and Cenni met us in the chapel. He pressed my hand in evident excitement, assuring me of eternal friendship and gratitude for standing by his side at this turning-point of his life, whereupon I returned his protestations with equal feeling. The bride, in a dove-coloured travelling-dress, with a wreath of orange flowers in her blonde locks, and a costly lace shawl as a bridal veil, was an exquisite image of love and modesty. On seeing me she bash-fully hid her face in her hands, exclaiming, "Oh! what

will you think of me ?" and to Siegfried, imploringly,
" Pray let me go back to the house ! My God, what a
step you have persuaded me to ! Pray let me go
back ; oh, pray do !" But Siegfried tenderly held
her hands, and persuaded her to go to the good Father
Paphuntius, who was awaiting her in the shriving-pew
to receive the confession of her sins ; for, as a good
Catholic, she could not marry unshriven. So she
simpered and blushed a good deal, and went away to
where the Father, with clean-shaven face—evidently
a Ligorian, not a Capuchin—received her with a
benediction.

It was a splendid farce, and admirably acted by
almost all the parties. There were two bridesmaids
with somewhat rural complexions, and hands which
seemed to swell out of their number seven white
gloves, as did their robust waists from the tightly-
laced silk bodices. Of course, we called them
"Milady," and spoke French to them, although it
was easy to guess that they were dairy and garden
wenches, and the only language they understood or
spoke was the Slavonic. They blushed and giggled a
good deal, and did not feel very much at ease on our
arms.

The ceremony took place in the most solemn and
decorous way. Father Paphuntius delivered a very
impressive sermon on domestic virtues and the fear
of God leading to earthly happiness and eternal bliss.
Bride and groom kneeled down before the altar and
exchanged their vows, whereupon the priest bound
their hands together and gave them his benediction.

My hand itched, and I could hardly keep from loudly applauding the acting priest or the preaching actor ; but I did not forget that at least the place of comedy was really sacred, although profaned by a parcel of blasphemous roysterers, and so I held my peace and looked on.

After the ceremony, of course, everybody congratulated the new couple, and I added the opal bracelet to my compliments, and received in return a sweet smile from the fair bride. " You have robbed your collection of its most precious treasure," she said, and "It will be made more precious by your ladyship's acceptance " was my answer.

We wrote our names in an old register which was in the vestry. I presented the excellent Father Paphuntius with six gold eagles, and the vestry clerk was made happy with as many brand-new and shining silver florins, while the boy received six glittering quarters—all in the fashion of a real wedding. After that, the new Benedict gave his arm to his bride. Baron Muckicza and I bowed to the red-faced damsels, with the German phrase, " *Darf ich Ihnen meinen Arm bieten, mein Fräulein,*" to which they answered in classic Slavonian, " *Gyekujem peknye mladi-pan,*" which means, " Thank you very much, young master." Then we went, *per pedes apostolorum,* to the shooting-box, Father Paphuntius, of course, accompanying us, to feast at the wedding banquet.

The table fairly groaned under the sumptuous meal. The newly-wedded couple took the seat of

honour. I was placed to the right of the bride, and
Masinka, the dairy-wench, sat next to me, as became
her position as bridesmaid. Next to the groom sat
the priest, then Anyicska, the garden-wench and
second bridesmaid, and at her side, between the
two damsels (the table was round), sat Baron
Muckicza.

We were in excellent humour and rather hilarious,
and the affair was a very lively one. At all such
revels I have the peculiarity of never drinking anything but champagne. All other wine I despise and
scorn to drink. Siegfried knew this well, and had
given orders that, after the trout, champagne should
be served. The cork was drawn with a loud noise,
the wine foamed and sparkled in the glasses, but,
when the servant came to help me, I took the bottle
from his hands to look at the label; for there is a
difference in the fluid, and Röderer and Röderer is
not always alike. There are certain symbolical marks
on the bottles, well known to connoisseurs. On some
is a bee, on others an ostrich or an elephant. On
this particular bottle was a fly, and I threw the
bottle to the wall with such force that it broke into
shivers, and the foaming contents went splashing into
the faces of the company. The reverend Father had
just risen, glass in hand, to drink a toast to the happy
couple, and Siegfried said, reproachfully—

"My dear fellow, you begin it too early; the bottle-
breaking business comes after the drinking, not before
it."

"All right," said I, grumbling, "but if you have a

physician as your marriage witness, don't treat your wedding company with wine marked with a fly. I know the effect of that poison."

He smiled mischievously, and, turning, he said in Hungarian, which the Father did not understand, "Don't spoil the game. You'll have another mark; this is for the Capuchin. I want to 'jump' him."

"Indeed!" I thought. "Well, I'll 'jump' you both." The mock priest was standing with his glass in hand to begin his toast, when I turned to him and asked—

"Is it not you, my dear Seestern, that plays the Capuchin in Schiller's *Wallenteins's Camp?*"

The man stared at me, and fell back into his chair, with the classical quotation "*Ha, ich bin erkannt!*" The bride shrieked, and, bounding from my side, ran out of the room. The rustic bridesmaids stared at each other, and asked, "*Csoeto?*" ("What does that mean?") and Siegfried's fist came down hard on the table. "*Sacré de Dieu!* This is treachery!" and taking hold of my arm, he asked, "Who was it? Who has betrayed this little joke?"

I looked him innocently in the face. "Why, my dear Siegfried, it would be unnatural if an old Vienna theatre-goer like me did not know Seestern, the famous comic actor. I am no country cousin to be cozened in that way."

"Well, evidently we have made the reckoning without our host," said he, grumblingly. "But it is a pity. Such a capital joke it would have been, and you would have laughed most. Still, it can't be

helped, so we'll make the best of the spoiled game. I
see the prima donna has thrown off her *rôle*, so you
had better go after her, Seestern, and see her safe to
the château. Your monk's cowl is a protection in
itself. Don't look disconcerted; you can come back.
Our revel does not end yet; it has hardly begun.
You, Muckicza, my dear boy, go out and get in the
boys. Tell them the hunt is over; the game has
broken fence."

By this time one of the Slav girls had stuffed her
pockets with French candies and confectionery from
the table, and the other drank off the champagne
from all the glasses near. Now Siegfried looked at
them, and imperatively motioned to the door. They
hurried out, and "my dear friend" Siegfried and I
were face to face, alone. His face wore a gloomy expression, and he said, in a courtly manner—

"Sir, I am at your service. Do you feel offended
by this joke?"

I laughed outright. "I offended? Why should
I? Nothing has happened to me."

"But it would have happened. We intended to
give you a little 'jump.'"

"And why?"

"Oh, for nothing! Only you look so funny with
that gorilla beard you wear on your face."

"Indeed? And pray how should I 'jump' as your
marriage witness?"

"Has not the person who warned you betrayed
the whole scheme?"

"Never you mind. I am not offended; quite the

contrary. I like such practical jokes, and have taken my revenge beforehand. I have played you an equal trick: I have given my resignation as a candidate this morning."

"You cannot mean it! Tell me, are you in earnest?"

"Dear me, no! I am joking; I told you so! But the thing is irrevocably done, all the same."

"But how could you do it without consulting the party!—without telling me! Thunder and lightning! this is no child's play, but a high game; and there are thousands staked on it! How dare you play fast and loose with us, after all the expenses you have caused us?"

"Oh, if I have a hand in such a game, I generally play it in the proper way!" I said, taking out the wallet with Siegfried's bills, and putting them all in a row on the table. "You see, this is the way I ventured to do as I did."

He tried to play the offended man. "Sir, it seems you do not know——"

"Oh, everything, my dear count!" I said, laughingly; "only don't let us make much ado about nothing. We have both had our joke, and now allow me to beg you for my piece of pasteboard, on which you had the kindness to lend me twenty thousand florins. Here, pray, let me hand you your money. I have it ready for you."

He gave me my card, but refused the money. "It is paid already," he said. "The amount is included in these bills."

At that moment Countess Diodora's footman came in, and Siegfried asked if he had come to look for Countess Cenni. "No," said the man, "Countess Cenni is in the château"—("What a good runner she is!" I thought)—"but her ladyship, the Countess Vernöczy—Diodora—is very ill, and begs his honour, the Dr. Dumany, to be kind enough to come and see her. The ranger has saddled his horse, and is waiting for the prescription to take it to town at once."

That was an honour indeed, and I lost no time in following the man, and left Siegfried utterly amazed. "Why, Nell," he said, "you can work miracles! You are a Cagliostro, and exercise some powerful, mysterious influence! You must be congratulated on this victory. Fancy Aunt Diodora consulting a physician! having a man enter her maiden sanctuary! It would not be believed if I told it!"

At the portal of the château I hesitated for a moment. I had grown suspicious, and suddenly it occurred to me that this might be some other little practical joke, and part of the programme; but I dismissed the thought as base. The countess was a woman—a sick woman; deception in that line was impossible, at least in my profession. I could not be "jumped."

In the château everybody went on tiptoe, as usual when Diodora had her nervous attacks, but I did not heed that. My step was as firm as ever; the reverberation of the physician's step is soothing to the patient, and fills him with hope and assurance.

The servant conducted me to the room in which

Countess Flamma sat; the adjacent room was that of the sufferer. Flamma sat reading before the lamp when I entered. She laid down the book, got up, and extended her hand. "Diodora expects you impatiently. She is more excited than ever, and has just driven out Cenni because she smelt of wine."

"So Cenni was here already, possibly for the sake of an *alibi*."

"Don't speak of that! She told me all that has occurred. Have you drunk wine also, or is your breath pure? Bend down a little, so. You are all right, and I'll take you to Diodora; only wait here a little."

She went in, but returned instantly, and beckoned me to follow her into a boudoir lighted by a lamp with a shade of green glass. Rich tapestry hangings divided the apartment. Flamma drew the hangings partly aside, motioned me to go near, and left the room, softly closing the entrance.

So I was here on that sacred spot, the first and only male being alive who had ever been granted the privilege of seeing the sublime Diodora on her couch. Only her head and arms were visible—such arms as might have been lost by the Venus of Milo and found by this, her divine sister. The thick tresses of raven hair were uncoiled and scattered in rich skeins on the pillows and the coverlet. One of the silken coils fell down heavily to the carpet, and another was thrown high over the sculptured ornaments of the mahogany bedstead. It was an *embarras de richesses* rarely met with; and in the rich and precious braids the ivory fingers were clutched, dishevelling them, tearing at them, in the excess of pain. The beautiful face was pale and lustrous, the eyes bright and glittering, surrounded by broad, dark blue circles; the lips were parted, and the breath came short. Her hands were hot and dry, and the pulse beat intermittently. When I laid my hand on her head and my thumb pressed against the crown, she groaned—"Yes, there it is. Hell itself, with all its tortures!"

My hands went down on her neck, between the *musculus cucullaris* and the *sternocleido mastoideus.* "Ah, that is the way the pain goes down," she sighed; and when I asked, "Will your ladyship give me leave to make use of my skill?" she answered, "Don't call me 'ladyship'! I am no countess now; I am nothing but a suffering animal, and you may call me what you please. Give me the title of dog, so you can help me."

"Then pray sit up first, and let me gather and secure your hair; it hinders my movements."

She obeyed; and, while I gathered the loose tresses and coiled them around the head, the coverlet slipped down unnoticed, and the lace nightgown, torn open by the restless fingers, revealed the marble bust and shoulders; but for the physician, in the execution of his professional duty, female charms do not exist. The warm, soft, creamy skin is nothing to him but epidermis, *stratum mucosum Malpighii;* the white, sculptured neck only the *regio nuchœ,* and then comes the *regio scapularis,* the *deltoidea,* and then the *sacrospinalis.*

What a fuss they make about that ascetic who

resisted the temptations of the flesh when tried by the evil spirit in the shape of Lilith ! What would that famous saint have done, how would he have be- haved, if he had been called to rub this soft, velvety, odorous flesh, the fascinating, peerless body, with his hands ? Who knows if then the Catholic Church had not boasted of one saint less ? Indeed, indeed, we modern physicians have more of the saint in our disposition—in general, of course.

The effect of the treatment appeared at once in soft, voluptuous sighs of relief, deep and long-drawn ; in the magnetic showers of the body I recognised a sure token which that mysterious disorder in the veins, lymphs, and nerves reveals in the ganglia. A firm pressure of the biceps with full fist, a pressure of the thumb against the *rhomboideus*, made her ex- claim, "Oh, that has done me good !" Then she began to shiver, the body ceased to be hot and dry, and perspiration set in. She laughed involuntarily, her teeth chattering with cold, and then she sighed again, and said, gratefully, "I feel as if you had saved me from drowning in an ocean of hot oil." I was at the *regio palmarum*, rubbing her hands and fingers, cracking each of them. "Thank you," said she ; "that will do. I feel much better."

But I told her that my work was only half done as yet and had to be finished, or else the attack would return. The object was to gain regular circulation of the blood throughout the whole body. This is no witchcraft, but plain mechanical aid to the action of the live organism.

But now that her sense had returned, her bashfulness returned also. "Could not the remaining part
of the treatment be executed by a woman?" she
asked.

"Yes, if she has studied anatomy, visited the
dissecting-room regularly, and knows every particle in
the structure of the human body; otherwise, a quack
may do just as much mischief with the pressure of
her unskilled hands on the outside of your body as
with a bottle of quack medicine to your inner system.
It is hard to make you open your eyes to the fact that
the organic structure of the human body is a more
wonderful, much more admirable work of creation
than the starry heaven. When, at a word, the
muscles of your face move to a smile of pleasure, or
your eyes are filled with tears of joy, sorrow, or compassion such a complicated machinery is set in motion
that no mechanical iron structure on earth can be
found half as involved or half as complete; and a
person not thoroughly acquainted with the qualities
and parts of this wonderful apparatus will prove a
tormenting executioner, not a healing physician, to
the sufferer. Be patient, milady, the physician at the
bed of his patient is of the neuter gender—just as the
angels are."

"Then—be an angel!"

I did my duty. The *musculus risorius* was
moving already. A happy smile played on her face,
the pale face regained its colour, and then the involuntary smile gave way to involuntary tears. After
this she fell asleep; so deep, so peaceful was her sleep

that the *aponeurosis plantaris* did not disturb her, although there are few or none who are able to undergo the process of having the soles of their feet rubbed.

She slept, and there she lay in all her sublime beauty, like some wonderful marble statue, the image of a goddess. I took the coverlet, on which the Vernöczy crest—a nymph rising out of a shell, holding apart her long, golden hair—was embroidered, and covered up the fair sleeper, folding the blanket well on the feet to prevent evil dreams. Then I let down the curtains to shut out the lamplight, and left the room.

On the thick, soft carpet, my step was noiseless, and Countess Flamma was not aware of my presence. I entered the room in which she sat before a little table, her palms clutched together, her pale, beautiful face bent over a book. It seemed to be a very interesting book, for she was entirely lost in the contents. I waited until she finished the page, but she did not turn the leaf, but re-read the same page again and again. "Countess!" I said, deferentially. She looked up and hastily closed the book. The silver filigree cross on the purple velvet cover betrayed the prayer-book. What prayer was that of which she did not tire, but read it over and over repeatedly?

She gazed at me in evident wonder, and her eyes sparkled like two shining orbs. "You have returned?" she exclaimed, as if in doubt of my bodily reality.

"Countess Diodora is asleep," I said, "and will not wake until the morning. Pray, take care not to disturb her."

"And—you—you—did not remain—there ?" pointing to the room I left.

" I have done all I could, and my staying would be of no use to her. To watch her sleep would do no good to her and be tiresome to me."

From the shooting-box shouts of revelry reverberated up to us. "You are going back to them ?" she asked.

" No. I have finished my business with Siegfried, and told him that I had revoked my nomination."

"You have really done it ?"

"Certainly. I have also paid the election expenses up to date, and thanked Siegfried for his good intentions. Henceforth we shall be friendly neighbours, but not friends. Now give me leave to say good-night to you. To-morrow morning I'll drive over to pay a professional visit to Countess Diodora."

"Don't go home now," she said, holding my hand ; "the night is dark, and something might happen to you. I have prepared a room for you here in the château, with auntie's permission, and you will stay. Henceforth, whenever you come to Vernöcze, you will come straight here, not to the shooting-box."

The blood rushed up to my face, and then back to my heart with a throbbing sensation. A tingling noise like the sound of bells was in my ears, and for a moment the whole universe seemed to have but one real fixed star—the fair, pale face before me. " Will you stay ?" she asked, with a sweet smile and a pressure of her hand ; and I ask, Is there on earth a

Cicero or a Demosthenes so eloquent as the pressure
of a woman's hand when it speaks?

I thought I knew all. I had sounded the mystery
of her warning to me, and in that moment of overwhelming bliss I do not know what I did. Had I
kissed her hand? Had I said anything? given a
promise or received one? I do not know; but that
my head was dizzy, and my heart filled with a world
of joy, that I remember.

# VIII.

## A BITING KISS.

THE valet conducted me to the room assigned to me, and carried my orders to my coachman to unhitch the horses, and send up my necessaries. "Will it please your honour to take some tea?" asked the valet.

"Thanks," said I, "I won't take anything. But you will greatly oblige me if you will send me a bowl with warm water; I want to shave."

"Certainly, sir. The chambermaid will fetch it at once."

I had resolved to shave. Good-bye to Chauvinism and national peculiarity! I wanted a smooth, clean face, as I had had before I had given way to vanity and political ambition. From this day on I ceased to be a clay figure in the hands of juggling quacks. I was Dr. Dumany again, and would remain so for life.

As I sat before the mirror, looking at my own face, I could not repress a smile. That beard of a few weeks' growth lent me an appearance that was nearly akin to that of a gorilla. I took a pair of scissors and clipped off the hair; then I prepared the soap and razor for shaving the bristles. A woman, whom I took to be the chambermaid, set a bowl of water before me, and, as I am not in the habit of looking

closely at chambermaids, I said, "Thank you," prepared
the lather, and commenced shaving.

The woman was yet standing beside me, and, as I
thought she was waiting for orders, I said, without
turning—

"Much obliged, my dear; you need not wait. I
shall not want anything this evening."

"May I not send you a cup of tea?"

I started, and the razor in my hand gave a great
jerk, happily not into my face: the woman I had
taken for a chambermaid was Cenni.

"Oh," I said, "it is you!"

She laughed, and said, with a mock obeisance,
"Yes, sir." But, looking at me in the mirror, she
laughed again, and said—"Only go on. I am waiting
for the Byron face to appear again, when these
stalks are swept off. We can talk a little meanwhile."

"Indeed? But, you see, there is one more forbidden
subject between us. There are four now: the step-
ladder, the Sultan of Morocco, the sea-dove, and now
Father Paphuntius."

"It's astonishing how sharp you are; almost as
keen as your razor. Only take care, you may cut
your own skin!"

"Not likely. My hand is skilled in using knives.
Am I mistaken in supposing that you have come to
ask for secrecy on my part?"

"Not altogether. That was a part of my motive
in coming."

"You magnanimously promised me a kiss for

keeping the other secrets. What will be my fee for this ?"

"A bite, and yet a kiss. It will hurt you, and yet it is meant as a caress—like those biting kisses which some over-fond mothers bestow on their little ones, and make them cry."

"Thank you, I am ready to accept it, and shall do my best not to cry."

"Don't be too sure of that. Take care of the blade in your hand! I half think I ought to postpone my revelations, because as long as this shaving process serves you as a pretext for making grimaces, I cannot clearly detect the real impression my words are making on you. Would you mind laying down that razor for a while, and leave off making faces and holding the tip of your own nose ?"

"Impossible. I have heard of Janus having two different faces—one for peace, smooth and smiling sweetly ; the other for war, frowning and threatening, and clothed with a grizzly beard. But I myself always show an honest impartiality to friend or foe."

"Oh, I daresay that you condemn and despise me. for, foolish and conceited as you are, you scarcely know how to distinguish between friend and foe. You think the misfortune that little pleasantry would have brought upon you highly important, whereas, if carried out as intended, it would have saved you from real harm and real degradation."

"What ? If I had played that game to the end and had caused you, the pretended bride of another

man, to elope with me, it would have been to my
advantage? Is that the quintessence of cynicism, or
sublime *naïveté?*"

"No. It is plain truth, and you will find it out
with a vengeance! Only then it will be too late for
repentance. You have been told that I lent my aid
to play a trick which would have made you the
laughing-stock of all your acquaintances. I tell you
if you had only gone on, unforewarned, you would
have come out a hero and the master of them all.
Only then you would have known me as I truly am,
and not as I choose to appear. I have been slandered
to you, and you think me a she-devil at least, because
I like a joke, and look everybody in the face, and not
up to heaven like a saint, or down to earth like a
sinner. I also look like a bold word, and am no more
a hypocrite in words than I am in deeds; and, first of
all, I never make use of calumny to gain my own ends.
I know who has told you that I was a Satanella.
Flamma, the—'angel.' Of course, everybody who
is acquainted with us will tell you that she *is* an
*angel*, and that I am a devil at least, because I have
cat's-eyes, a sharp tongue, and a quick temper, whereas
she has the face of a Madonna, the disposition of a
nun, and—she knows how to keep her own counsel.
Her mouth is only opened when necessary to her own
purposes; in such a case she does not recoil from the
basest slander. Do you think I did not watch you
two at that rose-bed? That I did not notice the
glitter in your eye, the excited shaking of your hands?
And do you know why she did it? Because the day

before I had boldly told you to win Diodora. That she could not forgive me, and do you know why? You remember your answer. It was when you told us the tragic story of your friend and the moral, that you were wary of the caprices of aristocratic heiresses. Now—she thought—if this is so? Here is a girl without a penny of her own, with a mock title which does not belong to her; if he disbelieves in heiresses, he may believe in her, and that is a state of things not to be endured. Let us spoil that little private game of Miss Nobody, because we have a reason for wanting the light-headed, easily-deceived fellow for ourselves. But do you know that reason? Can you guess it?"

The knife was at my throat literally; but she laughed a short, harsh laugh, and continued—

"Ha! ha! You come from them. You have been called to the divinity to admire her in her sublime loveliness, and you have treated her as clay, and played the *rôle* of the Messiah, Who drove out the demons by the touch of His hands. How she must despise you—nay, hate you—for that proof of your preference for Psyche over Anadyomene! How that sweet-winged creature, Psyche, must have pressed your hand, and looked up to you with a sweet, promissory smile as you kissed her hand and professed yourself her most obedient slave for ever after! Although you ought to remember your friend's story well enough! When you told it, you said, 'I am nothing but a runaway doctor, an expelled Member of Parliament, and a Slav king'; now you shave your

face and say, 'I am a marvellously powerful man, and
endowed with magical charms. I shall be a king of
hearts!'"

My face was smooth and clean. I poured some
*eau de Cologne* in the bowl of water, dipped a sponge
into it, and washed my face, drying it with a soft
towel. "Oh, you are quite handsome enough!" she
said, mockingly; "you can show your Byron face;
'I come, I see, I conquer,' is written on your forehead.
But now I am not jesting; and listen to me, or repent
it until your dying hour! If you succeed in winning
the divinity you may be a slave, but a cherished slave.
You will not know the blessing of love, but you will
also be free of the pangs of jealousy and of shame.
But beware of the angel! I tell you, if that rose-scion
which you both inserted the other day germinates
and comes to bloom, deadly despair will be your lot,
and the angel's rose will kill you with foul poison!
Beware, I say! Cut that scion while you have the
opportunity, and then go to the end of the world to
be safe from the angel's revenge! Remember, I have
warned you!"

She had gone to the door, but at the threshold she
turned and said—"I have given you the biting kiss I
promised. Much good it may do you!"

With that she went out, but her biting kiss had
not hurt me. My heart was full of hope and joy.
This girl's impotent jealousy had convinced me of the
reality of my happiness. I was beloved, and I loved
again; and could the venomous tongue of a jealous
woman incense me against an angel like Flamma?

True love is like pure gold, and the acid of calumny
does not destroy it, but gives new proof of its value.
I loved Flamma, and Flamma loved me.  This was
enough of bliss, enough to keep me all night in a
waking dream, in a transport of exquisite joy.

## IX.

### WHO IS THE VISITOR?

I WAITED impatiently for the daybreak. At the
first dawn I was up and dressed, and taking long
strides on the garden path. How long would it be
until the ladies were up, and willing to receive me?
Even the servants were asleep yet. I strolled on
aimlessly until I found myself unexpectedly at the
dairy, which was quite a grand establishment, where
twenty milch cows of the Aargau breed were milked
daily, and a delicious cheese manufactured. Siegfried
had told me some time before that, as soon as the railway was extended to the neighbouring town—a prospect which was expected to be realised shortly—he
would have a branch laid on, at his own expense, to
his dairy. Anyicska and Masinka, the two bridesmaids of last evening, met me at the gate, and were
very officious in showing me in, and while Anyicska
brought me a cup of excellent sweet milk, Masinka
brought some spongy rye bread, fresh from the oven,
upon a salver. Of course, this was offered as a bribe
for my secrecy on the topic of last night, and I promised them not to tell Countess Diodora how they
had been employed at the mock wedding. Poor
things, why should I betray them for obeying orders?
So I graciously accepted my hush-money, which was
less subtle and more substantial than that offered by

the fair bride herself; and they told me that the revelry had lasted almost until cock-crow. They all had capital fun. The Father had sung highly amusing songs. The girls had been called back after my departure, and then, with the other companions who were called in, the merry-making had reached a very high pitch. Of course, Cenni had not returned to them.

As I gave them my promise of silence they thanked me, and in return they told me that, with my smooth face, I was a much handsomer-looking fellow than last night, with that beard on my cheeks and chin; and I was conceited enough to pocket the compliment and believe in its truth.

Breakfast was served to me in my room. The ladies were up, but Countess Diodora was too weak to preside as usual at the breakfast-table. I requested the honour of paying her a professional visit, and was told that she would be glad to see the "doctor."

The room in which she received me was a magnificent *salon*, with a balcony in front. When I entered, the doors and windows were wide open; the rays of the sun darted through the filmy lace curtains; it was a "*tableau en plein air*" that met my eye. Countess Diodora, in a mauve-coloured silk dressing-gown, rested on a settee. Before her was a little Venetian mosaic table, and on it a tea-tray. Diodora seemed to be in excellent spirits, and looked beautiful; the suffering of last night had not told on her complexion the least bit. She wore a black lace

scarf to conceal her hair, which was still in the state
in which I had coiled and pinned it, except that a
great ornamental tortoise-shell comb, of yellow hue,
had been thrust into it. Opposite to the countess, on
two embroidered stools, sat the two girls, engaged in
finishing the Japanese sunbird; and in the balcony
door stood Siegfried, smoking a cigarette, and blowing
the smoke—in consideration of his aunt—out of the
door. I thought it would have been more considerate
still if he had not smoked at all. As I entered, the
thought seemed to occur to him that the business
of smoking would be best despatched on the balcony,
so he escaped the difficulty of looking me in the face.
Cenni also found a pretext for retiring; she took the
tea-tray from the little table and left the room with it.
Countess Diodora, Flamma, and myself remained in
the room. I asked the countess how she felt, and
whether she had enjoyed a peaceful sleep, and she
answered, with rapture—

"I slept deliciously, as I never have before
since my childhood; and I had such delightful
dreams! I fancied I was a child again, and rambled
in the garden chasing butterflies. You have worked
miracles, and henceforth I shall believe in you as in an
oracle. I revoke all I have said against your profession and science, and confide myself entirely into your
hands. The first touch of your hand had a magic
effect on me, and afterward I felt as if you had taken
my vile body of clay from me, joint by joint, with the
witchcraft of your fingers, and given me a new, better,
and more perfect form. I felt as if you had lent me

wings, and that now I could rise with you up above the clouds, captivated by your mesmeric influence upon me. Moon and stars seemed to remain far below me, and you were guiding me up to a strange world, full of unknown and eternal bliss. Oh, why cannot this transport of exquisite pleasure last for ever?  Indeed, indeed, I do not know how to express the gratitude I owe you!"

Diodora said this to me in the presence of Flamma, and in the hearing of Siegfried, who, on the balcony, could hear every word through the open door; and, as she said it, her great Juno-like eyes rested on mine with an expression of enthusiastic admiration.  Yes! such might have been the look which the goddess bestowed on poor, silly Ixion as she lured him on and then—left a cloud in his arms.

But do you know why that look failed to infect me as it had Ixion?  Because I had been inoculated against the infection by another look last night—a look from the violet eyes of Flamma.

I rose from my seat, and, throwing myself into an attitude befitting a ceremonious announcement, I said—

"Countess, to be of service to you is a happiness to me.  Pray dispose of me.  If I can convert your pains into pleasures, I shall consider the happy result as the highest reward.  Your ladyship's gracious words at this moment inspire me with boldness; so much so that I feel encouraged to lay the hidden secret of my heart, the cherished wish of my life, in your hands. If you deign to accept my confession and grant my desire, you will bind me to your service for life, in attaching me to your family."

I shall never in my life forget that proud, repellent lifting of her head as I spoke. Diana might have looked so at Actæon, although, poor fellow, he had never come so near to the virgin charms of that Olympian lady as I to those of the queenly virgin before me on the preceding night. Her forehead seemed to gain in height, her eyes retreated behind the lashes, her lips were pressed together, and her nostrils dilated. In looking at me her chin doubled, and she seemed the personification of haughty disdain.

"My dear doctor," she said, with proud emphasis on the "doctor," "it seems you have misinterpreted my words. I have never thought of encouraging you in desires such as you this moment expressed."

I bent my head deeper still. "Dear countess, allow me to say that the misconstruction is on your side. I did not intend the bold request which you seem to impute to me; I simply beg leave to ask for the hand of your niece."

Her whole disposition seemed to change on hearing this, and she broke into a long, ringing, scornful laugh—the laugh of offended vanity, of angered pride; such a laugh as women use to mask their disappointment and jealousy, and the rising of their temper.

"Ha! ha! ha! Ah! ha! ha! The little Cenni! Ha! ha! So it is true, and I have guessed right? Ha! ha! ha! And the little fool has run out; she guessed the object of your visit. Ha! ha! ha! It's wonderful! My niece, the little Cenni—Countess Cenni! Oh, what a perfect match! Ha! ha! ha!"

I did not disturb the explosion of her mirth. As a physician I knew that it impaired the health of a nervous woman if she was interrupted in her vagaries. At the sound of her laughter Siegfried re-entered and asked, "What is it now?"

Diodora explained, laughing hysterically, that their dear, common friend, Dr. Dumany, had just now asked for the hand of little Cenni.

"Very well," said Siegfried, "serves him right. Let him have her, by all means!"

"I beg both your pardons," I said, "but it seems to me as if the misunderstanding between us is becoming chronic. I very much admire, but have no intention of marrying—Miss Klara."

"Ah!" Like Semiramis she stood before me. "Who has told you that there was such a person—a Miss Klara—existing in this house?"

Retreat was impossible. I looked at Flamma, and she answered with an encouraging nod; so I replied to the countess's imperious inquiries—

"Lady Flamma."

"Yes, it was I," said Flamma, rising from her seat, and stepping to my side.

"You shall pay dear to me for this!" cried Siegfried, with a threatening look; but I took her hand, and said—

"Pray compose yourself. This lady stands under

my protection. I have done myself the honour to ask
for her hand, and I wait for your decision."

"Show the Devil your finger, and he will take your
hand; treat a peasant with kindness, and he will
think himself your equal," said he, with a sneer.

"Siegfried!" said Diodora, "I beg you not to
forget that this is my room, and that my guests are
not to be insulted in my presence. This affair does
not concern you in the least."

"But if he is impertinent?" growled he.

"Perhaps the count might be more careful in his
choice of language," said I, proudly, "if he would consider that a Dumany fought as a knight and a soldier
under the national tricolour at Mount Thabor, while
the first Vernöczy was still serving as a humble
shepherd on the Verhovina."

I was sorry for this as soon as I said it, for I had
offended Flamma also; but the bitter pill had the
desired effect, inasmuch as the whole aristocratic
family regained their usual lymphatic composure.

"Flamma," said Diodora, coldly, "have you given
this gentleman the right to claim your hand?"

"Yes."

"Then—I do not object," and she motioned with
her hand. I understood the gesture, and extended
my hand to Flamma. She accepted it, and I bowed
and kissed her hand. That was our betrothal.
Siegfried took out a cigarette, lighted it, and blew the
smoke at the chandelier.

"I had other intentions concerning Flamma's
future," said Diodora again, "but, since her choice has

fallen on you, I am satisfied—at least, I do not object.
Only I beg of you not to delay your nuptials. Have
them celebrated as soon as possible, for I intend to go
to Heligoland—to try the baths."

To Heligoland !—that was the place I should have
gone to, if I had listened to good sense—and to
Cenni.

"Certainly," I said; "I am only too happy in the
prospect. If you will give me leave I shall hasten to
Szepes-Váralja, to the bishop, for a dispensation, and,
as soon as I am in possession of that document, I shall
return, and we can have the ceremony performed the
day after my return."

"Then I should also wish," said Diodora again,
"that the wedding might be altogether a simple
family affair, with no strangers as witnesses."

"Your ladyship expresses my own wishes."

"If so, we might have the ceremony performed
here, in our chapel."

I remembered Father Paphuntius. "No, I'll have
nothing to do with that chapel."

Siegfried smiled as he guessed the reason of my
embarrassed silence, and then Flamma smiled, and
Diodora also. At last, as a smile has a soothing
effect on everybody, we all laughed. "No," said
Diodora, "I was not speaking of the park hermitage.
We have a chapel here in the château, and if
we do not invite too many we shall have room
enough."

"I shall invite no one but a single witness as my
best man."

"But do not ask me to fill that position," said Siegfried; "for I am invited to go buffalo-hunting in Volhynia, and shall start to-morrow."

"There is something else," said Diodora. "After the wedding ceremony I shall hand you over Flamma's dowry, which she has inherited from her grandfather. It consists of a million of florins in good bonds."

I bowed in silence, looking at Flamma.

"No; this is a matter which concerns you as well as her, and you must know that her grandfather laid down the condition that if she, guided by whatever motive, should release herself from the bonds of the Catholic religion, she should lose everything, and surrender the inheritance to collateral relatives."

"I cannot think that such an event could take place at any time."

"Time will show."

There was a long pause, and I thought best to take my leave. I turned first to Flamma, who laid both her hands in mine, and, looking up to me, asked me softly to return soon. Then Diodora languidly extended her hand to me, and I bowed over it with cool, studied politeness, and as I looked up I saw that Siegfried thought fit to shake my hand in honour of the new relation between us. He even went so far as to embrace me. "God bless you, my dear—cousin," he said, laughingly; but, thank God, he did not think it necessary to kiss me!

A week later Flamma and I were married. Everything went on in the regular way. No objection,

P

no obstacle was raised. The ceremony was held in Vernöcze in the afternoon, and the same evening I was free to take my bride home to Dumanyfalva. From one of the great portals I drove with Flamma; from the other, Diodora and Cenni started on a trip to Heligoland. Siegfried had gone to Volhynia six days before.

If you think that with this marriage my story is at an end, you are mistaken; it has hardly begun. It is a strange story, and not pleasant to dwell on; but you shall judge for yourself.

# X.

## AFTER THE WEDDING.

So overwhelming was my happiness that I sometimes fancied that it was all a dream, and that I
should wake to find myself in my former condition.
In one short week I had had my old mansion re-
furnished in a style worthy of the high-born and
gently-reared bride who was to inhabit it; and I
thought what joy it would give me if she should walk
through the halls and chambers of her new home, and
find everything arranged to suit her own delicate and
refined taste, and answering all her requirements as to
beauty and comfort.

And then I had dreamt of the first supper we
should eat at home at our own table; each dish an
inviting delicacy, deliciously prepared; and yet we
should hardly taste of it, our palates thirsting for
different feasts.

And now this dream had become a reality, and I
looked at my beloved, and tried to catch a glance of
her beautiful, downcast eyes. I had as yet never
enjoyed the privilege of a kiss from her lips, and I
was longing for one; but when I tried to draw her
close to me, she whispered, "Don't, we shall be
observed by the servants!"

At last the meal was over, and we rose from the
table.

"Pray lead me to your work-room. I have yet to hand you over my dowry."

I laughed. "Time enough for that a week or more hence. No? Well, any day you please; but not now." Still she persisted.

"It has to be done this evening. I can't keep it any longer. You did not accept of it from Diodora, so you must take it from me. It is no longer my own —it is yours."

"Dearest, there is no such distinction existing! Since this blessed morning neither of us can claim possession of anything that is not common to both alike. What is mine is all yours, and what is yours I claim all for myself! For the marriage tie has made us one for ever!"

"But pray come," she said again; "I have the chest with the securities here with me, and I should like to have it all over."

I sighed and obeyed. At the door of my study she left me for a moment, returning instantly with a rosewood chest, richly ornamented with silver. On one of her bracelets a tiny filigree key was dangling; with this key she opened the chest, and then, stepping back, she said—

"Convince yourself. The contents must amount to exactly one million of florins."

"I am quite convinced," I said, "and accept it as correct."

"That you shall not. Let us take out everything, and reckon up the amount." With that she took the papers out herself, and I had to sit down, take slate

and pencil, while she dictated to me the value of each
bond, its title, and, looking into every one, she satisfied herself that the coupons were attached to it.

In the abstract it may seem rather a pleasant occupation for a married couple to reckon up a million of
money as their joint property; but, in this concrete
instance, to spend the wedding-night in a study,
making pecuniary computation, is the pinnacle of
pedantry.

At last it was done; and, as I computed it, I made
the total to be one million and twenty-five thousand
florins.

"How is that possible?" she asked.

I had to explain to her the fluctations of the
market price in relation to the nominal value, which
was the basis of our computation.

"Then let us look for the market-price of the
bonds as it is at present. I know it is to be found in
every newspaper," and with that she took one up
from the table, looked for the exchange report, and
dictated again, "Hungarian real estate bonds, 85;
Lower-Austrian, 88; Transylvanian, 82, etc."

This time we have thirty thousand florins less than
the million.

"How is that possible?" she asked again.

"Dearest," said I, "let that be! What does it
matter if——"

"But it does matter. My grandfather left me
exactly one million; neither more nor less. So I
must find out this balance of thirty thousand, also."

"Maybe, at the time when he bequeathed this

money to you the price of these securities was higher than at present," I suggested.

"That is possible. But then there ought to be some list, or something else relating to it. Let me look it over again."

Great heavens! she took everything out again, and searched for a last year's exchange list. A crumbled yellow newspaper clipping was found, and then the whole process had to be repeated again; and now thank God, the million came out even! I drew a great sigh of relief; but I had triumphed too soon. She asked for pen and ink, and, as I got up from the seat before the writing-desk, she sat down and wrote on each of the bonds, deeds, obligations, mortgages, etc., her own name—"Flamma Maria Dumany of Dumanyfalva, _née_ Countess Vernöczy of Vranicsa," in a clear, almost masculine hand.

"What is the use of this, dearest?" I asked.

"You know," she replied, "all these papers, as yet, bear the name of my grandfather, and we could not realise upon them as they are. I must first write my own name upon each."

"But we do not want to realise on them."

"That you don't know—at present."

"But there would be time for this on some future day."

"No. Pray compose yourself. I have to finish this now."

And she did finish it. On two hundred different securities she wrote, in bold, large letters, her full name, and I stood there and looked on in helpless despair

At last there was an end of it. She put the papers in the chest again, handed me the key, and begged me to lock everything up in the safe. I obeyed, in the ardent hope that at last I had done with papers and accounts.

"There is something else I have to hand over to you," said Flamma, as I stepped nearer; and, drawing from the pocket of her dress an envelope, she handed me an official-looking document, fastened with tri-coloured tape, with a large official seal upon it. It was a power of attorney from Flamma Maria, Countess Vernöczy of Vranicsa, to her husband Dr. Cornelius Dumany of Dumanyfalva, giving him full authority over her dowry, consisting of real estate, bonds, etc., to the amount of one million of florins, and authorising him to sell or retain or use the aforesaid securities according to his own need or pleasure, and without previous consultation with any person, his wife included.

"Dearest," I said, "this is very generous of you; but there is no need of any such document to give me proof of your confidence."

"I did not intend it as such a proof."

"Then what was your intention?"

"To give you no cause to accuse me of meanness. You shall not say that I left you on your wedding-day without a shilling in your pocket, as your friend was left on the Isle of Wight."

I gazed at her, at the pale face that was even paler than usual, and cold and inanimate as a block of ice.

"Flamma!" I cried, "what does it mean? How am I to take this?"

"As a confession. That other man has made me —his—wife."

"Flamma !"

She stood there, pale, cold, statue-like, and her voice sounded like that of an automaton. I felt like one stupefied, like one who had meant to enter the gates of paradise and found himself in a sea of fire and brimstone.

"Who is the man ?" I stammered.

"Siegfried."

"And why did he not marry you, if——"

"Because he is married already. His wife lives in Egypt, and he cannot get a legal divorce from her."

"And why have you married me ? For we are married. The ceremony of this afternoon was real, not a comedy like that other ? "

"No ; we are married. When that—misfortune— happened to me Siegfried promised to marry me to some distinguished gentleman who might give me a good name and an acceptable position, so that the marriage should need no explanation."

"When was that ?"

"Three months ago."

"At the time I arrived from Vienna ? "

"Yes."

"Was that the reason for his instantaneous proffer of friendship ? "

"Yes."

"And for that reason I was nominated for Parliament ? "

"Yes, but that also was the cause of your first failure. It was Siegfried who bribed the witnesses against you. He wanted to crush your pride, draw you closer to him, bring you into close connection with and dependence upon our homes and us."

"So it was all a conspiracy?"

"Yes."

"And Cenni's mock-marriage and your betrayal of the scheme?"

"Were meant to win your confidence."

"So Cenni co-operated with you?"

"She had to. At first she opposed it, and meant to win you for herself. She is a poor girl, and dependent on Diodora's charity; and she had to give way."

"And Diodora?"

"It was she who designed the whole plot. Her sickness that night was simulated in order to bring you near me, and to encourage you to the proposal."

This whole discourse, so closely resembling a cross-examination, had altogether the appearance of such an interrogatory as a magnetiser would address to his subject; and the answers I received were given with the plain, involuntary precision characteristic of hypnotised persons. She stood there before me, with her hands clasped in each other; that seraph-face of hers, that seemed the type of innocence and purity, without a tinge of colour, although her dreadful confession was enough to paint the cheeks of the most degraded woman with the colour of shame. She seemed to have no bashfulness, no sense of shame.

and to be wholly incapable of realising her offence.
And I had not believed in a Devil! Here he was
before me, in the shape of this fair woman, who had
tempted me with her angel's mien to sell my soul for
her, and now she was dragging me down with her to
eternal damnation! And the other one had warned
me! She had told me with that "biting kiss" of
hers that this seeming angel was no angel, but a
Devil to kill me body and soul. She had told me
that this fair rose was full of foul poison, and her
warning had filled me with vain conceit and enhanced
my love for my executioner. I saw it now. Cenni
had meant to make that elopement real; and if I had
taken her she would have given me her love, as this
one had given me her accursed million. Money to
pay for my honest name, money for my lost life and
happiness, money to bribe me to the endurance of
these hellish tortures!

Impossible! I cannot believe that human nature
can be so vile, so miserably cunning and treacherous.
This is some evil dream, some test, perhaps, of the
sincerity of my love and trust in her.

"Flamma!" I said—"dearest! do not continue
this ugly jest. I cannot hear foul words come out
of your pure mouth;" and I tried to take her
hand. But she drew back.

"I have told you the truth," she said, with a repellent gesture.

The truth! The truth! This shameful, horrid
confession was the truth? Like an idiot or a lunatic
I stared, gazing before me, with scarcely a thought in

my stunned, aching head. A Calabrian dagger lay
before me on the table. I had taken it from the
museum, and used it for paper-cutting. Upon the
steel blade was graven, in golden letters, "*Buona
notte;* and "*Buona notte! buona notte,*" I kept
incoherently murmuring.

"Have you no other question to address to me?"
she asked, in a tremulous voice.

I shook my head, and pointed to the door, and, like
a wooden puppet, she turned and disappeared through
it. At the moment when her back was turned something like a flame flashed through my brain and body.
For an instant I felt a mad impulse to rush after her,
and with one bound bury this two-edged knife in her
heart. Yes, in her heart; but from behind, just as
they had stabbed me unawares, like assassins. My
better self kept me back. My Uncle Diogenes rose
before me. "Never quarrel with, never hurt a
woman!" and my professional instinct was awakened.
I should then have destroyed two lives; with the
guilty I should have slain the innocent—a life which
was in God's keeping as yet. Now the door closed
behind her, and I had let the only opportunity for a
deadly revenge upon the woman who had tricked me
pass by neglected. Had I killed her at that moment
I should have washed off the stain she had brought
on my name in her own blood. "Look," I might
have said, "she was led astray by another man, and I
have killed her; it was my right and my duty!"
This I could no longer do. She had escaped, and
would live on safe and unharmed, and I should be

dead and buried alive. I remembered now how confused they looked, Cenni and she, when I related to
them the story of my friend, and how I had prided
myself on my own prudence and good sense! And
the trap was already laid for me, and I, who had
thought myself safe from every such danger, here was
I, on my wedding night, left alone, insulted, degraded as he was. No, not quite. He had had no
money, and I had received a million. I had been
paid for my disgrace, bribed for my infamy with
money!

Great Jehovah, Whose vengeance is mighty,
lend me Thine ear! No! Thou art too just and upright, I'll have nothing from Thee! Turn from me! I
will none of Thy advice, none of Thy heavenly patience
and magnanimous mercy! That marble-hearted
woman had said to me, "If you deny God, He will
forgive you, for He is infinitely good and merciful;
but if you deny the Devil, he will be revenged on you!"
and I had seen the devilish light in their eyes. I had
shuddered and shunned them, and yet I had plunged
headlong into the abyss which they had opened at my
feet.

But now they had conjured up the Devil before
me, I felt that in my own breast they had awakened a
demon quite as cunning and wicked as their hoofed
and horned idol; and we would see whose teachings
would prove more destructive! Only, cool blood!
Let me not betray myself; let me consider how to act,
and then keep my own counsel. Shall I go to
Volhynia after that man? Hold him to account,

invite him to face the muzzle of my pistol or the edge
of my sword? He is a ruffian and a notorious duellist.
I am a bad shot and an indifferent fencer. He is
perfect in both; it is his profession. Naturally, he
would kill me, and where would be my revenge?
Should I kill myself? Die the death of a suicide,
and be spoken of as a lunatic who had crazy fancies
because his fortune had turned his head? And what
would be the result? Flamma would perhaps faint
away for a few seconds, have bad dreams for a week,
wear mourning for six months, and—would be none
the worse for being a widow, whereas I should be
laughed at as a silly fool. Shall I sue for a legal
divorce? "*Si fuerit dolus?*" Had I not had enough
of notoriety? Enough of laughter, calumny, and
ridicule? Must I drag my honest and hitherto
respected name through the mire, and become the
laughing-stock of every fop throughout the country?
No, anything but that! Help me, thou worser self,
thou Devil in my own breast, help me to find some
revenge worthy of a Devil's teaching! Give me death,
for it is death I crave; but such a death as will give
me peace and rest and honour in my grave, and to
those others remaining here on earth, shame, sorrow,
and remorse! I am a dead man from this accursed
night forward, but I can, at least, choose the manner
of my corporal death, and woe to her who has driven
me to the choice!

When the morning dawned my scheme was
complete, and it was a scheme that did honour to my
special demon. I would die, but fame and glory

should write my epitaph; and dead, I should be remembered by this woman with lifelong sorrow. She shall never be happy; and in remembering me, her soul shall be filled with bitter repentance for the misfortune she brought on me. She shall yearn for me, shed bitter tears for me, and fret away her life in despair. This should be my revenge.

# XI.

## MY SCHEME.

NEXT morning I said to my wife—"We cannot stay here. Our next year must be spent in travelling in foreign parts, and we shall start for Paris in three days. You had better make arrangements accordingly."

"My arrangements are made, for I have not unpacked my things yet. So everything is at your command," was her answer.

I left her, and drove over to the county town to my solicitor, and told him to borrow as much money on my property as he could possibly get from the financial institutions. As a pretext I told him that I had the intention of buying lands. He advised me to wait, for he had learned for certain that in a year's time Siegfried would have to sell out. His estates were mortgaged over and over, and matters were going very ill with him. If, then, I should add to the million my wife had brought me, the money I had and the money I could at any moment raise on my property, I should be able to purchase the Vernöczy estates.

This was a revelation that for a moment made me hold my breath. It would be something to tear that water-nymph on the Vernöczy crest from over the portals of the château into the mire, and erect the

Dumany crest on the front of the proud old castle.
But that feeling passed, and with it the temptation.
It would be no revenge on her to let her live as
mistress on the estates of her forefathers, and, first of
all, I craved revenge on her.   More than that scoundrel
who had betrayed her and then flung her to me, I
hated her, Lilith, the tempting devil in the guise of a
seraph !   But I said to the lawyer, " Very well "—that I
would consider about it, and not buy anything at
present; but that he should raise the money, all
the same, and send it for me to Paris, as well as the
funds I had inherited.   Perhaps I might have use for
the money there—at any rate, he must send it.   Then
I took the rosewood chest with my wife's dowry, and
sent it by mail, and under the usual guarantee, to a
well-known banking firm in Brussels as a deposit.

Three days after, we were on our journey to Paris.
I had taken the Swiss route, for in those days it was
the safest way to escape the obstacles and annoyances
which on the road through Germany were thrown in
the way of travellers to France.   War was, so to speak,
floating in the air, and was each moment expected to
break upon the two leading nations of the Continent.
At such a time the railroad termini are naturally the
centres of exciting scenes and noisy demonstrations;
but the Swiss republic was neutral, and the southern
part of France was quiet.   So we arrived in Paris
unmolested; and the great crowds in the boulevards,
and the multitude of detectives among the people, gave
us the first notion that something extraordinary was
occurring.

At first the demonstrations were all in favour of peace. Labourers in blue blouses were marching up in compact masses on the Place de la Concorde, carrying white flags and signs with the inscriptions "*À bas la guerre*" and "*Vive la paix !*" Public speakers delivered long orations on the horrors of war, and protested against the ambitious, fame-hunting tyrants who drove their innocent, peace-loving subjects into bloody combats to feed their own greed for glory and power. But their speeches were all blown to the winds. Bellona is a fair woman, and the more she is slandered to her admirers the more ardent and impassioned is their love for her. In vain did the orators protest that France was all for peace, and would not be dragged into the perils of war. The soil was thirsting for blood, and the day after our arrival in Paris the declaration of war which Napoleon had issued against Prussia was publicly announced.

I had been informed of these events long before they happened, and on them my whole scheme was built. When the public enthusiasm was highest, and the shouts "*À Berlin !*" loudest, when throngs of people crowded through the streets, singing the "*Marseillaise*" and "*Le Départ*," I mingled with them, bent on business.

During our journey I had shown my wife all those polite little attentions which are due to a bride on her wedding tour from her husband. Now I was looking for a residence for her. I found a handsome, palatial-looking house, exquisitely furnished, which had been hastily abandoned by a German diplomat at the first

Q

rumour of the war, and was now in the market, with its
carriages and horses, servants, and everything. The
bargain was made, and, as I took my wife to her temporary home, she seemed to be struck with the delicate
consideration which I showed her. I saw by her face
that she wished to protest against this excess of
luxury, which was not in keeping with our means.
But perhaps something in the expression of my
face warned her to be silent; perhaps it occurred
to her that as she had given me full power to do
what I pleased with her dowry, I had acquired the
right to squander it—if it suited my whims—on
herself.

When she was comfortably established I said to
her—"I have offered my services as an army physician
to the French Government, and they have been accepted. I have received my commission from the
Duke of Palikao, and shall start this evening for my
destination."

"If it is your wish, I cannot oppose it," was her
answer. What a meek, obedient wife she was!
Whatever I said or did, it was, "Pray please yourself.
Whatever you think best will satisfy me." She never
showed the slightest increase of temper, never offered
the least resistance to my arrangements. She was the
same quiet, pale, silent, sylph-like being as she had
been when I first knew her, and I wondered that she
had not changed. We had been married only two
weeks, but to me it seemed as if seven hard winters
and seven fierce tropical summers had passed since
that time, and had taken the marrow from my bones

and every spark of hope and brightness from my
soul.

"I have left you forty thousand francs in the safe;
they will last you until the time of my return. You
need not deny yourself anything you wish," I said.

"Thank you. I shall manage the money carefully,
and shall not spend more than is strictly necessary.
I am of a saving disposition."

These were our parting words, and we exchanged
no others. I went to H——'s banking-house to draw
the money my solicitor had sent me, and when they
inquired whether I wanted checks or bills of exchange,
I asked for the latter, because, as I said, in time of
war the Government might bring in a *moratorium.*\*
"What," they laughed, "the Napoleonic Government
bring in a *moratorium!* *Tête carrée!*" The latter
was meant as a compliment for me.

By the next express train I went to Brussels, and
then straight to the banker to whom I had sent
Flamma's million. I opened the chest in his presence,
and convinced him that it actually contained good
security—bonds and deeds for the sum of one million
and twenty-five thousand florins par—and asked him
for an advance. The banker put seventy-five per
cent. of the nominal value at my disposal, and I
handed him the power of attorney from my wife, and
a written authorisation permitting him to sell the
securities without notice in the event of my failure to
repay the loan at a certain date.

\* A governmental act of mercy in regard to the payment of
debts.

This money, with a part of the funds which my solicitor had sent me, amounted to two millions of francs. With this sum I went to a well-known and trustworthy stockbroker, and instructed him to speculate with the whole amount in French Government bonds for a fall.

"Do you intend to throw this money in the gutter?" said the man, eyeing me critically.

"That is my own business, I presume," said I, calmly.

"Have you ever speculated on the Exchange before? Are you versed in these manipulations?"

"No! Never!"

"Do you know the situation of the Money Market at present?"

"No."

"Then grant me leave to inform you by giving you a few data. All French securities are rising in value. Paris is enthusiastic for the war. The money-chests of the financial ring are open to the Government. The French military force is fully equipped, ready to begin hostilities, and stationed at the Rhone, whereas the Prussians are caught unprepared. Bavaria will remain neutral, and the Danes are preparing to break into Schleswig-Holstein. The sequel of the war can be foretold with such certainty that a Paris financier offers, to any one who will accept it, a wager of two hundred thousand francs against one hundred thousand that on August 15 the French will march into Berlin."

"Well, you may take up that wager, also, for me."

The agent shrugged his shoulders, and accepted my offer for a bear speculation. We agreed that from time to time we should communicate with each other in cipher. Telegrams were to be forwarded through H——'s Bank.

From Brussels I returned to Paris, and procured all the necessary surgical instruments at my own expense. Next I bought three waggons with strong Trakene horses for my own transport and that of the invalids, furnished myself with all utensils requisite for camp hospitals, and then, under the protecting ensign of the Geneva Cross, I joined the regiment of the French army in which I had enlisted as volunteer camp-surgeon. My scheme was clear now. I was a dead man. I was seeking Death in his own realm, where he reigned supreme, and it was impossible not to find him there, if one really sought him. So I should die, but not the death of a suicide, despised, misjudged, forgotten, but a death on the field of honour and glory, as a hero and a martyr of science and philanthropy. And that accursed money which was given me as a fee for my disgrace would be blown to naught, as my body would be by a merciful Krupp shell. When the news of my death reaches that woman in Paris, she will try hard to discover what I have done with her fortune—and mine! But let her search ever so thoroughly, she would find— nothing! I had left no trace of my operations, nothing from which she could regain one penny. Then she would be compelled to come down from her height, return to Hungary, and live a lonely, miserable

poverty-stricken existence on my Slav kingdom,
which I had mortgaged and ruined. She would have
to struggle against poverty and want, and, by daily
care and close economy, would have to pay from her
scanty crops the heavy debts I had incurred. All day
she would pine and toil, all night she would sigh and
grieve. And in her dreams she would call me back,
and ask me where I had buried the treasures. Her
priests would fail to console her, and she would become superstitious, and resort to clairvoyants and
mediums for the solution of the torturing mystery.
But no prayer or curse will reach me, no incantation
of conjurers or spirit-rappers will call me back. The
dead do not return, either for promised kisses or for
promised bites.

## XII

### SEEKING FOR DEATH.

To tell the truth, on my arrival at the camp I felt
like an apprentice in the presence of his masters.
French surgery in general occupies a foremost place.
French camp-surgeons have acquired skill and
experience in their great military expeditions ; there
their studies receive the finishing-touch, whereas the
little skill and practice which I had came entirely
from the clinic and the dissecting-table.

But, nevertheless, I was very cordially received by
the old, experienced masters of the profession, to
whom I stated that I had come, as a voluntary apprentice, to aid in the work of philanthropy as best I
could. My immediate superior was old Duval, who
had served as camp-surgeon at Sebastopol, and I
succeeded in acquiring his good graces. He asked
me if I had ever been on a battle-field before, and I
answered, a little ashamed, that I had never had
that opportunity. In spite of my descent from the
chivalrous Hungarian nation, I know the sound of
the cannon only from hearing the salutes fired on
our King's birthday, or other occasions equally
peaceful.

"It does not matter," said the old man, encourag-
ingly. "You will get over your first irritation at the
noise, and then you will feel as much at home and as

safe as in your own study. There is not the least danger for us. We hoist the Geneva flag with its red cross, and every civilised foe respects that ensign. After the battle is over, and the enemy has fled, beaten, shattered, and in disorder, we carry our ambulances to the gory field, and take up the wounded, friend and foe alike. The severely injured we attend to at once, dressing their wounds on the spot, and then we place them all on our beds, and take them to our hospital-tents for treatment."

This had been the old man's practice in many wars. The French had invariably been victors and masters of the field; the enemy had retreated, and then the French had taken up the wounded and nursed them faithfully, whether friend or foe. That a time could come when the French would be driven from the field, and the enemy would take up the wounded, was deemed preposterous and out of the question.

We were attached to Marshal Douay's corps, but, unfortunately, I did not receive the privilege of participating in the first battle at Saarbrücken, where old Dr. Duval's experience was confirmed; the Prussian advance was repulsed, and the victorious French gathered up the wounded.

The first wounded soldiers whom we treated were foes; one an Englishman, the other a German from Baden. Both were officers in the German army. Three daring officers from the German camp, on horseback and in full uniform, had galloped into the heart of the French camp in broad daylight; there they had cut down the sentinel, ordered food **and** drink, taken notes as to the camp, the position and order of the forces, the number of the batteries, etc., until at last the French awoke from their illusion, and recognised them as foes. They retreated firing, cutting their way through the French lines, killing two French officers, one of whom, as he expires, finds strength enough to return the fire, and one of the three, the Englishman, falls shot in the abdomen. A second, the Badener, is hewn down from his horse; but the third escapes unhurt, and cuts his way back to the German camp.

This incident I regarded as a bad omen. The French were so confident, so presumptuous, that they neglected the outpost service. Next day the Germans attacked Marshal Douay at Weissenburg with three times his force. This was the fault of the French, who ought to have attacked the Germans with an overwhelming force, instead of waiting to be attacked by them.

The French fought heroically against the crushing superiority of the Germans, vainly hoping that the report of the cannonade would attract assistance from a corps stationed in the neighbourhood of the battle-field; but in this heroic fight their lines were sadly decimated. At first they fought in the village, then they were forced out by the Germans, and had to defend themselves among the vineyards and the thickets. The soil was saturated with blood, and the dead and wounded were lying about in ditches, copses, and everywhere.

"Sir," said I to Dr. Duval, "to-day the enemy will be master of the field, and he will gather up the wounded, unless we prevent this by picking them up while the fight lasts. Now, while the balls are flying about, is our chance! Give me leave to go there with the ambulance."

"With all my heart! Try it if you have a mind to."

"If I had a mind to?" Why, of course, I had come for that; it was the opportunity I had craved, the chance for the immortalising cannon-ball to send me up to heaven and glory! So, taking the twelve men who were given me as aids, I started off with the ambulance to the scene of the battle.

There is not the slightest braggadocio about this. Soldiers, even in the hottest ardour of battle, will carefully avoid firing at the life-saving corps, which is distinguised by the sign of the red cross. But it is impossible to prevent an exploding shell from sending its splinters among them, and on that eventful day I had occasion to watch the course of these splinters.

The firing did not cease for a moment. The roar of the artillery, the cracking of the rifles created a deafening noise; the hoarse, grating sounds from the French mitrailleuses, in particular, made a horrible accompaniment to the dying groans of the wounded. But the French mitrailleuses had found their match in the Krupp cannon. These fire no balls, but some fiendish contrivances, longitudinal, cylindrical projectiles, which explode as they alight, and scatter their deadly fragments far and near.

All the injured men whom we took from the field were wounded by these splinters. As we toiled, the hellish projectiles were flying over our heads; but my experienced aids worked with the coolness of the harvester when he hastens to save his crops from the threatening rain. They knew well that these messages of death were not sent to them, but to the French artillery, which was opposing the advance of the Germans. All this while I felt that indescribable intoxication which is sure to overtake every novice. I stood there in the terrible realm of death, in the presence of the awful Moloch, Hamoves, the angel with the scythe. I felt a chill, a shudder, and I bowed down before the omnipotent Lord of life and death, the Almighty Ruler of the universe.

This short-lived sensation of terror every novice has to overcome. Nor is anyone spared the humiliation of this experience. The eye can hardly perceive anything of the effect of the shots, for the cannon-smoke envelopes the surrounding objects in a thick cloud of fog. The Prussian infantry were crouching down, and, while creeping and cringing thus, they were pressing forward. Nothing but the smoke of their rifles betrayed the level of their faces, and the French infantry were hidden in ditches, behind bushes and trees, and firing from these vantage-grounds. Only the Zouaves and the Turcos might now and then be recognised by their red caps.

While the artillery was pealing, the bugle was sounding the commands. All at once a strange

drumbeat was heard from beside us, and the veteran
sergeant at my elbow said—

"Sir, we must get out of this with our beds at
once. Cavalry is advancing."

"Cavalry of the enemy?" I asked.

"Brother and enemy is all one in such a case. If
we are in their way they will crush us under their
horses' hoofs, without observing what body we belong
to."

So we hastily picked up our beds with the wounded,
and retreated with all speed behind the line of battle.
We had hardly reached security when, from both
sides, the cavalry advanced, both friends and enemies.
The earth shook with the stamping of the hoofs,
"*Quadrupedante putrem crepitu quatit ungula
campum.*"

Avoiding our right wing, a regiment of Prussian
hussars was galloping towards us; a regiment of
French chasseurs on horseback, under command of
the commander-in-chief, Marshal Douay, in person,
was dashing from the hills to meet them. The strong
west wind was blowing clouds of dust in the faces of
the French, the backs of the Germans. All at once
the Prussian regiment divided itself, wheeling to right
and left; behind them a whole battery of artillery
appeared, and a powerful discharge saluted the chasseurs.

The shells made a fearful gap in the French horse-
men, but still they dashed bravely on, shouting wildly,
and giving the enemy's artillery no time for a second
shot. The Prussians wheeled swiftly, and hussars,

battery and all, fled before the lines of the French chasseurs. We thought this wild retreat meant victory for the French, but we discovered that it was only a ruse.

When the clouds of dust had dispersed, we saw that on the battle-field horses, struggling in deadly convulsions, and men in the throes of death, were strewn thickly around. We hastened thither to save whom we could, but, oh! what an awful sight it was! Man and beast piled in confusion and crushing each other. The neighing of the wounded horse mingled with the last prayer, or the death-groan, of its rider. Maddened horses, with their dead or wounded riders hanging in the saddle, were galloping on, while the less-injured soldiers, who had been thrown from their slain horses, or were struggling to extricate themselves from beneath them, were cursing and swearing, and invoking God and Devil for vengeance on the Prussians.

Among those who were fatally injured was Marshal Douay himself. As the old sergeant drew him out from under his horse, the blood rushed from an awful gash on his neck. "*O, mon général!*" sobbed the old soldier, trying to close the gash with his pocket-handkerchief.

"Don't cry!" said the dying chief, hoarsely. "Go shout to them '*En avant!*' in my place."

It was a fatal command, this "*En avant!*" The French chasseurs had pursued the German hussars to a hop plantation, which proved to be full of concealed Prussian sharp-shooters. At this point the hussars

attacked the chasseurs in the rear, while the sharp-
shooters received them with a volley from their quick-
firing rifles, and a general onslaught was begun upon
the brave corps.  The chasseurs endeavoured to break
into the hop field, but such a plantation is a terrible
fortification, with its walls of vines fastened to other
walls of stout poles, and behind each a hidden foe
with a quick-slaying weapon.  The whole fine corps of
cavalry was destroyed then and there.

The fall of the commander-in-chief, Marshal
Douay, had decided the fate of the battle.  When
finally, all too late, MacMahon arrived with his troops,
Douay's unfortunate command was shattered, and the
battle of Weissenburg lost.

## XIII

### MY DISCHARGE.

In spite of this terrible disaster, the retreat of the
French troops was accomplished in good order, and
but few prisoners fell into the hands of the Prussians;
even those few were mostly Zouaves and Turcos, not
real French soldiers.

That we had really been beaten was not believed
by anybody. Everybody was inspired by the conviction that the Weissenburg disaster was nothing but
an incident. A comparatively small defensive force
had been attacked by an overwhelmingly large force
of Prussians, and was compelled to retreat for the
moment; but the fight had been only a trifling
prologue to the great battle to come, or else was part
of a deep-laid plan which would secure to us the final
victory. So it had been at Solferino, when Benedek
had been allowed to attack and disperse the French-
Italian troops on their left wing, while at Solferino
itself the Austrian army was destroyed. So it would
be here. It was supposed that this slight victory was
allowed to the Prussians, so as to divert their attention from the movements of MacMahon and Bazaine,
who were certain to crush them all at their first
encounter.

Next day the Emperor himself and his young heir-
apparent appeared among us, presenting to each of

those who had distinguished themselves at the battle
of the preceding day some badge of honour. At the
recommendation of old Dr. Duval, the Chevalier Cross
of the Legion of Honour was pinned to my breast, and
the reporter of a Paris newspaper wrote a flourishing
item about the heroic and self-sacrificing Hungarian
surgeon. When I read it, I thought of that woman in
Paris, and what she would think of these reports.
Perhaps she would say to herself, "So he is not everywhere the same coward as he was here! He has
some pluck, some physical courage at least."

But in vain did we wait for our revenge upon the
Prussians. After Weissenburg came Spicheren, then
Wörth. Everywhere the German force was stronger
than the French, and it turned out that their artillery
was better than ours. MacMahon was cut off from
Bazaine, and in the gigantic battles at Bézonville and
Gravelotte, Bazaine, with his force of one hundred
and fifty thousand men, was driven back into Metz.
Strasburg was besieged, and MacMahon cut off from
the road to Paris.

In every battle that was fought the Prussians remained masters of the field, and it was always they
who took charge of the wounded. Of course, each
corps was in ignorance as to the fate of the others,
and if one was beaten or repulsed, it was fully convinced that the other had meanwhile been victorious
elsewhere. The Paris newspapers and the Bourse
supported and increased that belief. One evening,
after a forced march that very much resembled a
regular flight, we arrived at a certain town. I entered

a café, and being very curious to learn something of
the present state of the Money Market, I looked for a
newspaper, and here it was :—"Paris. Extraordinary
Upward Movement! Rate of interest raised to 68-15,
and rising rapidly. News of great victories!"

"Well," I thought, "my two millions are nicely
exploded by this time." Underneath I read in large
letters, "The Prussians severely beaten by MacMahon!
The German Crown Prince captured and made
prisoner by MacMahon!"

That very day we had been compelled to leave our
entire baggage in the enemy's hands and run for our
lives, so to speak, and here they are talking of the
German Prince having been captured. That is how
they create upward movements on 'Change. But
could this last? Surely such lies would soon be exposed! How long was it possible to keep on in this
way?

How long? For ever.

After the massacre at Mars-la-Tour, MacMahon's
forces were practically scattered to the winds, running
aimlessly about, and, when coming into contact with
the enemy, hardly thinking any longer of resistance.
If a Prussian Uhlan was seen far off on the road
every man took to his heels. The infantry threw
down their rifles, the cuirassiers their helmets and
breastplates; the gunners cut the traces of the
horses, jumped upon their backs, and dashed on, without thinking of the fate of the rest. On horseback,
with a loaded revolver in hand, I had to keep guard
at the side of the ambulance carts, to keep the

R

marauders away from the wounded. Once I had a
narrow escape from being captured by the Bavarians.
It was at a skirmish of artillery. A couple of French
and a couple of German pieces were in position. The
French were quickly disabled by the Germans, and
even the head gunner was severely wounded. I took
him on my shoulders, and got him out of the line of
fire. The Bavarians sent another shrapnell shell after
us, and, as the projectile burst over our heads, I felt a
blow on the leather rim of my képi. "A shrapnel
splinter!" I thought, scornfully: "could it not have hit
me a little more to the right, and have done with me?"

After I had hastily placed the wounded officer on
the waggon, I jumped on horseback, and hastened
after the flying troops. Upon a wooden bridge that
led over a shallow rivulet the soldiers were crowded.
I did not stop to consider, but dashed on with my
waggons to the water. A detachment of Bavarian
hussars, guessing at my intention, was there to prevent
its execution. A young lieutenant of hussars was leading the detachment, and, placing the muzzle of his
revolver to my forehead, he shouted: "*Rendez-vous:
demande pardon!*"

"At last!" I thought, "here is my opportunity for
the glorious end. This fellow is the man I want," and,
turning my face full toward him, I looked coolly into
the barrel of his weapon. "Shoot, comrade!" I said.
"You'll get neither me, nor my charges, as long as I
am alive."

He gazed at me, as if scrutinising my features.
"You are not French?" he asked.

"I am a Hungarian," I answered.

"Kornel, and no doubt about it!" he exclaimed, taking hold of my hand and shaking it. "Don't you know me? I am Plessen." Sure enough, he was my favourite chum from the University; but we had not seen each other for years, and the last three months of camp-life had done more to change a man's outward appearance than whole years at home. "Go on, comrade," he said, with a farewell shake of the hand, "and may our next meeting be a pleasanter one! Good-bye!" With that he let me take my charges safely across the water and over the fields, avoiding the open roads, until finally, as night fell, I reached with my patients the camp at Chalons, and found my way to the camp hospital.

What a cursed, vile task old Duval had had all day! Nothing but sore heels and slight shrapnel scars in the rear!—and he embraced me and kissed me all over for bringing him now three cart-loads of real wounded men, with wounds got from sword-cuts, rifle-bullets, and gun-shots. "What an invaluable, brave fellow you are!" he said to me, handling each of my charges with the tenderness of a loving father; "but now you shall share the privilege of dressing their wounds, and assist me in the necessary operations." This was a privilege indeed, and for a while we were very busy. When we had finished, he put his hand into his pocket and said, "Now, my boy, I will also present you with something."

I thought he meant to give me one of his utterly wretched cigars; but no—it was a paper, and, on handing it over to me, Duval said, "It is your discharge, my boy; you are free."

"My discharge?" I asked, offended, "and why, pray? Have I not done more than my duty? And if so, how have I merited this disgrace?"

"I am afraid that it was just your extraordinary ardour that brought it on you; that's it, you have done more than your duty; and as you are a foreigner, it is natural to ask, Why have you done it? Why have you exposed your own life, contrary to custom, picking up the wounded where the fight was the hottest and the balls flying thickest? True, you have by this course saved the lives of many that would have bled to death, or been otherwise lost; but it is a marvellous thing that you could do all that and escape unhurt. The fact is, you have always come back with a sound skin. Can you explain this miracle? Can you tell me, why you, a foreigner, took the risk of such imminent danger for—Hecuba—that is, for wounded French soldiers?"

The old man was right. I could not explain it, for I could not tell him that I had regarded their great national calamity as a means of carrying out my petty suicidal designs and giving them a decent cloak. I never thought of it before; but now I had to acknowledge that my conduct looked suspicious to strangers. What will be their suspicions, I thought, when they learn that I have talked German with a Prussian officer, and shaken hands with him? Would this not give new matter for their suspicions, and was it not natural in the vanquished to believe in treachery?

And then I thought what a self-conceited fool I had been to think I could command God Mars to afford me a disguise for self-murder. "Why," he said, "do you suppose these great national conflagrations are kindled to cook your meals on? What do I care for your family quarrels? If you are tired of life, take a rope and hang yourself on that willow, and there is an end of you and your paltry complaints."

As I stood there musing, old Duval turned my face around and exclaimed—"Look! look! Your forehead is wounded."

"A mere scratch with a shrapnel splinter," I said, bitterly, "not worth plastering." I took from him the letter with my discharge, presented him with my camp outfit, instruments, horses, etc., and kept nothing but one of the waggons and a pair of horses for my journey homeward—that is, to Paris. This was now the speediest way of travelling, for the railways were all occupied with the transport of troops.

Before I left Chalons, I entered a café and drank a cupful of some black beverage that was called coffee, although I think it tasted of soot, and read one of the Paris newspapers—the last that had arrived the same day.

A dazzling glare of light was visible through the windows, arising from the valley. It was the burning camp. The Emperor had given orders to burn all tents, since there was not time enough to strike them and carry them off. So everything was left to be consumed by the flames, while the men fled for their lives.

The newspapers in the coffee-house were going
from hand to hand, and were eagerly devoured. At
last I obtained one. I found the following report in
large letters—

"The Prussian army scattered! Two hundred
Krupp guns remaining as captures in the hands
of the French! Commander Moltke a prisoner! Bismarck fatally wounded! Price of rentes, 1 franc 25."

If this were true, one part of my scheme had succeeded. The two millions were annihilated. But
what of the other part? I was still alive, and death
would not come to me without disgrace and ridicule.
What a position to be in!

## XIV

### HOME! SWEET HOME!

It was damp, disagreeable, dirty weather when I arrived in Paris. It had rained for the last few days, for usually after great battles stormy weather sets in. The poets will have it that heaven washes away with tears the blood spilt by man. Scientists say that the gas freed by the combustion of so much gunpowder, together with the detonations at the explosions, brings on the rain. The fact is that after all great battles rain is sure to follow.

As I alighted from the one-horsed vehicle that had brought me to the door of my residence, my own porter asked me whom I was looking for at this house? I answered "Myself," but found it difficult to convince him that I was his master. At last he let me in, and rang the bell three times as a signal that the master of the house had arrived.

The valet met me at the ante-chamber, and stared at me with mouth and eyes wide open; but no wonder. I must have cut a handsome figure, with that torn and perforated red képi on my head, and the dirty, blood-smeared cotton handkerchief around my forehead. My face was blackened by exposure to the sun and wind, and had a grizzly beard of three months' growth upon it. My uniform was dirty and torn, and above it was a rubber cloak with a hood, while on my

feet were a pair of rough, high top-boots, with spurs.
By my side I had a sabre, a revolver, and a bag for
bread and bacon—not a very gentlemanly appearance,
by any means.

"Is madame at home?" I asked.

"Yes, sir. Madame is in her boudoir."

"Then tell her, monsieur has come home, and
afterward see that a fire is kindled in my room. I am
cold and damp."

The valet was a very humane and obliging fellow.
He asked me to step into the *salon*, where a fire was
burning already. I was forcibly struck by this proof
of democratic condescension. Fancy his allowing a
fellow with such a robber's look, who had unexpectedly intruded into the house, to enter the luxurious, polished, gilded *salon* of—his own wife!

The fire was burning in the grate, and I went up to
it to warm myself, when the door opened, and, with
quick steps, there entered—my wife. She had entered
hastily, but, on seeing me she faltered, and stood
motionless at the door.

Well might she start at my strange appearance;
but, if I looked dreadful to her, her appearance was
positively loathsome to me. I had not seen her for
three months, and she had visibly changed since
then.

To another man his wife looks charming in that
condition, but to me my wife seemed perfectly disgust-
ing, horrid, abominable! I cannot find a phrase to
express the detestation that filled me as I looked at
her.

" You have come away from the camp ? " she asked,
in a low tone.

" I have been discharged," I answered.

" You ?　How could that be ? "

" They believed me to be a Prussian spy."

" Nonsense !　I have read so much of your courage
and daring, of the self-sacrifice which made you risk
your own life to save that of others.　The papers were
full of praise of your magnanimous conduct."

" That's it exactly.　They think a respectable
surgeon has no business to risk his hide or exhibit
sentiment.　So they told me to pack off."

" But you are wounded ! " she cried out, as I took
off my képi.

" A mere scratch, and already closed.　It's nothing."
And, throwing the rubber cloak from my shoulders, I
stepped nearer to the gate.

" You have been decorated ! " she said, pointing to
the " *légion d'honneur* " on my breast.

" Trash ! " I said, tearing it off, and with an angry
gesture throwing it almost into the fire.

She ran up to me, and held my hand.　"No ! no !"
she said : "I shall not let you !　Leave it on your
breast ! " and, snatching it out of my hand, she pinned
it in its place again.

" Well, let it be," I thought.　At least there would
be one spot on my body that was honourable.　But it
was time to change the subject.　For a soldier coming
home from the gory field of honour might speak to his
wife of his wounds and his deserts, but I ?　As I was
no real soldier, so my wound was no real wound, this

badge of merit not really merited, and—my wife—was
not really my wife. So I changed the subject, and,
like a conscientious family physician, I questioned her
about her health. My questions were purely professional, and she gave her answers in confidence, as
patients usually answer the questions of their *ordina-
rius.* I advised her as to the best way of avoiding
inconveniences connected with her present condition,
and so on. After the consultation was over, I asked her
if no letters had arrived for me during my absence.

"Only one—in the last day or two, and that has
been opened."

"By whom ?"

"By the police, I think. For a short time back all
letters coming from foreign parts are opened by the
police."

"Have you also read the letter ?"

I looked into it certainly ; but I have not read it.
It is written in cipher."

"Ah !" I thought, "the communication from my
agent to say that the millions have disappeared." But
I did not show any impatience to get at the contents
of the letter. I listened politely as she related to me
the events of her life in my absence.

After a while the valet announced that my room
was ready for me, and then she asked if I would not
dine with her ? "No, thank you !" said I, with an
inward shudder; "I am quite unfamiliar with your
civilised customs, and will thank you if you will
permit me to retire to my room."

In my room I found the letter upon my writing-desk. As I had expected, it came from my agent in Brussels. The key to the cipher code was in my pocket, rolled up in a cigarette; so that in case of my death on the battle-field some soldier or nurse might smoke the cigarette and unwittingly destroy this last clue to the mystery which surrounded my money transactions. The letter ran as follows :—

"Sir,—The two millions which you entrusted to my care have doubled themselves, and I hold four millions of francs for you. The decline is continuous, and will hold good for a considerable time to come. The Paris Bourse created an enormous rise by fictitious reports of victories; but the decline was all the sharper in consequence. The French are beaten everywhere, and if you will consent to let me continue in the present course, I shall double your money again on short sales."

Camp life had taught me to swear, and I was furious. Fate was mocking me, tantalising me. Instead of taking from me the accursed money which I had received in exchange for my life, my soul's salvation, and my honour, it doubled that money, and threw it back at me. But I would see if I could not get the better of blind fortune. I did not want that money, and would have none of it.

I sat down and wrote an answer on the spot. I gave the agent fixed instructions to speculate with the whole amount for a rise, and that immediately. As soon as I had translated this into cipher, I gave it to the valet to be posted.

Then I took out the rough fare I had been accustomed to during my camp life, the rye bread and bacon, and, slicing it up, I toasted it at the grate fire. Surely a man who had thrown four millions out at the window a few minutes before had a right to indulge in such luxuries.

But the cognac which I had been used to drink I could not relish at home. For three months I had drunk nothing but cognac. It is a powerful stimulant, good for fever and ague, hunger and thirst, influenza-cold, and, yes, the tremor before a battle. But here, at home, I wanted something I could not get there—a glass of clear, fresh water.

Oh, how I enjoyed it! How deliciously refreshing it was after so long a craving! Home had still a great treasure to offer me—a glass of clear, fresh water.

**What a precious, sweet home it was!**

## XV

THE street was very noisy, and a tumult of loud voices, shouts, etc., penetrated through the blinds, shutters, and doors into the room in which I sat. I took that to be the normal condition of a Paris street, for in large cities there is always some spectacle afoot to set the mob shouting. But I was mistaken. The valet, whom I had sent to the post-office to mail my letter to the broker at Brussels, entered hastily, his face livid with fear.

"Monsieur, save yourself!" he cried. "The mob is coming."

"Coming where?"

"To this hotel. A German diplomat lived here before you, and the people think this is his house still. Someone has given them a hint, and they have taken it up, and they are coming to storm and plunder the house. The residences of two bankers have been demolished in this way, only because their names had a German sound."

"Let them alone," I said; "I will talk with their leaders. Now go to madame, and tell her I beg she will retire to the winter-garden, and not come out of it in any case or for any noise."

The valet obeyed, and I girded on my sword again, put on my képi, and went downstairs.

The porter had locked the entrance, but a loud muttering and battering noise was heard from the outside.

"Open the door!" I said to the porter, and, sword in hand, I stepped out. What I beheld was the usual spectacle upon such occasions. A mob of all classes; labourers in blouses, dandies in tall hats, college youths, street boys, market women, and veiled "ladies" in flashy dresses and with painted cheeks, all huddled pell-mell in picturesque disorder.

The man who was battering at the door was a gigantic locksmith, with hammer in hand, and I believe that the only object he had in his battering operations was to make use of his hammer. As I appeared, those who were near the door, retreated a little, and some of them called out, "See, see! An officer of the army."

"*Citoyens!*" said I, in a loud voice, "in this house there is a sick woman, and whoever tries to break into this house will have his skull split in two."

Most of the *gommeux* retreated at these words, but the locksmith seemed to think resistance a provocation to an attack. "Ho, ho!" said he, beating his breast and swinging his hammer, inviting me to try the edge of my sword on his skull, while around him sticks and umbrellas were upraised against me with threatening gestures of all sorts of people, male and female.

I had to make an end of this, and that was only possible by showing them that I was not afraid of them, and, first of all, I had to silence that burly smith by a smart cut on the hand that held the hammer. I had just lifted my arm with the sword, when someone caught it from behind, seizing tight hold of both hand and sword.

It was Flamma.

"What do you want here? Why did you come out?" I asked her.

She stepped close to my side, and addressed the people. I could never have believed that that tiny, silent, shell-mouth of hers could be capable of such eloquence. "*Citoyens!*" she said, with a perfectly dramatic intonation and gesture, "you are are mistaken in this house and in us. We are no Germans, no enemies, but Hungarians, and friends to the French. Look at my husband! He has just arrived from the battlefield, where he has served the French army. He has repeatedly risked his own life to save that of your brethren. Look at his forehead! That wound upon it he received in the service of your country! Look at his breast! It is decorated with the star of the Legion of Honour! He——"

I was furious. What business had this woman, who, in her heart of hearts, despised me as an abject, greedy, dishonourable coward, a base wretch, who had accepted the most degrading position on earth for a money consideration—what business, said I, had she to speak fair of me before this crowd?

"Madame," I shouted, "go into the house! I do not want your speeches! Let go my hand, I say! I want to drive this rabble away!" But she clung tightly to me, and, seeing that I could not free myself

of her, I caught her up in my arms, and carried her
to her room. There I threw her upon her couch and
said—"Don't move from this bed. You are trifling
with your life!"

"Then stay here with me," she said, beseechingly;
"don't go back among them!"

"Nonsense, I am able to protect and save you
from a drunken mob, but from an attack of convulsions
I could not save you! This might cost you your life."

At this word I fancied I saw a smile of contempt
on her lips, and it occurred to me that she thought I
feared for her life, because, in case of her death, I
should have to return her money. "I wish they
would come and tear me to pieces in her very presence,"
I thought, in the bitterness of my heart; but, to my
surprise, no one came. The next minute or two
furnished an explanation. I heard the sound of a
bugle, then the clatter of horse-hoofs; the Imperial
Guard itself had cleared the street of the mob. In a
few minutes the shouts and threats were silenced, and
the crowd had moved on to other quarters. Immediately afterward I heard voices in the *salon*, and, telling
the woman to keep quiet and not stir, I entered the
*salon.*

A police officer was talking with the valet. I
thanked him for ridding me of my unpleasant visitors,
who would undoubtedly have done harm to the
furniture of the house, if not to our persons.

"Oh, that is past," said he, "but there is something
else amiss; and I may tell you at once, sir, something
that is very serious!"

"Serious to me?" I asked.

"Yes, the police have certain knowledge of the fact that you keep up a cipher correspondence with some-body in Brussels. You have received a letter a day or two ago."

"I know it. The letter had been opened by the police."

"Exactly. You have answered that letter, also in cipher, and the letter was posted not quite an hour ago."

"And the contents of this letter are already in the hands of the police?"

"Yes. Will you have the kindness to give me the key to the cipher?"

"Sir," said I, "you know well that every corre-spondence has secrets which cannot be disclosed to a stranger!"

"I assure you that the Police Department is just as silent with respect to the secrets that are entrusted to it, as the tongueless stone lions on St. Mark's Square in Venice."

"And what will be the consequence if I refuse to give you the key?"

"If they offer to shoot me," I thought, "I will not tell."

"If you refuse, you will be conducted to the Belgian frontier without a moment's delay."

"No, thank you," I thought; "I'll have none of that."

So I invited him into my room, and together we solved the contents of both letters.

The first was that of the agent, the second was my answer, which consisted of the following words :—

"The French will be victorious ; invest my whole fortune, all the money you hold of mine, in buying for a rise."

The tears rushed down the cheeks of the police officer. That a foreigner had so much confidence in the French cause as to stake his whole fortune on it was completely overpowering to him. He pressed my hands in silent acknowledgment, when I could have laughed in his face, and was silently applauding myself on the comedy I had played.

"It is all right, sir," said he, taking his leave; "but since you are a true friend of the French, let me give you a bit of honest advice. Don't stay in Paris beyond to-day at the utmost. To-day we command ; to-morrow, God knows who may fill our place. Go to-day, while you are free to go; to-morrow it is possible that I shall follow your example."

I thanked him heartily, and gave him my passport for revision. In an hour the passport was returned to me in proper order, and at daybreak we were sitting in a railway carriage. My wife confessed that she felt very happy in being able to leave Paris; she had been very uncomfortable and ill at ease there.

## XVI.

### DAME FORTUNE.

IT took us two whole days to reach Brussels. All the railway trains were crowded with soldiers and refugees fleeing from Paris, and at every station there was some delay. Special trains had to be waited for, and at every town the passengers had to leave the carriage, show their passports, answer all questions, and open all trunks and valises for examination by the police.

For me this exasperating procedure was rendered more difficult still. The wound on my forehead betrayed me for a soldier of some sort, and a strict command of General Trochu expressly forbade soldiers to leave the country. Of course, I had my discharge; but, when I showed the document, it took them always a good while to consider which command of General Trochu should be respected—the one which bade me go, or the other which directed me to stay.

At the border I was detained for exactly four hours. Again my luggage was searched; again I had to convince them that I was no runaway soldier, no foreign spy, but a lawfully-discharged volunteer camp-surgeon of foreign birth; and I had to give my word of honour that the lady with me was really and legally my own wife.

When we finally arrived at Brussels, late at night, we could hardly find a lodging. All the hotels were crowded to the doors, and only with difficulty, and by the aid of a very liberal tip, was I enabled to procure a back room on the third storey. I took my wife to the elevator, to be carried to the room, gave orders for her supper, etc., and went down to the café to drink a glass of hot punch.

The place was crowded to suffocation, in spite of the lateness of the hour. Every newspaper was being read by five or six readers at once. Something very important seemed to have happened, but the noise was so deafening that it was utterly impossible to catch a word of the news.

I begged the waiter to let me have one of the papers.

"Never mind, sir," he said, smilingly; "these are all afternoon editions. If you will wait till your punch is ready, I will manage to get you a fresh paper moist from the press."

I rewarded his good offices with the expected money gratification, and some minutes later the hot punch and a moist copy of the morning *Indépendance* were before me. The price of the copy was five francs.

As an experienced reader of Continental news-papers, I began my reading on the last page, devoted to the telegrams. I found one from Arlon, stating that MacMahon's position was very good. He was posted behind fortifications, which were stored with provisions for three hundred thousand men. Yesterday's engagement had ended in a triumph for the French.

Another telegram came from Mézières, according to which yesterday's battle had ended fatally for the French, who had been forced to the Belgian frontier by the Prussians. The Emperor was with MacMahon. The line of battle extended from Bazille to La Chapelle. Three thousand French soldiers, with five hundred horses, had been driven across the Belgian frontier, and had there surrendered.

A gentleman sitting near me, evidently a Frenchman, politely begged me to show him the telegrams. "Oh," said he, "these are old ones, brought over from the evening papers. Let us look at the front page," and, turning the leaves, he pointed to a few lines printed in large letters, "Sedan, September 2, 8 p.m. MacMahon's army has surrendered and laid down its arms. MacMahon is severely wounded, and General Wimpffen has taken command in his place. The capitulation was signed by him. Napoleon has personally surrendered to the Prussian King."

The French gentleman had fallen from his chair in a swoon. He was carried out into the fresh air to recover. This incident caused a sensation in the room ; everybody inquired for the cause of the swoon, and I gave them the newspaper, which was eagerly devoured, until one gentleman leaped upon a billiard-table and read the news aloud to all.

I went up to my wife. She had thrown herself on the bed, without undressing, for, as we had only this single apartment for both of us, she could not undress before the stranger who was—her husband. I begged her pardon for disturbing her, but I thought she would be interested in the important news. Of course she was! All the sleep was gone from her eyes in a moment. She sprang from the bed and came to me.

"See how kind Providence has been!" she said. "If you had not been dismissed, you also would be a prisoner now. So what seemed an evil has been converted into a benefit."

At the first moment I felt inclined to share her views. For, indeed, it would have been a ludicrous end to my little private tragedy if, instead of the coveted death, I had experienced a few years of tedious inaction at Mainz or some other German fortress.

So that, considered from this point of view, I had indeed had a fortunate escape, and out of the fancied evil had come a certain good. "But if evil may change into good," I thought, "I wonder who can repair my marred and blackened life? Is there any Providence powerful enough to convert this evil into a benefit?"

I gazed at Flamma, and wondered how she would look if I were to tell her that her million had ceased to exist, that this catastrophe, which had dragged a monarch from his throne into captivity, had also cost her her sole fortune, the inheritance of her grandfather, and had thrown her upon my mercy? "Goodnight!" I said to her. "Try to sleep a little. I will go and look for some private lodgings. We cannot stay in this place." She thanked me, and, if I remember rightly, she extended her hand to me; but I contrived to avoid taking it, and left her to her own company.

I descended again to the café. Nobody was there except the staff of waiters. Everybody else had gone to the Bourse, I learned. 'Change open at four o'clock in the morning! is not that extraordinary? Certainly, but so are the events which are occurring. The spacious halls and corridors of the Exchange were brilliantly lighted all night long, and were filled with a throng of brokers and "matadores." Curiosity took me there also; but I had literally to fight my way in. My fists had to procure admission for me. In the large hall this fighting for room was general; and as for the noise and uproar of voices, the blockade of Spicheren must have been a symphony in comparison.

I promised twenty francs to one of the servants of the establishment if he would fetch me Mr. X., my broker, from the *coulisses.* I handed him my card. It was an hour before the good man could emerge from the crowd. His silk hat was crushed, his coat-collar torn off, the bow of his necktie was dangling at the back of his neck, and his waistcoat had lost four buttons; but he was radiant. As he caught sight of me, he ran to meet me, shook my hands, embraced and kissed me, and fairly went into ecstasies over me. Was this man mad?

"Sir!" he cried. "My friend! my hero! You are a sage, a prophet! At the news of the catastrophe of Sedan a tremendous rise has set in on 'Change!"

"Rise!" I exclaimed, astonished.

"Certainly, and what a rise! If the French had simply been vanquished we should have had a tremendous fall, but at the news of the surrender values are rising enormously. You are a wonderful man! How you have scented it all! Let me go back to make millions! Your money is all invested for a rise. To-day

we shall take lunch at Tortoni's at twelve o'clock sharp.
I shall bring you home eight millions. Let me go, or
I shall leave the lappet of my coat in your hands."

With that he ran back to the orgies around the
golden calf. I let myself go with a crowd that was
thronging out—possibly the beaten speculators—and
was borne by the current into the street. I was completely stunned at the results of my determined efforts
to lose that money, and felt for my head to make
sure that I was not dreaming. Could all this be true?
Could ice be kindled into flames, and could flames
freeze to ice? How was I to believe that all my
curses could be turned into blessings, and that out of
misfortune Fortune herself should arise?

By this time the morning had dawned, and I went
into a café to get some tea. With the tray a newspaper was laid before me, and, sure enough, I read—
"General rise! French values mounting and greatly
in demand! Money in abundance!"

So it was no dream.

Until noon I sauntered about in order to kill time.
At precisely twelve o'clock I was at Tortoni's, and
found my broker already expecting me. He had
ordered lunch: Four dozen oysters, woodcock, arti-
chokes, giardinetto. Wines: Chablis, Château Lafitte,
Grand Vin Mumm, etc.

"Wonderful victory!" said he, taking my hand.
"*Écrasant* defeat of the *contremine!* Sir, Napoleon
has capitulated before King William; I capitulate
before you. You know more of the psychology of the
Money Market than I!"

I to know the psychology of the Money Market? was not that excessively absurd?

"It is easy to understand," he continued. "You are home from the French camp. Evidently you have not gone there to plaster sores or set broken bones, but to have an opportunity for watching the development of the situation, and the movements of the forces. Oh if all 'matadores' would only be as prudent! But this course requires pluck, courage, and perfect coolness. You already knew that MacMahon was hemmed in, and that the Emperor shared the same fate. It was easy to foresee the ensuing surrender, and you made use of the means provided for your escape. You gave me instructions; I have carried out your order, and here is the result. Four millions are the prize of this one day."

"But how is it possible?" asked I.

"Pray don't try to play the simpleton before me. Of course, you had calculated that, with the capitulation and the capture of the Emperor, the war was at an end. The French have no organised armies left, and are, therefore, compelled to make peace. The Stock Market anticipates the conclusion of peace, and forces up French securities. What shall I do with your eight millions?"

What? I hardly knew. Throw it into the ocean; it would come back to me, like the ring of Polycrates. Nay, not like that, for it kept hatching, and came back like a hen with a brood of chickens—that is, millions. This odious money sticks to me like so many burs, and I cannot get rid of it. Fortune is called a goddess. To me she was a "She-devil;" her gold was choking me.

"Did you come from Paris alone?" asked the broker.

"No; my wife is with me."

"Have you found comfortable quarters to live in?"

"A back room on the third storey. I am looking for private lodgings."

"Well, I will tell you something. A banker, who was on the bear side, offers his residence for sale, in order to pay his differences. His house cost him four hundred thousand francs. We could get it for half the amount, and you could move into it at once."

"Take it, by all means."

"But what shall I do with the balance of the money? This glass to the new landlord!"

We clinked glasses. What a powerful agent money was! Only last night I could not find a room to sleep in, and now I was practically the owner of a palatial residence in Brussels. But what should I do with the rest, the seven million eight hundred thousand francs?

"Speculate with the whole amount for a fall," said I to the agent, determined that this time the hateful money should be lost for ever. Mr. X. set down his glass and looked at me. "I beg pardon, sir, but—perhaps you are not accustomed to spirits? The champagne was rather strong."

"Wine does not affect me. I am quite sober."

"Then, in all politeness, I would advise you to consult a specialist; perhaps you are suffering from the mania of contradiction or some other mental disease."

"This is my own affair. You do with my money as I instruct you. Put all the money left, after paying for the house, on a bear speculation at one week."

"Then, pray, give me permission to take out my percentage first; for in this transaction I take no share. You have pulled out the devil's forelock and shaved off his beard, but he won't give you his hoof and tail also. Give me my percentage, and handle your money yourself."

"Your percentage you may take when you please, but with the rest do as I tell you; speculate for a fall at the end of a week. I have no time to go on 'Change, as I must be off to Paris."

"Paris? You are going back to Paris? Sir, your reason must be disturbed. Why, revolution has broken out in Paris. Don't you know of it?"

"That's exactly the reason for my going. My wife has left her whole wardrobe, her silver, jewellery, pictures, and tapestry in Paris, and I am going to take everything away before it is destroyed."

"But, sir, this is foolish! Here are eight millions. Surely you can buy a new wardrobe and jewellery for your wife with this money without carrying your head to the guillotine."

"Will you allow me to judge of my own affairs?" said I, angrily. "I must know best what I ought to do."

After that my man put the tip of his forefinger to his nose, and exclaimed: "Oh, so!"

I looked at him with tight-shut lips, giving vent to a slight "H—m, h—m!"

At that he raised his eyebrows, lifted his fat finger with a warning gesture, and smiled mischievously; whereat I shrugged my shoulders, and the mutual understanding was perfect. Of course, it was natural in the owner of eight millions to have, besides his legal wife, another illegal wife, or mistress; and as in case of danger an honest man's first duty is to save his own wife, I had of course done so; but, like a real gentleman, I was returning to the place of danger in order to save my other wife as well.

That was the meaning of the mysterious winking and smiling and hemming, and I did not think it worth my while to undeceive him. Let him believe whatever he likes; what do I care for his opinion?

The same day I obtained possession of the house, and took my wife to it. She was greatly astonished at its splendour, but ventured no remark. I asked her if she had any money left out of the forty thousand francs, and she answered that she had only spent half of it. That showed good economy. Not to spend more than twenty thousand francs in three months was the quintessence of thriftiness. I told her that the house was at her disposal, and that she might arrange everything to please herself. I was compelled to leave her on urgent business. She did not ask me what business I had, nor where it would take me. Neither would she persuade me to stay.

I reached Paris much sooner than I had expected. As soon as I had passed the frontier I had donned my uniform again, and was very wise in doing so. All those who had hindered me when leaving the country

were now very officious in assisting me to reach Paris.
The sight of my uniform, my wounded forehead, and
the *légion d'honneur* was enough to put them
entirely at my service. In Paris I was surprised at
the change of the appearance in the public streets.
Over every porch, on every house, a large tricolour
flag was displayed; the military embraced and
fraternised with the people. I saw the Imperial Guard
hacking at the imperial eagle over the barrack-gate
with their swords—the same swords which they used
two days before to drive off and disperse the mob at
my door.

My own residence had undergone a similar change.
Like the caterpillar which has developed into a gay
butterfly, it had put on wings, and from the balcony,
above the porch, on all sides, great tricolours were
hanging, with the legend " *Vive la République !* "

So it was already a Republic, and only the other
day it had been an Empire. And all this had occurred
without the shedding of a single drop of blood,
without the least disorder! It was just as though a
handsome widow should remarry the day after her
husband's funeral. The new Government was already
established, and the satisfaction over this performance
was enough to sweeten the pang caused by the catastrophe of Sedan.

In the streets no policeman, no detective could be
seen. The National Guard watched over the public
order, and the foreigners, who, under Palikao's reign,
had been the victims of so many molestations, were
left in peace. Yes, large placards, in big red letters,

invited all foreigners who were true friends of liberty to enter the volunteer corps, which was called into existence for defence against the tyrants. It was enough to show some exotic trait of dress or appearance to be literally embraced on the streets by fair ladies.

So it was in vain that I had come to this place to get rid of my head. There was no guillotine, no barricade, not the slightest opportunity for cheap martyrdom; and as for the volunteer legion, why, that was a veritable life insurance corps.

I could not get myself killed. But my millions had another chance of annihilation. The rise was lasting for days, and all Europe believed in a restoration of peace.

On the sixth day, the limit I had given to my broker, appeared that manifesto of the French Republican Government which proclaimed that the war would be continued until all resources were exhausted. France would never rest until she had driven her enemy from her soil.

This proclamation was a deathblow to all hopes of peace, and destroyed all calculations and expectations. That a tremendous decline in values was the consequence will be readily understood.

So my Hell-born millions had hatched again, and returned to me doubled. Dame Fortuna insulted me! She was a demon—a Devil!

# XVII

## LIGHT AT LAST.

AT this I gave up that Quixotic fight against windmills, and said to my own familiar spirit, my little inward devil—

"My dear little demon, I find you are a much more cunning little devil than I thought you to be, and I shall begin to listen to your advice. What the devil shall I kill myself for, when I have got sixteen million francs of ready money? Is there any need of my final surrender to you as yet? First, I'll see what services you'll do me still. The money I got by following your suggestions, but the suicide speculation was a failure. Evidently there are other devils more potent than you. Now let me see. If I judge correctly, I can spare you altogether, dismiss you with good references, such as, 'A fine little demon, very cunning, very devoted and submissive.' It would be easy for you to find another master, and I could well spare you. Why, with sixteen millions there is no need of my being unhappy, and giving way to despair; with so much ready money, I have Fortune at my command. She will come at my bidding. If every husband in France who is not beloved by his wife were to enlist against the Prussians, daring Death and Devil alike, the Prussians would very soon find their way home again. And if she has insulted, betrayed me with another man before she became my wife, I can revenge myself now, and why not? When

Father Adam quarrelled with Mother Eve, he found consolation with Lilith, the dark-skinned Hashor, the almond-eyed Anaitio, the silent Mylitta. So, my dear little demon, I can't see of what use you can be to me any longer. I am tired of going death-hunting, and not fool enough to play a game of shuttlecock with a lump of gold. Then what's the use of my keeping you?"

"Ha-ha-ha-ha-ha!" laughed he. "Fancy your sending me off when you stand most in need of me and my advice. My dear boy, you were never so much my own as at this moment. You are tired of death-hunting? Very good; live on, drink deep of the fountain of life, drain it to the dregs, and much good may it do you! You have wealth and therefore power, and you will become just such a dare-devil villain as the man who has caused all this pother. You will betray innocent, confiding maidens, deceive loving friends, ruin families, and beget unfortunate, ill-starred beings. You will become a heartless libertine, a selfish sensualist. You will mock at God, mock at the Devil; and when you are all alone, you will dread and despise yourself. You will do evil for evil's sake, and rejoice at the despair of your brethren. Oh, you can't spare me now, my boy; you want me more than ever!"

I did not enter the Franc-tireur legion, although its captain was a countryman of mine, a chivalrous Hungarian: if I am not mistaken, his name was Varjassy. I returned to Brussels, and remained there.

My broker, Mr. X., came to me, quite submissive, doing penance in sackcloth and ashes. Again he called me sage and prophet, and finally asked me, "What next?"

"Nothing," I said. "We will not go near the Bourse again. We have made our booty; don't let us run the risk of losing it."

"You are certainly wise!" he said, admiringly. He took his own proportion, and bought property with it. The last time I had heard of him he had established a great dairy and was manufacturing an excellent cheese.

I had become a fashionable dandy. I was a member of the Jockey Club, was seen at the theatres and at all fashionable places of public entertainment. I opened my palatial residence to fashionable society, and took my wife to all social amusements fitted to her station in life. I took pride in the elegance of her toilette, and was jealously careful that her equipage should outshine all others.

Still I cannot say that this constant, tender consideration and attention to her affected her in my favour. On the contrary, I found that of late her glance had a troubled, I may say, puzzled expression when it rested on me; and when occasionally I entered her room unexpectedly I saw that she hastily concealed in a drawer a small and well-worn note-book. I supposed she was calculating what this expensive rate of living might cost. If she only computed what I spent officially, so to speak—that is to say, on herself and the household—she must have made it some four hundred thousand francs. The income on her million of florins would amount, at the utmost, to one hundred thousand francs, so she must naturally have come to the conclusion that her securities were scattered to the winds.

At that time the rosewood chest with the bonds, in

exactly the same condition as when she had given them to me on our wedding night, was in my own possession again, and locked up in my safe. It had been my first care to take it home from the banking-house where it had been deposited. I had repaid the amount of the loan, received the securities, and found them all in excellent order.

By this time the period of Flamma's confinement had arrived, and a son was born. I had made her a proposition to postpone the christening for a month, and only then to give our aristocratic family connections at home information of the happy event. She consented, and by the time the christening took place she had fully recovered her health and beauty, or, rather, she had become more beautiful than ever; for, from a girlish maiden, she had developed into a blooming woman.

The little boy we christened William James. He was a well-formed, healthy child, and I myself had conscientiously selected a nurse for him.

When at last no harm was to be feared from excitement, and Flamma's health was fully established, I wrote her a line that I should like to have some conversation with her on money matters that afternoon. She wrote me in reply that I had anticipated her own wishes, and that she would be ready to receive me.

At the appointed time I carried the rosewood chest with her dowry to her room. I found her engaged with the same worn-looking note-book that I had already noticed, but this time she did not hide it upon my entrance. She offered me a seat, but I set the chest on the table in front of her, and, looking her in the face, I said—

"Madame, to-day it is seven months since that eventful evening on which you made me certain confidential disclosures. At that time I did not make any remark on the subject, because the state of your health was such that, in my capacity as a physician, conscientious scruples prohibited me from creating in you any excitement which might prove fatal to yourself and to another being. You will not refuse to bear witness that I have paid you all the care and attention which your condition required, and that I have done everything that was possible, under the circumstances, to save you from emotions which might be injurious. I have nursed you conscientiously, and omitted nothing which I thought necessary to your health and that of your child. But now your health is fully established, your child is christened, and I have given him an honourable name and a good nurse, which is all that he requires for the present. Now the time has come when I may express my real sentiments to you. I shall even now forbear to reproach you. In this whole baneful connection between us the fault has been mine alone. It was my boundless vanity, my absurd conceit, which led me to believe that a beautiful, wealthy, and high-born young lady would choose me, of all men, for her husband, without any secret motive or hidden reason to prompt her. I ought to have known my own worthlessness better, and not yielded to a flattering self-conceit. You see, I acknowledge my fault fully, and I own that I have deserved my punishment. I have no accusation against you. You were desperate; you had to save your reputation, and you did not stop to consider what it might cost me so long as it served your purpose. Of course, the pride and honour of Countess Vernöczy were of much higher importance than the life, the honour, of an insignificant fool like myself. Moveover, you paid for the services you had procured with admirable magnanimity. You placed your whole dowry at my disposal. But now your honour and reputation are saved; so is that of your child. There is no need of my suffering longer for a fault for which I have bitterly atoned. Now, pray, let me restore to you the money which you placed in my hands on that memorable night. Let me beg you to take slate and pencil, and convince yourself of the entire correctness of the amount."

She looked at me as if mesmerised, and mechanically she obeyed me. I opened the chest, took out the papers, and, as she had done on the night of our wedding, I dictated to her the titles of the various deeds and securities, and she wrote as I dictated.

The amount was correct. "You see that the coupons are inside," I said; "those of last year and those of this year also. Not one has been touched."

"And our household expenses?" asked she, breathlessly.

"Were liquidated by me with my own money. Now, pray, take the property out of my hands, for this is the last time that we shall ever speak with or behold each other as long as we live." She gazed up at me, trembling in every nerve. I continued—

"I shall leave you to-day, and you will never learn whither I have gone or where I am. Like the criminal

escaping from jail, I shall change my name, and
deny the term which I have served at your side. I
shall possess no name, no home, no family. I shall
be a stranger and an outcast, wandering to and fro
for fear that the acquisition of a settled residence
might betray my abode to you. And now, there are
three roads open to you. You may return with your
child to the old home of the Dumanys, my poor Slav
kingdom. There you may live, secluded from the
world, bringing up your child and teaching him virtue,
honesty, and useful employments. You may dole out
alms to the poor, and in this mournful solitude
pray to God for happy oblivion or the still happier
news of my death. This is one of the roads open to
you; it is the stony path of virtue, dreary and tiresome. The second path is the flowery one. You
may throw yourself upon the waves of life, drink deep
of the cup of pleasure, not troubling yourself with
scruples as to what is allowed and what forbidden.
Your youth, beauty, and wealth will carry you up to
the pinnacle of pleasure—only beware of the conse-
quences! I, the husband, shall be separated from
you by whole oceans perhaps, and shall not be here
to legitimatise the result of a *faux pas*. There is still
a third way—a divorce; and I authorise you to commence your suit. Only, you know, this way is tedious,
and requires great sacrifices. Monetary sacrifices
also, for we cannot get a divorce without being converted to Protestantism, and in that case, according
to your grandfather's will, you are obliged to give up
your dowry—this million. But you have also to give

up the Church and the religion in which you were born and brought up, and which has given you consolation in despair, and the saints whom you are accustomed to invoke to your aid. Still, the road is open to you, and I will give you four hours to make your decision. If it should be for a divorce, I am ready to go with you to Transylvania to procure a divorce under the Unitarian laws."

As I finished she rose from her seat, her cheeks aglow, her eyes burning. "I know a fourth way," she said, catching her breath.

"And that is?"

"I will not let you go!" she cried, taking hold of my arm with both hands, and clinging to me with her trembling body.

I broke out into a bitter, scornful laugh. "Countess," said I, "do you believe that there is in the world an interest, a sentiment, a spirit of magnanimity or of cowardice, which is powerful enough to hold me in jail now that the time for which I have sentenced myself has expired? That there is any power existing which could tie me to your side, if but for another day? Well, I have read the hate, the contempt, the scorn in your eyes, and you were justly entitled to those feelings; but you cannot wish me to endure these daily pangs and lacerations of my wounded self-esteem for ever. You cannot ask of me to live on at the side of a woman who hates me, despises me, and scorns me, simply because it would suit that woman to retain her present position. No, my lady! Even my ample stock of weak foolish indulgence is at an end. I go, and I go for ever! Not even in Paradise do I wish to meet you again. And if you go to salvation, I shall go to perdition to avoid you!"

The effect of my cruel, insulting words were marvellous. They did not seem to hurt or offend her; she seemed to delight in them, drink them in like some sweet, delicious nectar. Her face, her eyes, her attitude spoke of exultant admiration, of triumphant joy, of ecstatic delight.

"True!" she said, "it is all true that you have said. Only what I have felt for you was never hate; it was love warring against contempt, and contempt fighting against love. Yes, I have despised you; for I was told, and I believed it, that money was all that you cared for, and your own words have confirmed me in this opinion. Do you remember, after you had told Cenni and me the story of your friend, you spoke of the qualities of the girl whom you might marry? She must be young and beautiful, and wealthy and luxurious. Young and beautiful—I thought—to suit your vanity; wealthy and luxurious—because you loved wealth and luxury; and your conduct after our marriage hourly convinced me of the correctness of the supposition. You accepted your position without a murmur. I was burning with shame and humiliation, ready at a word to fall at your feet, and make you a confession which would cleanse me from the burning stigma, remove from me the brand of shame. But you accepted the money, and asked no questions, and I left you in despairing contempt. Our married life was much too luxurious to undeceive me, and I believed that you were making use of my money to feed your appetite for pleasure. When you protected me against danger, nursed me in my odious condition, I thought, 'All is well to him as long as he can keep the money. He fears for my life, because, in case of my death, he would have to restore the money.' The comfort, the splendour, the costly presents, dresses, and jewels which you bestowed upon me were so many accusations against yourself. And yet how I longed to be able to respect you! When the newspapers spoke of your undaunted courage, of your disinterested and indefatigable activity, your self-denial, generosity, and discreet modesty, how my heart yearned for you! How my soul cried out to you, 'Why are you not the same to me as to the world? Why are you brave, generous, disinterested, and self-denying to them, and not to me? Why am I, of all persons alive, condemned to know you for a cowardly, avaricious, and selfish man, when, in spite of all that, my heart burns for love of you?' And now you have thrown off the hideous mask you wore, have shown me your real face, shown me how much I have misjudged you, how I have sinned against you! You give me back that money untouched. You have not even spent the interest of it, and now I see how I have wronged you in accusing you of greed. All your tender care, your delicate attention, your patient indulgence were given to me out of your magnanimous sense of duty, the heavenly generosity of your soul! And now that I know you in all the glory of your goodness, now that I have found my ideal in you and

my love has grown into worship, now you tell me that
you are lost to me for ever, that you will not be mine,
and I must choose the paths you point out to
me. No, sir; that is impossible! You cannot cast
me off, now that I love you! I have sinned against
you, caused you insufferable pains, infinite tortures;
but my whole life shall be given to atone for those
sins by meek submission, dutiful obedience, ardent
love. I cannot choose between those paths you have
shown me. I do not want to be consumed by the
fires of sinful love, nor to freeze in the ice of solitude
and self-abnegation. I want to be happy, and to make
you happy. I want to love, and I do love you!"

"You have a child."

"That child! That living stigma which was
branded into my flesh by a miserable assassin! I hate
it so much that I will never kiss it, never pray for it.
Its very sight is loathsome to me! I have given
birth to it, but shall never love it as a mother!"

After this tempest of her emotions she threw herself
against the door, barring it against me as though
to say: "The way through this door, the way that
separates you from me, leads over my body."

I looked at her, and the sight of her deep and real
agitation summoned me to a silent condemnation of
my base hypocrisy. What was I but a cunning
dissembler, coming here to play a great part before
her, making believe that I had not touched her money,
when I had time and again risked it in speculations?
And the very house she lived in, the comfort and
splendour that surrounded her, were the result of the

profits her money had acquired. How dared I make
a parade of my generosity, when all the time I had
been scheming for her ruin and dreaming of revenge?
Truth and sincerity were all on her side; the halo of
virtue around my head was false.

And she loved me! She confessed that love with
the frank truthfulness of her nature—confessed it in
words that sent a thrill of delight through my whole
frame! And I, who am burning for love of her, I stand
here like a pagan idol, in stony indifference, looking
down at the bleeding heart which is held up as a
sacrifice to me. No, I am no stone! Avaunt, Hathor,
Mylitta, Baaltis, I am none of yours! And thou too,
vile, wretched Dissimulation, I cast thee forth!
Depart from the presence of this true woman!

I went to her and took her hands. "If your boy
is not to have the love of a mother, he shall have that
of a father instead. I shall love him dearly and be a
true father to him."

As I said this, she broke into passionate sobbing,
and, crouching down at my feet, she threw her arms
around my knees and wept bitterly.

"No," said she, "do not lift me up, for my confessions are not yet ended. I have asked you for
mercy heretofore. I now ask you for justice; for a
righteous judgment! I have never been the degraded
wretch you believed me to be, have never been
the mistress of another man, never listened to his
words of love, so help me God! Siegfried was not
my betrayer, he was my assassin! He made use of Diodora's and Cenni's absence from the house, at a time

when a slight illness had prevented me from accompanying them, to drug my wine at the table, and during the lethargy caused by the soporific potion he slew my soul! Devil as he is, he took a devilish revenge, because I had shown him my contempt and abhorrence."

Before this I was down on my knees, covering her eyes, her hair, her face, and her mouth with my kisses; weeping in the excess of my love and happiness. "Why did you not tell me this before? Why not on the night of our wedding?" I asked.

"I intended to! Do you remember that I asked you if you had no other question to address to me? You said 'No,' and pointed to the door. For a few moments only your eye had rested with a fiery glare on a two-edged dagger which lay upon the table. If you had carried out the wild promptings of your wrath, if your hand had raised the dagger against me, if only a single word or action had given me proof that you were the man I wished you to be, and not the wretch who accepts the money which is offered in return for his name and honour, I should have spoken. Oh, how I have longed to do it!"

I pressed her to my heart and kissed her again. "You are innocent," I said: "as innocent as that poor child himself. You have not sinned; others have sinned against you. And now that you have confessed to me, let me also confess to you, and, if you can, forgive me!" I told her all—my evil designs, the monetary speculations, my suicidal purposes, my moral cowardice. She listened, shuddering, but, when I had finished, she nestled close to my heart and kissed me passionately. She had forgiven.

\*　　\*　　\*　　\*　　\*　　\*

After this we decided to leave Europe and go to the New World—to America. My old Slav kingdom I did not care to keep; it was best to give up everything, and wipe out all memory of myself. So I left it to be sold in payment of the debts I had accumulated. In the New World fortune clung to me with the same persistence. Whatever I undertook was sure to succeed, and all my enterprises were fortunate. So, in course of time, I became the "Silver King." We came to Europe on account of little James, who all at once ceased speaking and became a mute. We tried American physicians, but to no purpose, and so we came to Europe in order to consult the best professional talent. Now you know all. You know how it was possible for the little son of a South American nabob, after regaining his lost speech, to speak Hungarian, and you know who taught him to speak that language. The child has never loved anyone but me, and no one has loved him but myself. And I love him truly and with all my heart. For to him I am indebted for all my present happiness; not only for my wealth, for wealth alone is not happiness. A man may be happy without wealth, and be very unhappy with it; but I owe him this.

He took a photograph from his pocket-book, and showed it to me—four laughing little cherub heads, peeping out of a bath-tub, like birds from the nest. "These my little James has brought me," he said, with tears of joy in his eyes; "if he had not come, these would not have come either. So, you see, my dear friend, I was thrown into Hell and fell into Paradise."

\* \* \* \* \* \*

"I beg your pardon," said I to Mr. Dumany, as he finished his story, " but I am curious to know what became of Siegfried ? Would you mind telling me ? "

" Oh, he is a very famous man at present, and fills a very honourable position. He is engaged as horse-tamer in the Paris Hippodrome, and they say that he is excellent in ' jumping.' I have not seen him yet, but I hear he has a good salary, and is a general favourite. He is very much praised and admired by those who have seen him. I think it highly creditable in a man when he lives honourably by means of his ability and talent."

By this time the dawn had greeted us. Through the chinks of the closed shutters the rising sun was stealing, decorating the wall-tapestry with rings of golden red, adding radiant circles to the smoke-wreaths of our cigarettes, and sending long glittering darts into all the corners and behind the curtains.

Presently, breaking the monotony of our voices, which punch and cognac had made hoarse, a sweet, silvery voice chimed in, " Apácska ! Apácska ! " ("Papa ! Papa !") and a little unfledged cherub was peeping out from the bed-curtains. " You may come to me," said Mr. Dumany, smilingly, and, in an instant, little James was out of bed, and, barefooted, in his little nightgown as he was, he ran to his father, shouting with glee, climbing up into his lap, and throwing his little arms caressingly around his neck, laughing mischievously the while. At the noise of this babbling and laughter, similar sounds were heard in the next room, just as in a bird's nest when one little fledgeling chirps all the rest join in, lifting the little heads and trying the winglets.

"Reveille is sounded," said my friend, with a happy smile. "I have to go and muster my troops; this next chamber is their bedroom."

But the muster was postponed, for the commander-in-chief arrived—the mother. She was in a plain, dark dress, but her beautiful face bore a soft expression of happiness which I had not seen the day before. "You are up yet?" she asked.

"And you are up already?" asked her husband.

"Yes. I have been out to my confessor's. You have made a clean breast to your friend at home; I have done the same in the confessional, and I have come home much happier than I went, and I truly hope much better." With that she bent down to the child, and kissed it tenderly.

"I have been an unnatural and undutiful mother," she said, in a low, trembling voice, "and if you, in your generous pity, in the overflowing kindness of your nature, had not taken this poor innocent to your heart, it would not have known the tender love, the sweet care of a parent. Father Augustin has shown me the great, black sin in my breast. How can I hope for mercy from Heaven if I mercilessly lock my heart against my own innocent offspring? How can I hope for love and respect from my other children, if I withhold a mother's love from this one? Oh, my dearest husband! here in the presence of your friend, whom you have made cognisant of our past sorrows and trials, I thank you from the bottom of my heart for the love you have borne my child!" And before he could prevent the action she had bent down and pressed her lips to his hand.

"Flamma! dearest!" he said, overcome by his emotion, "you have been the truest, the most considerate, most loving, and most dutiful of all wives and mothers; but this day you have filled my cup of happiness to the brim. This one drop, the mother's kiss to the sweet innocent, was wanting. This day shall henceforth be kept as a high holiday, as this little darling's real birthday, for it has given him a mother."

He held up the boy to her, and at the sweet, inviting smile and the opened arms the little one threw open his arms also; one of them he drew around his mother's, the other around his father's neck, and then he showered a volley of kisses and caresses on both. Never in all my life have I seen a picture more lovely and beautiful than this.

"Come, my little one," said the mother, after a while, to the child, "it is too early yet for you to rise. Come to your little brothers and sisters and sleep awhile longer," and, nodding sweetly to us, she disappeared, with the child on her arm, through the tapestry *portière* that led to the children's bedroom.

The "Silver King" silently pressed my hand as I said—

"Sir, you are the happiest man on earth, nor can all the crowned monarchs of the world compare to you in wealth!"

"Yes," he said, after a while, "I am very happy. But I owe you an explanation, before I take leave of

you. You may think it singular that a man who is
the father of a family should disclose such intimate
secrets to a friend of whom he knows beforehand
that he will make public use of the disclosure, and relate to his readers the events he has learned. But, you
see, so much has already been said about my wife and
me—the fantastic imagination of one half of our fellow-
creatures has invented so much to feed the idle curiosity of the other half, that the plain truth will serve
in general as a cooling sedative. There are different
versions afloat as to how we got our money. Some
say that I was a general spy of the Prussians, and
that my money was a fee for the information furnished,
or, in plain words, the betrayal of the positions of the
French forces. Others say that my wife had been the
mistress of a King, and was enriched by him, and
that she still draws a life-pension from the Civil List;
while superstitious fools will have it that I have sold
myself to the Devil, and am supplied by him with
infernal ore. Against all of these the disclosure of the
plain truth will be the best defence. Human I am
and have been, and human have been the temptations and trials that have beset me. The only
Devil to whom, for a time, I sold myself, was the
demon in my own breast—a poor, feeble spirit, and
long ago subdued by the more potent angel of love and
peace."

**THE END.**